ALIENS IN MY GARDEN

Aliens in My Garden

Jude Gwynaire

PRODIGY GOLD BOOKS

PHILADELPHIA * LOS ANGELES

PRODIGY
GOLDBOOKS

ALIENS IN MY GARDEN

A Prodigy Gold Book

Prodigy Gold E-book edition/October 2018

Prodigy Gold Paperback edition/October 2018

Copyright (c) 2018 by Jude Gwynaire

Library of Congress Catalog Card Number: 2018954883

Website: http://www.prodigygoldbooks.com

Author's e-mail: jude.gwynaire@ntlworld.com

ISBN 978-1-939665-73-7

Published simultaneously in the US and Canada

PRINTED IN THE UNITED STATES OF AMERICA

ALIENS IN MY GARDEN

1

Do you have a garden?

Has it shown you the Thing yet?

Not all gardens do the Thing, of course, and even with those that do, not everyone can see them do it.

My garden does.

Look—this is my garden. Overgrown grass, flowers, the vegetable patch—the shed, the broken swing, the trees down the far end with dark leaves for shade. Nothing special. Nothing to worry about, right? An ordinary garden…

There are people who say the whole world grew out of a garden. There are other people who say the whole world is *still* a garden—a big round garden in the black and starlit backyard of space, big enough to be seen by the creatures who live out there, unaware of us all scurrying about down here, being important. Of course, if that's the case, then everything's relative. Maybe we only see the garden that's the right size for us. Maybe, beneath or within the garden we can see, there's somewhere else, with people and creatures living their important lives, as unaware of us as we are of them.

And maybe, if the sun's in the right direction, and you step lightly on the grass and think really tiny thoughts…

VZZZZZZZZZZZZZZZZZZZZZZZZZZZZZZZZZZZHHH-HHHHHHHT.

That's the Thing my garden does. It shows you the Garden underneath.

———————

Harper flapped, his wings practically fluttering, his heart hammering beneath his straggly, scruffy-feathered chest. He didn't know it yet —but soon, he would have new visitors in his garden. *Strange* visitors—stranger than any he had ever seen. Of course, it wasn't just *his* garden—the Garden belonged to many others…including a witch, a green man, *and* a wizard. So, maybe, the Garden was already a little strange.

Must tell Alditha, must tell Alditha, he thought, fluttering frantically. Really speaking, owls were meant to swoop majestically, only doing something as undignified as flapping when there was no graceful alternative. But Harper had never been good at being an owl. He'd nearly been thrown out of flight school as a chick, and it had taken him five tries to pass his hunting module. And as for talon care, many was the time old Master Woozlem had looked down the length of his stern, hard beak, then turned his head away in despair.

Harper gulped. *Where am I? Oh no, I must be lost again…*

Navigation was another owl thing at which…well, he wasn't exactly *bad*, but he needed to really concentrate to get it right. It was all the flight dynamics and four-dimensional mapping on a moving landscape. He shuddered. It was like doing hard sums in your head while somebody threw a planet at you and expected you to move out of the way.

He'd come from Mill Bottom, around the fringe of Nettle Wood, then flown north, through Rosemary Chase, where the warm summer smells had calmed him for whole minutes in the lands of the East Garden—just shy of the Downs, past the hedgerows, cornfields and jade-green meadows of Hogweed Town.

Sometimes, when he wasn't concentrating really hard on where he was going, Harper felt the Garden shudder and shimmer far beneath him, and then he'd gaze down and it would look unreal—a mad, enormous spooling-out of intricate, unravelling landscapes. A vision of unknown fields, rivers, hills and woodland that he had no hope of recognizing, as though the Garden was suddenly much bigger and stranger than it could possibly be—as if he were somewhere else entirely. And then, almost as soon as he looked at it, trying to work out which direction to fly, his eyes would adjust, and the world would shimmer and shudder again, and he'd be back in the Garden he knew, wondering where he'd been and where he was and what the meaning of it all could be.

He never told anyone all this of course, not even Alditha. He had quite enough to worry about without people thinking he imagined great swathes of Garden that couldn't possibly be there. Nevertheless, in his mind, it *was* his Garden—*Harper's Garden*—and he worried about it constantly. Harper was an unusual owl, for sure.

He looked down and around, trying to see where he was. Bright flowers clustered and seemed to giggle like schoolgirls with a secret. Harper blinked with sudden recognition—he was approximately six big fields and a meadow due west of the South Garden. Taking into consideration the 20-degree curve on the 1.7% upward grade that he'd encountered by the orchard at Coxton, and the unexpected headwind over Foxy End, he was still quite pleased with his efforts. However, somewhere along the line, he *had* missed the periphery of Blue Dragon Forest, for the distant towers of Skoros Castle were already visible on the horizon.

The thought of the castle made his heart beat faster again, made him flap harder and more determined.

Just you wait, wizard, he thought. *Just you wait till I tell Alditha what you're up to.*

Even as he had the thought, he saw Alditha's cottage come into view. As the Garden's leading white witch, she made sure the cottage was always neat and tidy, whitewashed, thatched and welcoming, so it stood out of the undergrowth, a solitary dwelling. People knew witches liked their peace and quiet, and while Alditha's reputation was white, you didn't want to take the risk of getting on her dark side.

He slowed his flapping, concentrated as the cottage loomed larger, closer.

Glide, he told himself. *Glide like an owl…*

He shot in through the open kitchen window, put his feet down too soon, and tumbled head over wings, somersaulting in the air, and colliding with, in order, a heavy copper pan, a bottle of something sweet smelling and sticky and green, a large ball of thistle-fluff and a miniature haystack.

Landing was another owl thing he'd never quite got the hang of.

Still, he admitted to himself, *could've been worse.* He lay there upside-down, dripping in green goo, covered in thistle-fluff and hay. *Could've been much worse.*

'Morning, Harper,' said Alditha from the far corner of the kitchen. 'Having fun?'

He ruffled his feathers and swung his wings around, trying to get the working surface under his talons. When he stood up, the goo stuck to him, and the thistle-fluff and hay stuck to the goo. He looked like a badly built matchstick model of himself.

'You'll never guess what that wizard's up to now,' he cried, re-membering what he'd seen down at Mill Bottom, outside the Green Man's house.

Alditha looked up from what she was doing. Harper wasn't entirely sure what that *was* exactly, but it seemed to involve a silver ball, about as big as he was.

'Skoros? What's he done to upset you this time?' she asked, turn-ing to look at him as he waddled along the working surface. Normally he'd have flown over to speak to her, but covered in goo from ears to talons, he thought he might just drop like a stone if he tried.

'He's only gone and built a flying teacup, that's all. And now he's flying it about the place, scaring people silly. Gave the Green Man a real start, I don't mind telling you,' he announced.

Alditha raised one eyebrow at him. She had good, proper witchy eyebrows that seemed to work independently of the rest of her face. People said the eyes were the windows to the soul, but when Alditha raised one eyebrow at you, it was pretty much a window to her certainty that you were a blithering idiot.

'A flying…teacup?' she asked. 'Harper dear, are you feeling quite all right?'

———————

Skoros was a wizard.

His great great grandfather, Radzack The First And Only, had been a wizard.

His great-grandfather, Salu-Valek The Merciless, had been a wizard.

His grandfather, Malcontent The Peacemaker, had been a wizard.

His father, Subracken, The Broody, had been a wizard.

Wizards, every one of them. As he padded down the plush red carpet of the corridor of ancestors in what he'd been quick to rename Skoros Castle as soon as his father had accidentally blown himself to bits, their portraits all glared down at him in expectation. All except Malcontent, who smiled incongruously from his portrait as if he knew some great and wonderfully calming secret.

They all had wizards' robes, just as Skoros had. They all had wizards' hats, just as Skoros had—in fact, the hat had been passed down through the generations and was a little too big for him, so he had to keep pushing it up over his eyes. The soft, scarlet silk curly-toed wizarding slippers were an indulgence none of them had gone in for until Skoros himself. But from their glaring faces, and even Malcontent's beaming face, one thing became depressingly obvious. They all had wizards' beards, just like-

Skoros *didn't* have.

He knew with every fibre of his being that he was destined to be a wizard, and not just any wizard either but one of those great, world-conquering wizards he'd read about in the family history books. But there was one fact he couldn't deny. Wizards had beards, and he didn't have one. He couldn't seem to grow one, no matter what he tried—and he'd tried a lot. He'd tried potions, and lotions, and gels, and sprays, and even on a couple of occasions, actual magic hair-growing spells.

He shuddered. The last time he'd tried that, it had gone badly wrong. The hair in his nose had twitched and started sprouting, and then, having got the idea, it had begun to grow, and grow, and grow, till it reached his feet in two long, spiky plaits. He had toyed with the idea of combing it round his mouth and trying to pass it off as a beard—but then he'd sneezed an enchanted sneeze, and the snot had flown all the way to the ends of his nose hair. Skoros The Bogey Face was *not* how he wanted to be known.

That was another thing, he grumbled to himself as he passed beneath the portraits of his illustrious wizarding ancestors, towards his secret room. They all had cool names—again, apart from Malcontent, who'd been a bit of a white sheep in the family.

Skoros didn't have a cool name.

Skoros The Even Mercilesser, he thought. *That'd be a cool name. Or Skoros the Garden-King, that'd work too. And I'd make everyone call me it. Not-*

He stopped at what looked like a wall, covered in circles, cogs and piston designs. He closed his eyes, remembering and not wanting to.

Not what She *called me.*

Against his will, Skoros closed his eyes and reminisced. Suddenly he was twelve years old again, in the *Old Garden Magic School* playground, staring at his boring, ordinary shiny school shoes.

'Well?' said the girl, impatient, making him snap his head up to look at her.

'Well…' He'd completely forgotten what it was he'd wanted, *needed* to say to her so badly that he'd waited till she was alone and tapped her on the shoulder. He remembered planning to ask her something, remembered asking the mirror a hundred times in the weeks leading up to this moment—but *what?* What was it he'd asked? His mind was blank. He felt the blood rushing to his cheeks, and his eyes began to search her face for some clue as if he'd find his answer there.

She humphed, began to turn away. The question hit Skoros in the forehead like a blacksmith's hammer.

'D'youwannagooutwithmeorwhat?' he yelled—too fast, too loud, and not at all like he'd practiced in front of the mirror.

She turned back to him, raised one slow, perfect eyebrow.

'I mean,' he gasped, 'would you…erm…do me the honour of accompanying me? Y'know…to the Midsummer Hallowe'en Dance. I mean…if you've got nothing else on. I mean, obviously, someone's already asked you, and…obviously, you're going with them. I mean, obviously.' He nodded, as the obviousness of it began to sink in for the first time.

She rolled her eyes. He saw Shadrach Michelthorpe sidling up to see what was going on.

'Oh Skoros,' said Alditha, 'don't be such a wet blanket.' And with that, she turned on the heel of her black leather boot and walked away.

Shadrach Michelthorpe began to laugh, a big belly laugh from the boy with the big belly. 'Hey, lads. Skoros is a wet blanket. Did ya hear? Alditha called him a wet, wet, wetty wet blanket. Prob'ly *wets his own*, eh lads? Eh?'

It took the crowd of boys a moment to get into the spirit of the joke, but Michelthorpe, who'd been the victim of the bully boys himself too many times, was not about to let the joke go, and slowly the fun of it spread, till most of the boys, and some of the girls too, were chanting it round the yard. 'Wet blanket, wet blanket, Skoros wets his blanket.'

Alditha turned around as the noise rose, and for a moment, she met his eye, a look of sorrow and apology on her face. And he snarled, turned, and stalked off to the school library to escape the jeering of the crowd.

Skoros opened his eyes. *Skoros the Wet Blanket* had been his name for the rest of his time in Magic School. *Well,* he thought, chewing his bottom lip, *we'll soon see who the wet blanket is.* He reached into the sleeve of his wizard's robe and pulled his wand from its holster. There were plenty of wands in the castle—the wands of his noble ancestors, all now held in cases, finally at rest. Each wizard made their wand—it was part of the ritual of apprenticeship. When it had been his turn, his father had directed him to some of the most magically powerful trees in the Garden and told him to feel which one called to him.

Skoros had felt nothing. It was as if even the trees had heard about him and weren't going to help him pretend to be a wizard when he had no right to be one. From that moment on, Skoros looked at trees and saw only firewood.

He had stayed in the family library for days, only emerging when his eyes were red with reading. Then he went walking in the castle grounds, until a beautiful song made its way to his ears. The sound of hammer on metal, the hiss and spit of hot steel plunged into water. The song of it sang to him, and he stumbled there, pulled by some powerful instinct.

In his mind, Skoros retraced a snippet of conversation from that day…

'Afternoon, Master Skoros,' said Grunde, the blacksmith.

'Get out,' said Skoros, without intending to be rude. 'Just get out, now. Please.'

'But your father's wanting this 'ere fireguard by mornin', Master Skoros-'

'GET OUT,' yelled Skoros, pinning the big man to the wall of his own forge unexpectedly. It had been the first time he'd ever raised his voice to anyone, and the power of it coursed through his veins. He met the smith's eye with something cold and imperious in his gaze, and eventually, the smith gave the smallest of nods. Skoros let him go, and the man skulked out of the forge. Skoros barred the door after him, then turned back to the hammer, the anvil and the range of metals around the room.

'Now then…' he said, and set to work.

He didn't stop for three days straight, ignoring hunger, ignoring thirst, ignoring the frequent hammering on the door and the yelling —first of the smith, and then of his father—to open up and stop this foolishness. But at the end of three days, Skoros held up his wand. It was steel inside, with tiny valves and pistons operating pin-wheels and thick, chunky stoppers. The casing was pure bronze, with curlicue designs in copper and silver. It had circular recesses along the length of the shaft and ended not in the traditional point, but in a corkscrew that made the tip of the wand hard to see.

Now Skoros knew he had found his magic.

He'd remade the wand several times since then as his skills had improved, boosting the power, adding some clicker-switches and a row of tiny rubies which lit up inside when the wand was activated. The corkscrew rotated now too, which delivered a more stable magi-cal field, and boosted the wizard's ego tremendously.

Back in the present, Skoros waved the wand at the decorated wall suddenly, and the cogs began magically to turn, the wheels to spin at different speeds, the pistons that had looked like decoration began to pump. One let off a small jet of steam, and the wall split into two halves. Skoros pulled open what were now a pair of doors to reveal his secret room. It was bronze from head to toe, the walls covered in thick strips of metal welded together with heavy rivets. Along the far wall was a mechanical marvel—another mass of pipes and pistons, dials and gauges, that seemed to have eaten a large dark mahogany desk and made it part of itself, as though it was slowly devouring everything in the room. A large wood and leather chair sat ready at the desk, its arms, too, riveted in bronze. On the right-hand side, welded into the enormous bronze contraption was what looked like a mirror, except the glass was pure black, reflecting nothing. Sticking out from the side of the mirror was a crank handle, while perched on top of the would-be looking-glass sat a sleek, black-feathered bird—much like a raven—with what appeared to be bronze feet and claws, and a silver beak.

'Rawk,' said the bird as Skoros came into the room. 'About time, too. Thought you were never gonna get here, Wet-blanket. Rawk.'

Skoros smiled his first real smile of the day. 'Razor,' he whispered, barely waving the wand at the bird. 'Sssh.'

'Raw-aaaaarrrrk.' squawked the raven, its eyes bulging as it felt an invisible grip on its throat.

2

The Green Man was flustered.

He was, like Alditha, accustomed to being left to his devices—
when you looked like a walking tree, as the Green Man did, but you
lived in a house, as he also did, people tended to wait until you called
on them.

Being woken on a bright summer morning by company, even
company as pleasant as Harper's always was, had rather thrown his
routine out of whack. He'd been delighted to see the owl of course,
for they hadn't run into each other for about six months; but still,
living alone, he'd gotten into the habit of rising late, breakfasting
long, and more or less ambling into the day. So, to be roused by the
sound of his favourite owl landing with a crash and a clatter and the
terrible scraping noise of claws along a particularly good oak dresser
had been, if he was honest, just a little irritating.

To have to find the kettle, and the tea, and the makings of a hos-
pitable beakful of breakfast for the bird when he'd barely rubbed the
sleep out of his eyes, had hardly improved his mood; but gradually, as
Harper had chattered on about Alditha this and Alditha that, and the
shelf-training of Dramm, Alditha's latest, and still rather mischievous

spellbook, he'd woken up more naturally, and felt the first few new leaves of the day sprouting on his arms and head and neck.

The leaves had quivered, though, when *the noise* had begun. At first, neither of them had heard it—Harper because he was chattering, and the Green Man because he was wondering just how long Harper intended to stay, while trying to look interested in the fact that Dramm still left occasional puddles of enchantment all over the place.

Now, his new leaves trembled and stood up on the back of his neck.

'Harper-' he'd said, suddenly serious, holding up a bark-covered arm. Then, in the momentary silence of Harper's pausing to take a breath, they'd both heard it—a kind of whistle, high-pitched and not unlike the sound the Green Man's kettle made when it was ready and wanted him to know about it.

The whistle came slowly down in pitch, getting lower and lower until it really wasn't a whistle anymore, but a sound like an unhappy cello, loud enough to shake the china off the owl-scratched dresser. Harper had hopped onto the Green Man's arm and together they'd gone to the window. And there, suspended some twenty feet off the ground…was a teacup. A large, round-topped, white-painted teacup, about the size of a small house. It seemed, somewhere before arriving in the Green Man's nook, to have lost the saucer that would normally have gone with it. It had none of the normal decoration you might expect to find on a teacup, but it did have the image of a large red star displayed on what they could only assume was its front side. The design had wings drawn either side of it, as though the red star, whatever it represented, could fly away if need be.

And now it was just sitting there, hovering, in a way the Green Man felt instinctively that a house-sized teacup shouldn't do. Harper, of course, had panicked, said it was some evil plan by Skoros to confuse and frighten them all. The Green Man had chuckled at that, and Harper had taken offence, going into a rant about how nobody took the wizard seriously around these parts, when they really ought to, and no good would come of him dropping teacups into people's nooks willy-nilly. And while the Green Man had done his best to distract his friend, even popping out a handful of juicy red berries for him to peck at, Harper wouldn't be mollified, and had flown off in a hurry, declaring that Alditha would understand, and she'd teach the wizard not to go dropping giant bits of crockery on people's heads.

So now the Green Man was flustered. If it *was* Skoros who had sent the teacup, then obviously he would have a reason for sending it, and that meant he could soon be receiving a wizard in his extremely humble home. Of course, if it *wasn't* Skoros, then he was about to have visitors, possibly strangers, in his still extremely humble home. The Green Man set to work, determined to make his home feel a little *less* humble to anyone not accustomed to his way of living. He touched a root-like finger to the dresser, and the scars of Harper's arrival disappeared.

'Ah ah,' he chided, as the dresser began to push tiny leaves up through its surface. He took his finger away, and the leaves sank back into the wood.

Next, he sent out roots and creepers through an open window, past a collection of empty wine bottles and round the solitary water butt, down into his extensive back garden, complete with workshop and distillery. Creepers crept, found a few buckets of paint, some with sticks already in, some with thick and dubious skins formed on the top. He picked them up and brought them indoors.

Of course, he thought, *there's the quick way…*

If he'd touched a creeper to the wood of his home, which was little more than an extended shed, the wood itself would have grown young again, filled with sap and vigour, and would have looked as though it had been freshly varnished.

…but the quick way is not always the right way, he chided himself, finding paintbrushes, dipping roots into paint buckets and stirring absent-mindedly. He had lifted three roots with rudimentary hands attached, two brushes clutched ready and a bucket of bright yellow paint set to go, when a new noise from the teacup startled him.

VSSSSSSSSSSSSSSSH.

It was as though the teacup was singing, and it quite unnerved the Green Man. So much so, in fact, that the creeper holding the paint pot quivered and flung itself into the air. There was a slow-motion moment, as the Green Man called out against the inevitable. He saw the yellow paint leap, like custard from a doughnut, out of the bucket. The bucket followed its trajectory, which was unmistakable. The slow-motion interlude stopped the second the yellow paint hit the Green Man in the face and ran all down his body, the bucket landing—*plonk*—on his head like a big wooden helmet. The Green Man, now feeling altogether more like the Yellow Man, lifted his new headgear and ran a hand over his closed eyes, then opened them and peered through the window again. In the side of the teacup facing his home, a big black slab of nothingness had opened up.

'...so down it came, whooooooooooosh, and just sat there, hovering like a, like a, like a *hovering thing*. A bloomin' teacup, Alditha.'

'And you're sure it's the Green Man you went to visit, are you? You didn't stop in for tea with Truffle Cremini at all?'

'No, of course not. What do you mean?'

'Well, as I've told you before, every time you stop in for tea with Truffle, you come back babbling like a loon. As I say, if he asks you if you'd like some tea, you just...say...no. Politely, mind,' she added, waving a finger in his direction. 'Last thing we need is the Fungi-folk thinking we're insulting their hospitality.'

'I haven't seen Truffle in *months*,' said Harper indignantly—or at least as indignantly as he could manage with his feathers stiffening up beneath his green goo, thistle-fluff and hay overcoat. 'It was *definitely* the Green Man. I mean they're not exactly lookalikes, are they? One's a talking mushroom, the other's a walking tree. Alditha?'

'Mmm?'

'What...' He tried to flap. 'What *is* this stuff?'

'Mmm? Oh. Wingbalm. I noticed your feathers were getting a bit dull. You're welcome.'

'And the *other* stuff?'

'Soft landing. Don't say I never do anything for you.'

'I shan't. I most assuredly shan't. Wait a minute—soft landing? What about the copper saucepan?'

'Ah. Well, yes. Call that an incentive to keep practicing your landings. Do you feel sufficiently balmy now?'

'I couldn't think of a better word.'

'Good then.' Alditha snapped her fingers in Harper's direction, and with a quick ruffle of wing feathers, the thistle-fluff and hay fell away. The green goo soaked into his feathers, and for the moment at least, Harper looked like all the other owls he'd ever known—plump of plumage, sleek of line and ready to take on the world.

'Blimey,' he said. 'It's not true what people say about you, you know, you're really quite nice.'

'Thank you, dear. You know, I think perhaps, if you're convinced this is Skoros trying something underhanded, I'd better go up to the castle and have a word.'

'No.'

'No?'

'Well, I mean…he won't be there, will he? He'll be in the teacup.'

'Hmm.'

'Oh, I forgot to mention—it had a thing on it.'

'A thing?'

'Like a pattern.'

'Ah. A patterny thing.'

'Yes,' said Harper, fluffing out his newly plump plumage. 'A patterny thing. Like a big red star with wings.'

Alditha's face was suddenly serious. 'A what?'

'A big red-'

'Yes, I heard what you said,' she snapped, turning away from him for a moment.

'Well pardon me for breathing, I'm sure.'

'A red star with wings, a big red star with wings...' Ailditha moved through the cottage, going from the kitchen down a short passage and turning right, into her library. Harper flew after her.

'A red star with wings...I've seen that symbol...somewhere.'

'And is it a good symbol? Do we like that symbol? Are we hanging out bunting and having a bit of a dance about that symbol, or...are we not?'

'Harper dear, there are many subjects on which I'll be delighted to talk with you at almost any hour of the day or night, but just for this moment, I'd be obliged if you'd honour me by shutting your beak for a minute. The grown-ups are trying to think.'

'I'll shut my beak then,' said Harper haughtily. 'Not another word. The beak is closed. Silence is beak-shaped.'

'A red star...with wings,' muttered Ailditha yet again, looking along the rows and rows of books, some magical, some just ordinarily interesting. On the end of one shelf, Dramm jumped up and down, trying to attract her attention.

'Dramm, sit,' said Ailditha, and the new spell book settled down, seeming somehow crestfallen, as though she'd kicked it.

'Not a single, solitary peep shall leave this beak until commanded to speak,' said Harper.

Ailditha rolled her eyes.

———————

Unseen, in Ailditha's kitchen, the silver sphere she had been working on cracked open precisely down the middle, a series of yellow lights appearing on its surface and beginning to blink.

———————

'Who's the wizard?'

'Raa...'

'And who's the annoying pet who could be put down without a second thought *by* the wizard?'

'Arr.'

'Good. As long as that's clearly understood.' Skoros pressed a button on the wand, interrupting its flow of metal magic, and Razor gasped.

'Raaark. One day you'll…raaark, go too far with…that.'

Skoros smiled, almost sweetly, at the creature. 'And on that day, bird, your problems will be at an end. Won't they?'

Razor said nothing, his tongue poking quickly through his beak to get some air.

Skoros eased the mirror towards himself, forcing Razor to hop onto another strut of the great machine. The wizard reached behind the mirror and pulled a brass lily with a neck like a question mark.

'Mirror, mirror, on the wall, who is the greatest wizard of all?'

The mirror stayed completely, silently black.

'Mirror, mirror on the—oh, wait a minute,' said Skoros, grabbing the crank handle that stuck out of the side. He turned it five, six, seven times before something caught in the monstrous machine, and the whole assembly seemed to come to life. Cogs whirred, pistons pumped, a greasy grey steam slicked out here and there between the joints. Slowly the screen of the mirror flickered from black into life.

The word 'Booting' flashed up on the mirror's surface briefly, then vanished, replaced by a service message: *Mirrors 8.1. Who do you want to spy on today?'*

The chugging of the great machine was growing louder in the small room, and Razor put his wings over the sides of his head. The mirror finally cleared to a series of different, moving views of the Garden.

'Mirror, mirror, on the wall, who is the greatest—wait a minute. What's that?'

'Unable to comply,' said a warm, rich female voice coming out of the brass lily. 'Please re-state your request.'

'Never mind,' said Skoros. He pulled a brass keyboard out of a compartment in the half-machine, half-desk and ran a finger over a smooth pad set into its base. He tapped the pad twice, and one particular view of the Garden filled the whole of the mirror. 'Razor, look at that.' The bird still had his wings over his ears, so Skoros grabbed him round the body and pointed him at the mirror. 'Razor, look at *that*,' he repeated.

'Oh, really?' demanded the bird. 'I hate this bit. Look at the angle, what kind of brain are you asking me to go into here? Is this a weasel or something?'

Skoros checked a series of flashing lights on the keyboard. 'It's RoboFerret 7, since you ask. And you're going in. I need to see what's happening there.'

The screen seemed to show an enormous well, teacup, essentially, floating in mid-air some twenty feet up, down at Mill Bottom. But that was madness, surely?

Skoros pulled a small brass skullcap from a drawer, with wires trailing from it, which he slid into special holes in the machine-desk. Then he fitted the skullcap onto Razor's head. A flat metal strip held in his silver beak. Skoros pressed a button on the wand, and tiny darts snapped snugly into holes in Razor's head, hidden by feathers. The bird went rigid in an instant, staring straight ahead, and the image on the mirror grew larger and clearer, as RoboFerret 7—an unfortunate creature wearing the same skullcap, and with the same darts permanently embedded in its brain, stepped closer, round to the front of the Green Man's house.

'Ahh,' said Skoros, recognizing the place. Yes, it was a giant teacup, with a slab of darkness opening up in the side of it and—wait, what was that? 'Closer,' he yelled, and the Ferret scurried nearer to the improbable floating crockery. 'A red star, with wings?' said Skoros to himself, rubbing his naked chin and wishing for the thousandth time he had a full beard to stroke at moments like this. 'I know that symbol, from...' He shrugged. 'Somewhere.'

The image on the mirror froze, interrupted by another service message. *Your battery is critically low. Either connect to another power source now, refuel, or switch off to conserve power.*

Razor sagged, suddenly free of the machine. He whipped the skullcap off with a beat of his wings, spitting the beak-strap out with a loud 'Ptui.'

'Ach,' growled Skoros. 'More power? So soon? But I just cut down an acre of the forest, what? Three days ago?'

'It's your power to output ratio,' said Razor, sounding smug. ''s'like flying. You're flapping madly to just about stay in the air. What you need to do is find a thermal.'

'A what?' asked Skoros as he flicked switches and pulled levers, shutting the great machine down. The chugging and growling and hissing subsided, slowly, as the power was switched off and the contraption gradually became just another piece of odd metallic art.

'A thermal, raaaark. Pocket of warm air,' Razor replied, as though he was explaining to a five-year-old. 'Then you can glide, and soar. More energy in, from the hot air, less energy out, cos you're not flapping about like a goose in a gale force. Raaark.'

'Hmm,' said Skoros. 'Interesting. Actually interesting. But what I really need right now is more trees to burn.' He snapped his fingers, and the bird flew quickly up to his shoulder, its metal talons curling and piercing the robe. 'Fortunately, of course, the Green Man is a practically inexhaustible supply of tree.'

'Inex-raaaark-haustible?'

'Not to mention tremendous fun,' said Skoros. 'You cut a branch off him, he grows another in its place. It's hilarious.'

'Raark. Reckon he'd find it challenging though, not burning up if you threw him into the incinerator.'

'D'you know, I have a feeling you're right.' Skoros pushed open the doors with their elaborate cog-work decoration. 'Let's go and find out,' he said, waving the wand idly behind him, and hearing the wall re-seal itself with the smooth noise of clockwork and pistons, as he and Razor strode back down the corridor.

The Green Man peered through his window. In fact, he'd been peering through his window since the slab of blackness had appeared, waiting to see what other tricks the floating teacup had up its sleeve.

There was a long hissing sound, and then a person stepped through the slab of blackness and stood there on the lip of the hole.

It was a slim person with a fringe of blonde hair all the way around its head, and remarkable violet eyes the shape of almonds. Its nose was tiny, just a snub of a thing. Perhaps, thought the Green Man, it had missed school the day they'd been taught about growing noses, and had learnt to make do with what it had. The Green Man was no expert when it came to people's ages, because he counted in rings, rather than years, but he would have hazarded a guess this one was more than ten, and fewer than fifteen. And it's mouth…

Its mouth made the Green Man smile, without quite knowing why. It seemed to be permanently trying to hold in a grin, and, at the moment, it was doing quite well at it.

The person looked around the nook, blinking its big almond eyes. The Green Man was no expert when it came to guessing these things either, but he thought, given all the evidence he had at that moment, that it was a girl-person. A she.

The strange girl-person was dressed in a tight one-piece suit—trousers and top all together, with a thick collar round her neck, and it all shimmered in a rainbow-colour. Whenever he tried to really see what colour it was, he got the impression of it changing, as though it was playing with him. In the middle of her hair she wore a simple hairband. It, too, was of a colour that did that run-away-and-hide trick whenever the Green Man really stared at it. He blinked. Colours had never hidden from him before. He wondered why they'd decided to start now.

She looked quickly around to left and right, then nodded. She pulled an oblong metal box out of a pocket he couldn't see. It looked complicated to him, lights flashing and winking and throwing colour on her otherwise pale face. She pressed a button, and with a deep fizzing noise, a slide made of blue pulsing energy appeared, leading from the slab of blackness to the ground. The girl checked again to see if anyone was watching, then-

'Wheeeeeeeeee.'

She slid down, giggling and gurgling all the way, kicking long, probably-girl-person legs in the air. Once she reached the bottom, she stood up quickly and pressed a button on the device. The slide disappeared. She looked serious now, her grin gone. Then she waved the device around, left and right, and spoke.

The Green Man, who had excellent hearing, listened in wonder.

'Nice going, Alpha. You've put us down in the wrong zone. There are no orbs here.'

Despite his powerful, branch-like antennae ears, The Green Man couldn't quite hear the response from 'Alpha', but the girl frowned, whatever it was.

'Well, next time, maybe I *will*,' she said. 'Right, let's get started. What? No no, we're here now. I'm not trusting you to do shorts hops. You'll probably hop us all the way into the next galaxy by mistake.'

Again, there was a pause while the girl listened to the reply.

'Yeah, yeah,' she said. 'You can talk about quantum fluctuations in the dimensional and spatial harmonics and the planet being "bigger on the inside" till the g'zunk come home. We all know your problem. Honestly, what kind of bio-mech doesn't know left from right?'

There was another pause, then-

'D'you mind? I'm trying to be all official and important here? Right. Commander's log, planetary phase, first entry. We've landed on the planet designated the Garden, though in the wrong location, due to a navigational error by bio-mech Grey Alpha Squiggle Wiiirm 456. Am surveying the area to discover and re- Yes, you did.'

The Green Man narrowed his eyes behind his open window, wondering what she was talking about.

'Are we where we're supposed to be? Have we made contact with the orbs? Thank you, didn't think so. So, I have to put it in the log, don't I, or they'll only ask questions. Now quiet, I'm nearly finished. Am surveying the area to discover and re-establish contact with the orbs. There appears to be a dwelling of some kind here, which is strange because there wasn't meant to be any significant life on this planet at all. Anyway, will investigate. Am hoping to make contact with some examples of the dominant life-form. Log ends.'

The Green Man darted back from his window, looked around his kitchen. The yellow paint had spilled quite far over his wooden floor. He sighed. The quick way wasn't the right way to do things like this, but with his visitor intending to knock on his door any moment, there was no alternative. He reached out some roots and touched the paint-spattered floorboards. The paint bubbled, turned to a soft yellow wisp of gas, and disappeared. He closed his eyes and blew out his cheeks, and the paint that had covered him simply dissolved, as he put out his brightest bark, and forced fresh foliage out of the top of his head and along his shoulders. The kitchen still looked a little too sparse to receive new friends, but he decided, on this occasion, they would have to excuse him.

He'd no sooner decided that than his door went ZZZAP and disappeared. The girl with blonde hair and strange violet eyes stepped over the threshold and held up a hand.

'Hail, Gardling,' she said. 'I bring you greetings from the Astarian High Council. I am Commander of the Scout Ship Gol HuR 87.' She waved her little box of tricks in his direction. The box spoke in a soft, velvet-covered voice. 'Arboreal life form with regenerative capabilities and some highly developed folkloric undercurrents. Basically, a tree-oid. Sorry to disappoint you, but it looks like we've discovered the Planet of the Woodentops this time.'

'Hail, noble tree-oid,' said the girl, quickly hiding the machine behind her back.

'Err…well, yes. Erm…hail,' said the Green Man. 'Around these parts, we say hello.'

'Hello,' said the girl with gusto and without a second thought. 'Are tree-oids the dominant life form in the Garden?'

'Err…' said the Green Man. 'Well, I don't know about dominant. Come to that, I'm not entirely sure about tree-oids. I'm called the Green Man.' He extended an arm-branch, so his hand went out towards her.

'Hello, the Green Man,' she said, grinning, but ignoring the hand. 'My name's Celeste. I don't suppose you've seen any orbs lying about the place, have you?'

3

Old Tom was a potato farmer. In fact, he was both a potato and a farmer, and he worked the land down at Mill Farm. He didn't want for much in life, potatoes generally not being given too much in the way of ambition, but when he'd seen the teacup streak across the Garden sky, he'd been seized with a strong desire. A desire to dig up the starball he'd found.

Most of Old Tom's life, since the days when he'd been Young Tom and had grown the roots and shoots that served him as arms and legs, had been spent digging. He'd dig by day and he'd dig by night. He'd dig by feel and he'd dig by sight. Many of the Garden's farmers hired Old Tom to work their land, because most of them didn't like digging at all, and digging was Old Tom's thing.

That meant he'd spent most of his days looking down at the ground, as spade or blade turned the earth inside out, as he dropped in seeds and covered them up and dug another hole before the last one had settled. He looked up if you spoke to him directly of course, and over the years he'd learned to be as sociable as a potato ever needs to be; but most of the time, if you talked to Old Tom for more than a few minutes, you got the feeling he was getting fidgety, and his eyes would start to drift to the floor, and you just knew that his mind had gone back to his favourite occupation.

Which made it all the more strange that a week before, while much of the Garden was going about its business, Old Tom had looked up suddenly. Walking home from a visit to Brangle the elf, he'd been meandering by moonlight round the outskirts of Blue Dragon Forest when he'd felt a change in the wind, and as he looked up, he'd seen what looked like lots of new stars in the dark sky, twinkling like diamonds and rubies and a rainbow of other colours, all winking at him to keep their secrets. And then, from somewhere in the middle of the jewel-coloured stars, he'd seen something coming towards him, something falling out of the sky, like a big dead bird with no wings to fly. Old Tom had run, as fast as his wrinkly old roots would carry him, away from the falling star, but it had overtaken him and hit the ground with a boom that knocked him off his feet and sent his finest straw hat spinning.

When he'd remembered which way was up, he'd seen the trench the star had made when it fell—it was about forty feet long and disappeared some six feet into the ground. And there, stuck at the bottom of the trench, had been a glowing silver orb, steaming hot and blinking with yellow lights that flickered a little while, then died.

'Well that's right peculiar an' no mistake,' he'd muttered to himself, stepping into the trench to take a closer look at the fallen star. The steam had stopped wisping up into the night off the orb's surface, and he was able to get close to it without any danger.

'Fallin' stars,' he'd said, rubbing his brow. Then a thought had struck him. Ragbag, the scarecrow of West Field, was always bragging about the strange things he'd seen, or found—a frog with three legs or a conker he swore was as big as his head, or some such stuff and nonsense. *Bet he ain't never seen a fallen star before though*, Old Tom had thought, smiling as he calculated how much rosemary ale he'd be able to winkle out of the scarecrow for a look at a thing like that.

Without another thought, he'd buried the orb right there in its trench, getting a good hard bit of digging done in the process, and taken note of where it was, between the two big trees, fifty paces from the sign that told people that trespassers ran the risk of being eaten or roasted by Sagar, the Blue Dragon.

But truth be told, Old Tom hadn't given the orb much more thought. He'd meant to brag about it to Ragbag the next time he'd seen him, but the thing about having potato where a brain should be was that even things you especially wanted to remember sometimes leaked out and disappeared until something particularly reminded you of them all over again.

Old Tom had felt the wind change again that morning, and had looked up in time to see a giant flying teacup streak across the sky, heading for Mill Bottom and the Green Man's nook. And then he'd remembered his fallen star, and been gripped with a certainty that he should go and dig it up. That this mysterious orb had something to do with the flying crockery that had just arrived in his world seemed obvious, for it wasn't every day—or even every year—that the skies surrounding the Garden had produced so many strange portents.

'Somethin's afoot,' he muttered as he stomped towards the burning-trespassers sign again. 'Somethin's a great big stinky-socked foot, so it is.'

When he saw the large round hole in the ground where his fallen star should have been, he frowned and pushed his straw hat further up on the brown-skinned dome of his head.

'Stinky blinkin' socks,' he said, staring into the hole. 'Some beggar's nicked me, Star.'

Alditha sighed and pulled her eyebrows together. Other than an itch she couldn't quite reach, there was nothing more irritating than knowing she knew something, but not being able to remember what it was. She stared at the bookshelves, hoping they would reveal the riddle of the red star with wings, but the harder she concentrated, the further away she seemed to be from finding the memory. She knew it was an old thing, somehow associated with a book with yellowed, oddly smelling pages, rather than anything she'd seen in the last few years. But when she tried to reach out and touch the memory, it skittered away like a mouse under the floorboards of her mind. Her shoulders sagged.

'You can talk again,' she said.

Harper said nothing.

'I said you can talk again.'

'Nothin' to say, particularly.'

'Oh, don't sulk,' she said, reaching out a finger and scratching him under the chin. He resisted for a moment, then turned his head, to let her get to just the right spot. 'Maybe if I saw it for myself,' she pondered, 'it might trigger the memory.'

Harper shuddered. 'It's Skoros, I tell you. He's up to something devious. Why does nobody believe me?'

'Oh I don't *disbelieve* you,' said Alditha. 'It just doesn't seem his style, that's all. He's always been one for grand gestures, granted. But flying teacups? Hmm.' She paused and thought, placing a long finger onto each side of her head as if for inspiration. 'Okay then,' she said suddenly, having made up her mind. 'Guess what? We're going to pay the Green Man a visit today. Won't that be nice for him?'

'Erm,' said Harper. 'He mentioned something about polite guests sending messages ahead of time, so their hosts can tidy up the place and make sure to get in some strawberry marshmallows and lemon curd biscuits.'

Alditha raised an eyebrow. 'I'm a witch,' she said. 'The normal rules don't apply to me.'

'I shouldn't think the normal rules would dare,' said Harper without thinking.

Alditha grinned a broad grin. 'Good.'

Harper flew out of the library, heading back towards the kitchen. 'I suppose you're going to make me go on that wretched broom of yours again, are you?'

'Only way to travel.' Alditha called after him. She went and stroked Dramm's cover. 'You be a good book while I'm gone, you understand?' Dramm jumped up and down, nuzzling his cover against her hand. 'Sssshhh,' said Alditha softly.

'Ha,' said Harper. 'So says you. I'm an owl, I am. Fearsome airborne king of the night. Well, morning. Well, y'know what I mean. I hate that broom. I swear it doesn't like M.'

He stopped suddenly. Alditha kissed a fingertip and planted it softly on Dramm's cover. 'Be good,' she whispered.

'Alditha,' cried Harper. 'Alditha, come here. You're really gonna wanna see this.'

She smiled. Harper was one of the dearest friends she had, but he did get his talons in a twist occasionally. 'What is it?' she called.

'It's...it's...well, it looks familiar,' he replied. Alditha rolled her eyes and went back to the kitchen, stopping suddenly when she saw it. The orb, the metal ball she'd found and had been trying to make sense of for days, had sprouted metal wings either side of its body and appeared to be hovering there, in her kitchen, without even needing to flap.

'Hello,' said Alditha when she'd recovered from the shock. 'Can we...help you...at all?'

The yellow lights on the orb flashed and it made a chittering sound.

'Is that a yes?' Alditha asked.

The orb made some more meaningless noises, then turned and shot out through the open kitchen window, at a speed Harper could only envy.

'Damn,' said Alditha. She grabbed the handle of her broomstick out of the miniature cone of power in the corner, barely stopping to recognize her cleverness in putting it on charge overnight. She grabbed her hat from the hatstand and jammed it firmly on her head, where, if it had the sense it was stitched with, it would stay until she took it off. She ran out of the door, threw the broomstick in the air and wasn't in the least surprised when it hovered there. She jumped up and threw a leg over the broomstick, crouching low over the handle for take-off. 'C'mon Harper, before it gets away,' she said, and the owl reluctantly perched on her shoulder.

'Please state your destination,' said the broom in a neutral, wooden tone.

'I don't *have* a destination,' said Alditha. 'Just, oh I don't know, just *follow that orb.*'

The broom slid forward, slowly at first, then it rose higher and higher into the air, moving faster all the time.

———————

'Can't,' said Skoros, scowling. 'What do you mean I *can't?*' His wand-hand twitched.

Gunkin swallowed, regretting for the thousandth time listening to his mother. 'Henchmaning's a respectable career for a goblin,' she'd said, over and over again. 'Plenty of prospects,' she'd added. She'd been right of course. Being the henchman to a wizard like Skoros did bring plenty of prospects. It was positively brimming with the prospect of being turned into nothing more than a pair of boots and a wisp of smoke, for one thing. Then there was the prospect of having holes drilled into your head and being converted into a Robo-Goblin. There were plenty of prospects of that, too.

Plenty of prospects. Thanks, Ma, thought Gunkin bitterly.

'Well?' Skoros demanded.

'I didn't mean "can't", as such, your magical eminence,' Gunkin groveled. 'You *can* chuck the Green Man in the furnace. I mean, course you can, someone as powerful as yourself. Only…'

'Only *what?*'

Gunkin gulped. He felt the sweat prickle on the back of his neck. Goblins generally didn't sweat—it wasn't something they usually had a need for. But since entering Skoros' service, Gunkin had discovered a talent for it.

'Only, why would you do it, lord? I mean, you cut down an acre of ordinary trees, nobody says a word, nobody much notices. You burn fifty acres, who really cares? You burn *The Green Man*, and no-one's really sure what happens. Y'know…he's connected to the seasons, ain't he? To regrowth and renewal and all that gubbins. You burn him up, who knows? Maybe all the trees die overnight. Maybe it stays Summer. Like, forever. Disturbs the fundamental…y'know…balance of things, dunnit?'

'The fundamental…y'know…balance of things?' Skoros scoffed. 'Believe me, Gunkin, when my plans are activated, no-one will care about the fundamental y'know balance of things, ever again.'

'Yeah, well, of course,' said the purple goblin, still sweating. 'When your plans get up and running that's all well and good, your lordship. But…till then?'

Skoros sighed. 'Perhaps I should throw *you* in the furnace in his place.'

Gunkin laughed, a high-pitched, nervous, stuttering laugh. 'Oh my lord, you're in a fine fooling mood today, oh my word aren't you though?'

'Raark,' said Razor.

Skoros tried to raise one eyebrow. It was something he'd never quite mastered, so both eyebrows raised at the same time, making him look more surprised than menacing. He sighed again. 'Very well then. You, Gunkin, you personally, and you alone, will cut me down two acres of trees while I'm out investigating the new arrival in our world. Cut them, portion them, and feed them into the boiler. Do it by the time I return, or I'll come looking for you. Do I make myself clear?'

'Oh yes sir, your lordship, absolutely, clear as raindrops.'

'Good then. See to it.' Then he swept out, heading to the stables.

'Waaaaaaaaaaaaaaaaaaaaaaaargh,' squawked Harper, clinging on to Aalditha's shoulder for all his talons were worth. It was rare for Aalditha's broom to travel lightening fast, but she seemed determined to catch the orb, which was flying, still without having flapped its wings even once, some thirty feet ahead of them, zigzagging around and over trees and buildings. In the occasional moments when he took a break from being terrified for his life, he had the distinct feeling the orb was *playing* with them, like a game of Chase The Mouse, only where the mouse was in charge of the game.

Hanging on for dear life, Harper felt the night air surge around him. Aalditha's cloak streamed out behind and flapped about his face, threatening to knock him off his precarious perch. The owl nestled himself into the hollow of the witch's slender back as they sped on, faster and faster, further north, towards Blue Dragon Forest.

Peering out from behind Aalditha's cloak, Harper saw the Garden change from a landscape of meadows, hills and open countryside mixed with the ornate lawns and flowerbeds of the South Garden, to one of unknown shapes and dimensions. Its magic worked deeper and stronger, and, suddenly, he could distinguish the broad treeline of Blue Dragon Forest ahead of them, merging with vast rivers and mountains, oceans and fairy castles. The interchanging masks of the Garden clung to the owl, and, for a moment, he felt like they were flying over unknown distant lands, wondrous and fair.

I wish my Garden wasn't so scary at times, he thought to himself. *Am I really the only one who can see all this?*

'Aalditha,' he said. Aalditha didn't hear him, she was focused on flying the broomstick and catching the orb. 'Aalditha.'

'What?' Aalditha yelled back, her voice caught by the wind and thrown away almost before it reached him.

'What do you *see* down there?' He almost screamed.

She laughed. 'Scaredy cat. It's only Blue Dragon Forest. So what? Sagar won't burn you or eat you while you're with me. Don't worry.'

Harper looked down again at the vast, unfamiliar expanse of geography spooling out beneath them—and at Blue Dragon Forest at the same time.

'Just that?' he cried, needing to be sure. 'Just Blue Dragon Forest?'

Alditha chuckled. 'That's my brave owl. Yes, it's *just* Blue Dragon Forest, absolutely.'

Harper hooted softly against her back. 'That's what I thought you'd say,' he muttered, far too quietly for her to hear.

Carefully steering her broomstick, Alditha swooped down, skimming the dark treetops as she did so. The smell of pine and damp woodland grew ever stronger as the forest appeared out of the swirling landscape below. Here was the beginning of the North Garden.

'Hang on,' she yelled back to Harper. 'I'm going to try something.'

Harper curled his talons into the fabric of her black cloak even further.

'Broom, broom, tried and true,

Make me magic's best lasso.'

Harper peeked out around Alditha's side, not liking what he'd heard. Sure enough, the broom slowed down slightly, allowing the orb to put a little more distance between them. Alditha gripped the broomstick hard, pulled it upward, then flicked it down. Harper saw a rope of golden dust zip out of the front of the broomstick, like a loop of power spooling out from the tip of the broom. It looped around the flying orb and tightened. Immediately, the broom sped up, forcing Alditha to grip on with her knees, and Harper to close his big eyes. They were dragged around the sky, up and down and loop-the-loop, till Harper wished he hadn't had *quite* so much breakfast with the Green Man.

'Waaaaaaaaaaaaaaaaaaargh,' he said again, and was mystified to hear the sound of Alditha giggling helplessly as they rode the sky, no longer under their control.

He dared to open one eye again to see what she was giggling about, but couldn't understand it. Then he saw the orb turn a fuzzy, glowing red. The colour grew deeper, and deeper as he watched.

'Errr…Alditha.'

'I see it,' she yelled. 'Did I mention you might want to hold on TIGHT?'

Suddenly the red colour flared, and the golden 'rope' of magic connecting the sphere and the broomstick snapped, falling away into sparkles.

The broomstick, which had grown accustomed to flying at the speed of the orb, shot past it, and Alditha lost control. They went tumbling head over wings over feet, time and time and time again across the sky, somersaulting wildly in mid-air. Through the chaos and the colour and the feeling really sick, Harper heard the broomstick speaking calmly.

'Turn around when possible,' it instructed them.

'Nooooooooo ppppppprrrrrrobnbbblemmm,' said the owl as they tumbled through the air.

There comes a point, when tumbling through the air, when it stops being something the air is willing to let you do. It decides you've had your fun, and drops you to the ground like a hot frog.

The air dropped them to the ground like a hot frog.

Alditha landed with an 'unff' and Harper, who had more experience at difficult landings, tucked his wings around himself and closed his eyes. He bounced along the forest floor like a pebble flung across a lake. When he finally landed, there was a soft, wet thud.

'Harper?' demanded Alditha, laying on her back with her hat down over her eyes. 'Are you alright, bird-friend of mine?'

Harper groaned. 'I feel like mouse-food.'

Alditha grinned beneath the brim of her hat. Then, as if from nowhere, she began to chuckle.

'Something funny, you broomstick-riding eyebrow-waggler?'

'We've lost it,' said Alditha through what were becoming gut-laughs. 'We've lost the orb. But did you see it *move*?' She burst into laughter again.

'I saw it nearly get us killed,' snapped Harper, struggling for the third time that day to find his feet after a bad landing.

'Let me guess,' said Alditha. 'It's Skoros' fault.'

Harper flicked his gaze around the patch of forest where they'd crashed. He hadn't thought of it till now, but it would be just the wizard's style to build something so monstrous.

'Wouldn't be surprised,' he said, and Alditha exploded into fits of laughter again.

'You have reached your final destination,' said the broom, and Alditha howled even louder.

Harper worried, though. It was alright for Alditha, she was a witch. Although she was generally a 'good' witch...a witch was still a witch. There wasn't much that tried to eat them. But there were plenty of things in Blue Dragon Forest that might decide a little *Harper* between meals was just the snack they needed to see them through till lunch.

There was Sagar, the Blue Dragon himself, for one. Harper found the floor of the forest quickly and narrowed his eyes, looking for anything that might be keen to nab itself an owl sandwich. He was probably safer in Alditha's company, but felt like leaving immediately. He was upset at her reckless behavior.

———

'I'm forgetting something,' said Celeste, frowning in a way that didn't crease her forehead.

'The gifts,' said Alpha, its voice a little tinny and muffled. Now he was closer, the Green Man could see that when the voice spoke, Celeste's headband glowed gently.

'Oh yes.' Celeste stuck her hand in a trouser pocket that seemed to be there only when her hand approached it. She pulled out a small satin bag, tied with a ribbon, and the Green Man watched her pocket disappear again. She held the bag out to him.

'Oh. Erm...thank you,' he said, curling branchy fingers around the bag. He opened it up. 'Erm...yes. Thank you, again,' he added. Inside were a small collection of perfectly round balls—some silvery-grey, others pulsing in colours that the Green Man couldn't quite make out. He smiled. 'What are they?' he asked, trying to sound polite.

Celeste shrugged. 'Just tokens from me to you, to show my squigirrrkle intentions on this planet.'

'Your what, sorry?' The Green man frowned at her.

'My squigirrrkle intentions on this planet.'

'That's what I thought you said. I'm sorry, what does-?'

'Alpha, run a tighter linguistic sub-routine,' said Celeste. 'What's Gardenese for squigirrrkle?'

There was a long moment of silence, before Alpha replied: 'Peaceful.'

Celeste frowned again, that same frown that never reached her forehead. 'Are you sure? Seems to lose something in the translation.'

'Confirmed,' said Alpha. 'Peaceful.'

Celeste shrugged. 'Oh well, there you go. My *pees-full* intentions on this planet.'

'Ah,' said the Green Man. 'Good. Best intentions, I've always thought.'

Celeste waited. She smiled. She rocked back and forth a little on her heels. Then finally she said 'Do you…have any tokens for me?'

'Ah,' said the Green Man, catching on. 'Oh. Errr…yes, I'm sure I have something. Do you like strawberry marshmallows? They're my favourite.'

'Alpha?' asked Celeste. There was another long moment before the reply came back.

'Strawberry marshmallows—no information.'

Celeste rolled her big violet eyes. 'Sorry about him,' she said. 'He tries hard, but he's a bit rubbish, as Greys go. I'm sure straw-berry marsh-minnows would be perfectly acceptable.'

'Mallows,' said the Green Man as he went to fetch some from his cupboard. He felt a pang of sorrow at having to part with his favourite treats, but he was a good host. He put the bag of little balls that Celeste had given him in the drawer where he kept his marshmallows, and offered the sweets to Celeste. She looked at them, then back at the Green Man.

'You *eat* them,' he said, taking one and popping it into his mouth. As always happened when he ate strawberry marshmallows, he smiled a big broad smile, and leaves grew fresh and deeply green along his arms.

Celeste blinked at him and took a sharp breath. The Green Man gulped. 'Oh, don't worry,' he said, trying to reassure her. 'I'm sure you won't grow leaves. Well, fairly sure, anyway. I have a friend, Harper, and he's never grown leaves from eating marshmallows, I promise.'

Celeste looked at him curiously, then picked a marshmallow from his hand, popped it into her mouth and chewed it, making a face.

'Mmm,' she said, still chewing, trying her best not to disappoint the Green Man. 'It's like eating a frrrninkle…only fruity.'

'A frrrninkle?' queried the Green Man.

'Alpha?' said Celeste.

'Nearest translation for frrrninkle…slug,' said Alpha, its voice coming through Celeste's softly glowing headband.

'There you are. It's like eating a fruity slug,' said Celeste, struggling to swallow the marshmallow. 'Sorry about the translation software. I really should upgrade it, but you know how it is—every time they release an upgrade you have to reboot your whole scout ship, and it does tend to fall out of the sky when you do that. Anyway, that's the diplomacy out of the way-'

The Green Man pulled his small collection of strawberry marshmallows back. He wasn't entirely sure he liked them being thought of as fruity slugs. He knew one or two slugs who wouldn't be best pleased with the comparison either. Still, if Celeste didn't want them, it meant there were more left for him. He had an idea and extended his hand towards the strange girl-thing again. He grew a single, small, pristine leaf from the top of his finger.

'For you,' he said. 'More portable than marshmallows.'

Celeste softly took the leaf from his finger and gazed at it, turning it over. It was one of his best and greenest, and it shimmered green and gold as she examined it. Then she lifted it to her mouth.

'No,' said the Green Man hastily. 'That's not for eating. That's part of me. You just keep it, and when you look at it, it will remind you of your friend.'

'Oh.' Celeste blinked those big violet eyes again. 'Thank you.' She slid the leaf down the outside of her tunic, and a pocket opened up to take it, then disappeared again.

'What's that?' she gasped, turning to look at the hole where the Green Man's front door used to be. The Green Man turned and looked. There was nothing there to see.

But Celeste could hear something approaching—a something that was loud to her ultra-sensitive alien ears…

4

'Bloomin' witches,' Harper muttered, stomping in the undergrowth extra hard in case Alditha was listening. 'Bloomin' wizards. Nobody listens around here, but that wizard's a bloomin' menace, with his hexperiments, and his whizzing balls of blitherin' doom and his bats-'

He stopped and shuddered. The bats. He leaned backward, scanning the leaves of the trees, looking for anything black and grey and whispery. Listening for the wingbeat of the wretched creatures.

Normally, he was good at leaning back, but he was having a distracted day, and he didn't realize what was happening till he began to fall backward. He scrabbled with his talons, managing to stay upright, and hoping Alditha hadn't seen him.

'Harper,' she called.

Harper didn't answer her. He wasn't ready yet to forgive her for laughing at him. Then he heard her sturdy boots coming through the soft undergrowth of the forest.

'Harper,' she called again, more urgently this time. 'Where are you, darling bird? Are you sulking?'

There she went again. He wasn't sulking. He was doing his job as her familiar and her friend, trying to warn her about the wizard and his flying teacups and his flying silver balls of speedy death and, and, *everything*. And she wouldn't take him seriously.

'Ah, there you are,' she said.

He turned his back to her.

'Are you scared?' she asked, softly. When he didn't answer her, she began to intone a soft, plaintive mantra with a strong agricultural feel. Quickly, her chant became louder, clearer, turning into a type of song. Then, as if reciting a prayer to the forces of nature, she slowly sang a little verse:

'Earth, water, fire and air,

Yours is the gown of the wanderer fair.

Myrrh, gold and frankincense, amethyst rare,

Ours is the crown of the kingdom to wear.'

As she finished singing, Harper felt a warm red glow surround him. He could even see the glow, just a little.

'Safe now,' said Alditha. 'Safe from everything in the forest.'

Harper didn't answer her for a long, long moment. ''cept the bats,' he said then.

'It's daytime,' said Alditha reasonably. 'Skoros' bats don't come out till nighttime.'

'Says the witch who thought it was a good idea to lasso a silver ball of death,' muttered Harper.

'You're not being fair,' she said, her voice hardening. 'We have no evidence it meant us any harm.'

'Is *it* lying abandoned in the middle of Blue Dragon Forest, then?' he demanded, turning to face her. 'Is *it* lucky to have escaped with its wings intact? No, it isn't, is it? That would be us, wouldn't it? And *it* would be the one who's whizzed off back to Skoros Castle to tell its master all about Alditha the witch and Harper the owl, the numpties it left bowling about the sky like a pair of prize conkers.'

'Thought you said Skoros would be in the teacup,' said Alditha. 'Besides, we have no evidence that Skoros built the orb.'

'Oh please,' said Harper, clacking his beak together. 'Who else creeps about making all those *metal* things?'

Alditha opened her mouth to reply, but then her eyebrows drove down in a thoughtful frown, and her mouth clamped shut again. 'That's a good question,' she said. 'That might be the cleverest thing you've said all day, you bright bird.' She stuck a finger in her ear and waggled it about, which Harper knew meant she was trying to re-arrange some things in her head. It didn't seem to work, and she pulled the finger out again and peered at it. Then she huffed and shrugged. 'I think you'd better show me this flying teacup,' she admit-ted. 'What do you think?'

'I think that could be insanely dangerous, that's what I think,' said Harper honestly.

'Well if it's insanely dangerous, you wouldn't want the Green Man to face it, would you?'

Harper whistled. He hadn't even thought about that when he'd flown off to tell Alditha the news. He'd abandoned his friend to the mercy of the wizard and his deadly flying teacup. He flapped his wings and landed on her shoulder, then turned around to face the same way as her.

Alditha patted his talons gently, then reached out her other hand.

'Broom, broom, tried and true,

Come to me; it's time we flew.'

The broomstick shot from where it had landed on the forest floor, straight to Alditha's hand, and she threw one leg over it, crouching forward.

'Oof,' she said. 'Next time we leave the cottage, remind me to bring my cushion. It's no fun riding a broomstick without a saddle.'

'Woo,' said Harper, still trying not to be too friendly. She'd won him with the idea of saving the Green Man, but her refusal to admit it was Skoros who was controlling the sphere still rubbed him the wrong way. As if it could be anybody else.

More slowly than before, they began to rise into the air, and as they cleared the treeline, Alditha steered the broom around in a big lazy circle.

'You have reached your destination,' said the broom, automatically pointing its front end towards the ground.

Alditha bent low over the broom and whispered to it. 'And that's quite enough out of you,' she said, 'or do we need to have the *conversation* again? You know, the one about *firewood*?'

The broom rose quickly again. It didn't say another word.

They were heading towards Mill Bottom when Alditha gasped and yanked the broom suddenly sideways.

'Whoah,' said Harper. He'd stopped paying attention to where he was again, so the sideways lurch took him by surprise. 'What the—?'

'Sorry Harper. I've got to check something out.'

'What? Where are- Oh nooo.' He realized with a sickening lurch that they were heading towards Skoros Castle.

'I've got to,' Alditha said, urgency forming ice crystals on her words.

'Got to go see the wizard? Well you can count me out, then. No way am I getting caught near that place.'

'There's something strange happening over there, look.'

'I will not,' said Harper, stubbornly closing his big owlish eyes. 'Something strange,' she says. 'Surprise, surprise. I don't know how many times I have to tell you this, but it's *Skoros*. Something Very Strange is what he does before breakfast. And breakfast is a big huge bowl of Strangeness. He has Weird for lunch, and Creepy for tea, with a few Despicable Evil bars in between.'

'Yes, yes,' said Alditha, clicking her tongue at him. 'But this is *really* strange.'

'Oh, as opposed to all the made-up strangeness I'm talking about, I suppose? Go on, say it, you think I'm just making things up, don't you? Well I'm not staying here to be called a liar and turned into bat-food, Miss High and Mighty, Ooh Look At Me, I'm A Witch. You're on your own.'

And Harper unhooked his talons from her shoulder and flew off, heading in the direction of the Green Man's house.

Alditha couldn't believe what she was seeing. Trying not to worry about Harper and his quick exit, she had been circling the wizards' castle for a good half an hour.

For all Harper's warnings, she'd known Skoros since they were at school, before her magic had even introduced itself to her. Everybody'd expected Skoros to become a wizard of course, but she remembered him as a lanky, pale schoolboy, too unsure of himself to be noticed if he hadn't been the son of one of the biggest wizarding families in the Garden. She'd sent a note when his father had died, had tried to express her sorrow for his loss.

He'd never acknowledged her letter.

She'd heard the rumours, the tittle-tattle that said he was involved in some unusual magic. From time to time, whole families of ferrets or birds or rabbits had come to her door, complaining that one of their number had been stolen away by 'the lonely wizard' and forced into magical slavery. Alditha wouldn't believe it. She usually explained that sometimes, bad things happened to good ferrets. It didn't seem fair to us when we loved those ferrets, or birds, or rabbits, because we felt the loss of them in our lives. But in the turning of the Great Wheel, everything was equal and everything made sense. Next year, new life would take the place of those we loved and the Wheel would turn again.

Now though, as she hovered at what was hopefully a safe distance from Skoros Castle, she wondered if there might not be something to the stories after all.

The castle, which, in memory of Skoros' father, she privately still thought of as Subracken Castle, was built on a high peak, poking up through a mass of dark, thick trees that had always threatened to strangle its walls and turrets. Skoros' great great grandfather had planted them, partly, it was said, because he liked to hunt things that went squeak and squished when he hit them, and a forest was the best place to find such creatures, and partly, it was said more loudly and by the old man himself, because if anyone had a quarrel with him they could go and get lost—and nowhere got you more thoroughly lost than a forest.

Alditha blinked. Anyone who had a quarrel with Skoros would have to work extra hard to get lost. The forest appeared to have been chopped down. There was not a single tree left within half an acre of Skoros Castle, meaning the wizard's home stood cold and looked naked on its peak, like a schoolboy who'd forgotten his PE kit, and was standing there all knees and embarrassment while the landscape laughed at him.

As she watched, she saw a tree fall on the border between the forest and the naked landscape. A few minutes later, another followed it. A few minutes after that, a third fell.

Alditha raised an eyebrow at the mysterious falling trees, and steered the broom downwards to investigate.

The Green Man was still listening, though he could hear nothing yet, despite his exceptional sense of hearing. However, Celeste seemed delighted with whatever it was she could hear. 'It can't be,' she said. 'Can it?'

The Green Man shrugged. He had no idea if it could be or not. But then, suddenly, he heard it too. It sounded like nothing he'd ever experienced in the Garden before.

There was groaning and wheezing and graunching and puffing and thudding and squealing and, probably, he thought, a whole range of sounds for which the Garden had never had to think up descriptions. And it was getting closer. Very fast.

It's coming here, thought the Green Man with a sigh. *More visitors.*

If he was honest, the Green Man wasn't happy about the idea. His stash of marshmallows and lemon curd biscuits was running dangerously low. But before he'd had long to admonish himself for the selfishness of that thought, the noise grew deafening. It added clanking and rumbling and hissing and grinding to its repertoire.

'Excuse me,' said the Green Man, moving past Celeste and going outside. She followed him quietly, waving her oblong instrument at the space where the door had been. With a zap that neither of them heard, the door reappeared.

The Green Man blinked. It was Skoros, but it was Skoros as the Green Man had never seen him before. He was sitting, high up on the back of a…a *thing*. It was a big, bronze, thing-that-definitely-wasn't-a-horse. It had clearly been *modelled* on a horse—four legs, broad back, long neck, tail. But the degree to which this monstrosity wasn't a horse was huge and mortifying. It was paneled in strips of bronze, with heavy rivets holding the strips together along its back and up its belly and chest. Where each of the legs joined the body were huge cogs that turned when it moved. Each of the beast's knees was an intricate shining flywheel, with wires running round it, feeding into what looked like pistons underneath. There were other whirring and ticking and whizzing wheels and cogs along the length of its body, sometimes punching holes in the strips of bronze, sometimes seeming to join them together and turning like clockwork. The most disturbing way in which this thing was not a horse though was that it only had one half of a face. The half it did have had been moulded by someone who clearly thought they knew what a horse looked like, but really, really didn't. And the other side—the empty side—was open to the air, showing pistons working inside the thing's head. Skoros was perched precariously on the moving thing's back, with his wizard's robes tucked into his riding boots. He sneered down at the Green Man, and even further down at Celeste.

'Hello, Skoros. Nice… erm… *thing* you've got here.'

'It's a horse,' snapped Skoros.

The Green Man blinked at it again. 'It really isn't, you know.'

'Its Horse 2.0,' Skoros explained quickly. 'Better than the original.' He pulled a lever at the front of the saddle, and the Horse 2.0 reared up on its hind legs, with a creaking, metal-scraping noise that made the Green Man shudder. The enormous front hooves seemed to loom above his head.

One wrong move and they could trample me to matchwood, he thought.

Skoros twisted a dial and the Horse 2.0's half-finished head raised. There was a horrible hissing sound, a gurgle, a dark, ominous bubbling noise, then twin jets of fire shot out of the horse's nostrils, setting fire to some petunias, and leaving a dripping, oily smell where the flames hit.

Skoros laughed. 'See? Better in every way.'

The Green Man's eyes widened in sadness. 'Unless...unless you like petunias,' he babbled.

'Oh, fab,' said Celeste. 'This is just...I mean, I haven't seen a retro-biological construct built from hand in aaaages.' The girl ran a hand up the Horse 2.0's leg. 'Mmm...bit clunky here and there, but I know how it is—you can't get the parts, right?' She looked up at Skoros, nodded at him. ''S'that why the face looks so weird? Ran out of plating, did you? Should try incorporating actual bio-elements next time. Trust me, bio-mechanoids are what all the universe is doing this millennium.'

Skoros straightened his spine, sitting stiffer in the saddle.

'*Love* what you've done with the quirky shape though. I mean it's not right, obviously, but still...'

'Big words for a child who lives in a *teacup*,' said Skoros.

'Mmm,' said Celeste, not listening, feeling her way around the horse, keeping a hand flat against it. 'Loose rivet there. And your hull stress is all to pot. Ride this thing anywhere near top speed, it'll shake itself to bits in about ten minutes. Mmm, what?' She looked up. 'Oh, the scout ship? Oh it's not really a whatever-you-said. That's just a randomly generated image, based on something native to this world. The Council orders us not to scare the local life forms. Oh that reminds me—have you seen any orbs around here recently. Metal? Round? Not in disguise? Erm...probably flying about making a nuisance of themselves? My name's Celeste, by the way. Hello. What's *your* name?'

Skoros was turning an unflattering shade of purple, infuriated at the child's refusal to be intimidated by his machine. 'I am Skoros. I am a wizard, thankyouverymuch, and I'll thank you to keep your grubby little hands off my Horse 2.0. You,' he demanded, pointing a thin finger at Celeste and narrowing his eyes. 'You understand the magic of metal? Then you are my prisoner. Get up here.' He twisted a handle, and with a grinding noise, the Horse 2.0 bent its knees, lowering to the ground.

Celeste blinked. 'Well, that's just rude,' she said, and twiddled a lever, pointing her oblong instrument at the Horse. There was a strange squiggle of noise, then with an urgent release of steam from underneath its tail, the metal creature rose again.

'Wait,' yelled Skoros. 'Stop. What are you doing?' He pulled his corkscrew wand from his robe-arm and pointed it at Celeste's head. 'You are my prisoner.'

'Don't think so,' she replied, and with an awful metal graunching noise, the Horse 2.0 began galloping backward the way it had come, Skoros' yells of rage drifting back to them.

'Stoooooooop. Stoooooooop, you metal…'

Celeste frowned at the Green Man. 'Strange man.'

The Green Man thought about agreeing with her, but then thought better of it—you never knew who was listening.

Celeste went and crouched by the burned flowers. She waved her device at them, and it beeped, just once. 'Alpha?' she asked. There was a long moment of silence, then her headband glowed.

'Thermic damage too extreme. Internal structures compromised beyond repair.'

Celeste nodded slowly. She stood up, faced the Green Man, cupped her hands and blew on them, as though blowing him a hundred sad kisses. 'Sorry for your loss,' she said. 'Must have been the landing pulse beam that did it. Astaria is in your debt for their lives.'

The Green Man was about to say it was Skoros who had burned the petunias, but he stopped himself. There was something about Celeste's solemnity that touched him, as though she understood the pain he felt.

'Now,' she said, 'I must get on. Clearly, the orbs are playing hard to get. I am glad I met you, Green Man.' And she extended her hand to him again, then turned away before he could shake it, marching off down the road, consulting her device, and occasionally firing questions back to Alpha.

This, thought the Green Man, as she disappeared from view, *has been a most peculiar morning.*

Then he heard a familiar noise. The noise of wings flapping frantically, a yell of 'Oh bother,' the rhythmic banging and screeching of an owlish body bouncing along a working surface and clawing its way along an old oak dresser.

Harper had returned.

———————

The orbs were flying higher, one from the east, the other from the west, aiming at a point where, had anyone in the Garden been able to see them through the clouds, they'd have worried they were going to smash together and explode. The eastern sphere was spinning bottom to top as it flew, doing backward rolls as it soared upward. The western sphere was spinning right to left, like a planet with a thousand days and nights passing by in half a heartbeat. They screamed silently up and up, and in a moment that bent mathematics all out of shape, they—didn't collide. Instead, they began to circle round each other, first the east round the west, then the west round the east, at a speed which grew faster and faster till they were invisible, just a steel-grey blur, glowing yellow, then red with heat as their movements sped up.

The red yellowed out to white, to blue, to sparks that spat from the spinning centre. Then the sparks grew arms—eight long, slow silent lightning bolts that stretched out across the Garden sky, like questing fingers, looking to point out six points on the ground. As the orbs spun, invisible, the lightning fingers wagged, slid streaky through the air, and eventually shot forward and touched the earth at eight points, the lightning crackling and steaming the ground. If anyone on the ground had been able to see it, it would have looked like a giant spider made of light, with a tiny spinning body suspended on eight long legs.

Then, in an instant, the legs vanished, and at each of the eight points where they had touched the ground, there was a small explosion, that threw earth up into the air.

Far, far above the Garden, the orbs vanished with a flash.

5

Something odd is happening in my garden.

Did you see it happen? The spinning thing?

I often see strange things in my garden, when it does the Thing it does. Sometimes—you won't believe this, but it's true—I think I see a tiny owl, flying around the place, no bigger than a bumblebee. I sometimes see black bats too, with wingspans no wider than a thumbnail—but when I think I see the bats, I close my eyes until they're not there anymore.

I've never seen a spinning thing before. That must mean it's new.

In any case, the spinning thing is gone now. It came shooting up out of my garden, like a speck of brilliant dust. It glowed like a diamond and it zipped up into the sky, so small I could barely see it at all. Then it disappeared altogether.

I wonder if that's a good thing, or bad.

What do you think?

————————

'Oi.'

Another tree creaked and groaned, then began falling directly in Alditha's path. She walked forward, the shadow of the tree growing long over her. At the last second, she stepped sideways, then carried on walking along the length of the fallen tree without breaking her stride. She patted its bark and drew her eyebrows together, ready for combat.

'I said oi.' Normally, whenever she said 'Oi' at someone they stopped what they were doing and looked up. Some of the Garden's brighter inhabitants had been known to run indoors and barricade themselves in their cellars at an 'Oi' from Alditha.

'Did ya now?' said a voice from behind the base of the most recently fallen tree.

Alditha grinned. The day was about to get interesting. 'I did, yes.'

'Are you my master then?' said the voice, the source of which she still couldn't see.

'Your master is Skoros, yes?'

'That's *Lord* Skoros, to you, stranger, Dark Lord Of All He Surveys, innit?'

Alditha burst out laughing. 'Is that what he's got you all calling him these days? Good grief. Anyway, what are you up to? Cutting down all these beautiful trees—what's that about?'

Gunkin stood up straight, his pointed ears emerging from the other side of the tree trunk, followed by his pronged nose and pointed chin.

'Oh, it's you, is it?' said Alditha. 'Gunkin Pimplebutt, as I live and breathe.'

'Lady Alditha, white-ish-if-you-get-her-in-the-right-mood witch of this parish,' said Gunkin, nodding slightly.

Alditha raised one eyebrow at the goblin's impertinent assessment. 'I know your mother,' she warned. 'They tell me you can talk the shoes off a horse or the teeth off a troll. What're you doing here, chopping down trees?'

'Henching,' said Gunkin, picking up his axe.

'Well, stop it at once,' said Alditha, her eyebrows arching.

Gunkin looked up at her eyebrows. He ran his tongue over his teeth. 'Make me a better offer,' he said.

'No.'

Gunkin flung his axe casually behind him—it landed with precision a foot from the base of the next tree along. 'Sorry.' He smiled. When goblins smile, it's a peculiar thing—unless they take the time to arrange all their teeth in a particularly friendly way, it looks like a mouthful of threats.

'What are you henching *for*?' demanded Alditha.

'For?' asked Gunkin. 'Well for money, innit? For a job. For...' He shuddered, remembering his mother's words. '...*career prospects*.'

'*Good* career prospects, are they? Fancy yourself as a career chopper-down of innocent trees, do you? Stop this foolishness at once, Gunkin Pimplebutt, or I'll box your ears for you.'

Gunkin took the time to arrange his teeth. 'It's not that I don't see the persuasive, shall we say, force of your arguments, Lady Alditha. But it's simple—if I don't stop, you'll box my ears. If I *do* stop, Lord Skoros, Dark Lord Of All He Surveys will box my ears—and my head—and send them to my mother for Midsummer Hallowe'en.'

Alditha's eyebrows went to war. 'What's he *need* all this wood for anyway? He can't be that cold, it's nearly Mid-'

There was a moment of odd silence. Alditha realized Gunkin wasn't looking at her anymore. She followed his eye line to the sky, where lightning-bolt legs were slowly making their way down towards the Garden. She squinted—there seemed to be a bright spot getting bigger and bigger in her way, like a moon growing out of nowhere. Alditha tilted her head slightly to the side and frowned at it, to get a better perspective. It was—it was heading straight for them.

'It's coming straight for us,' said Gunkin.

'It's moving slowly though,' said Alditha, squaring her shoulders and hitching up her skirt. She straightened her hat on her head, folded her arms and stared at the oncoming finger of light. 'I'm betting it blinks first.'

'You're barking mad, aren't you?' Gunkin yelped, looking from Alditha to the lightning and back again.

'What I am is either right or wrong,' said Alditha. 'Madness has nothing to do with it either way.'

Gunkin rolled his eyes. 'Look, I tell you what. How about I stop henching at once and come along quietly with you? Skoros, Dark Lord Of All He Surveys can chop his firewood, how about that? Only let's get out of the way of the lightning.'

'That look like lightning to you then, does it?'

'Well,' said Gunkin, frowning at it, 'mostly. It's a bit slow, I grant you.'

'Seen a lot of slow lightning before, have you?'

'Well no,' said Gunkin. 'Not as such, but-'

'So what does that tell you?'

The bright leg of light was getting closer and brighter and bigger as they watched.

Gunkin shrugged. 'I give up, what does it tell you?'

Alditha's eyebrows drove further down as she stared at the ball of light that was inching towards her face. 'Tells me it's Something Else Entirely,' she said, frowning under the brim of her hat.

'Oh, that's great,' Gunkin panicked. 'I'll tell them to put that on your gravestone, shall I? Lady Alditha, white-ish witch of these parts, killed by Something Else Entirely. That'll look good, won't it?'

The lightning, or the Something Else Entirely, was close now. The brightness of it burned Alditha's eyes to look at, but she wouldn't turn away, and she wouldn't step aside. She could feel the energy of it crackle and it made her nose itch. She took a breath in, and the air was warm with the lightning's touch.

There was a crackle, and a zap, and Alditha blinked hard, unsure what had happened.

When she saw it, she smiled in witchy satisfaction. 'See? What did I tell you? Something Else Entirely.'

'You cannot have known that would happen,' cried Gunkin.

'You're just- just- impossible.'

The lightning was still pulsing through the sky, but where it should have touched Alditha and turned her into so much witch-bacon in some sensible boots, it was as if the energy itself had stepped sideways around her, and thudded into the ground a foot to her left, and a foot behind her.

'I know,' said Alditha, grinning at him like a mouthful of sugar lumps. 'Annoying, isn't it?'

The spot where the lightning had hit exploded in a shower of earth and wood chips.

Old Tom was befuddled. To be fair to him, he was upside-down with his head in the earth and his legs in the air, which is enough to befuddle almost anyone. He'd watched the lightning amble down through the sky, and then suddenly jump the last ten feet, hitting the earth with a whumpf. Then he hadn't seen anything else, because the whumpf had turned the world on its head and pitched him skyward, landing him back to front with a thud.

Dig, thought Tom. *Dig, y'ol' fool, and dig now.*

He dug, using his powerful hands to push the earth away from his face. He did a backward press-up, pushing his legs back until they made contact with the soft ground. When he was standing the right way up again, he used his hat to wipe the soil off his face, and turned round to where the lightning had hit.

There was a crater.

A small crater, no bigger than twice his size, but a crater nevertheless. Old Tom walked up to the lip of earth and peered in.

His eyes widened.

'Stinky blinkin' socks,' he said, almost falling into the hole.

There, at the bottom of the crater, was another orb. Older-looking, not quite so complicated, and covered in earth and the occasional rather surprised worm, but with its lights already blinking. As he watched, the ball sprouted wings, and shot up out of the hole, flying fast and high till it was out of sight.

'Another one,' Old Tom said in disbelief. 'I've blinkin' lost another one.' He flung his hat onto the ground and stamped on it. 'Wretched bloomin' blinkin'…' he yelled and trampled the hat into the mud.

———

'Easy now,' whispered Alditha to Gunkin. 'Don't alarm it.'

Gunkin looked sideways at it. 'Alarm it?' he hissed. 'What in the name of Sagar's Satchel *is* it?'

Alditha grinned, not taking her eyes off the sphere that had flown up out of the hole the lightning had made. 'Something Else Entirely,' she whispered.

'Oh, deep. That's being a witch, is it?' said Gunkin. 'Saying something vague and meaningless and grinning at the same time? I can see why everyone's scared of you lot.'

Alditha raised an eyebrow. 'Anyone ever told you you're an annoying goblin?'

'Most people, since you mention it.'

'Good. Haven't taken the hint yet then, have you?'

'I'm working on it…'

Alditha shook her head. Then, ignoring Gunkin's response, she turned her full attention to the sphere. She was unsure about it, and, strangely, felt out of her depth.

She reached out a hand, gently, and whispered: 'Broom, broom, come to me; slowly mind—don't fret or flee.'

Slowly, like a cat stalking a mouse, her broom inched forward to her hand. Something told her she might need it close by. A witch's broomstick had many uses beyond that of aerial transportation, and the orb looked unpredictable.

'Hello,' she whispered to the sphere. 'You're not from round here, are you? What are you doing here? Eh? Tell Aunty Alditha. Where are you-'

'Ass… ass… asssssimilated. Language assimilated. Extrapolations now possible,' said the sphere suddenly, its voice low and tinny.

'Gooooood,' said Alditha, nodding at it. 'Now maybe we can have a proper chat, eh? I'd like that, wouldn't you?'

'Assessing,' said the sphere, followed by some clicks and whistles. 'Culture—primitive. Largely pre-industrial. Evidence of mytho-folkloric influences and sigma energy. Incantation suggests sigma energy regarded as ma-ma-ma-magic. Conclusion: the Sleepers have not awoken. Objective one—wake the Sleepers.'

With that, the sphere shot out its wings and zipped straight up into the sky.

'What the-?' said Gunkin. 'Get after it.'

'No point, believe me,' said Alditha, staring after it. 'Absolutely fascinating, though,' she murmured, more to herself than to the goblin. Then she widened her eyes. 'Wonder who the Sleepers are.'

'Y'see?' screeched Harper, sticking a wing up into the sky. 'It's the end of the world, I tell you. That mad wizard's finally done it. He's gone and killed us all.'

The Green Man looked up at the fingers of lightning strolling slowly down towards the ground. 'It's odd, that's certainly true,' he said.

'Odd?' said Harper. 'It's scrawkingly terrifying, that's what it is.'

'Well,' said the Green Man, 'if it helps unruffle your feathers, it looks like none of the lightning bolts are due to hit us. And it's rather sporting, going at that speed. Gives people plenty of time to get out of the way, you know?'

'Not the lightning,' Harper flurried. 'Who cares about the lightning? Lightning's normal. It's *that* I'm worried about.'

The Green Man looked. Then he coughed, just a little. 'Yes. Erm…forgive me Harper, dear friend, but you do appear to be pointing *at* the lightning.'

But he wasn't. What Harper could see was huge—it filled the sky, on all sides of the lightning. It was blackness, but it was full of horrors—seething off-white tendrils danced, looking for ways to come down and kill them all. Beetle-creatures the size of fields scuttled across the sky on legs that looked hard and darkly armoured, their mouths pouring, roaring threats to the world below. Hideous pink-brown faceless snakes slithered around the clouds, writhing blind, gaping maws ready to suck the air from the Garden

Harper closed his big eyes and tried to think sensibly.

Maybe you're just dreaming.

Maybe you're just dreaming.

Maybe you're just dreaming.

He opened his eyes again, and one of the snake things oozed its way past a particularly fluffy cloud.

Nope—not bloomin' dreaming. Waaaaargh.

Calm down, Harper. Calm down.

Whaddayou mean, calm down? he argued with himself. *The sky's full of monsters.*

Is it?

Wait—what?

Maybe it's like when you lose your way, and you see…things.

Harper squinted at the Green Man. 'You can't see them, can you?' he pleaded. 'I mean, what do you see?'

The Green Man frowned. 'I see some bolts of quite slow lightning, heading towards the ground. As I say, really quite odd.'

'And…erm…that's it?' Harper asked, feeling sick. 'Is it?'

The Green Man squinted at the sky. 'Yyyyyes,' he said eventually. 'Yes, that's it.'

'No horrible, squirmy roots and monsters and…stuff?'

The Green Man frowned. 'Nnnno,' he said, checking the sky again, then blinking at his friend. 'No, I'm fairly sure I would have noticed that.'

'That's it, then,' cried Harper, waving his wings about. 'I've gone bonkers. Doolally tap. Up the spout and round the twist and nutty as a squirrel's sandwich-box. Oh, what a terrible fate for a young owl in the prime of his wossname.' He hid his eyes with his wing. 'No,' he said. 'Don't look at me, I don't want your pity, old friend. I'll just go off somewhere on me own and never look up again, that's all. Don't trouble yourself.'

The Green Man made soothing noises at his dramatic friend. 'Would you like a marshmallow?' he offered. 'Everything looks better after a marshmallow, I always find.'

'No no,' wailed Harper. 'The sky's never done anything to hurt me, and now it's crawling with monsters. Goodness only knows what I'll see if I look at a marshmallow. For all I know, it might grow teeth and try and bite me beak off. Oh, that it should come to this,' he said. 'Struck down in me prime by that wretched wizard, flying his teacups around the place and turning me loopy.'

'I meant to say,' said the Green Man, 'you were wrong about that, you know. Had nothing to do with Skoros in the end—there was one of those…*girl* things in the teacup. Said her name was Celeste. Quite nice, really, in an oddish way. You should have seen what she did to the wizard when he came riding up to see what all the fuss was about, you'd have laughed yourself hooty.'

'A girl?' said Harper, peeping over his wing. 'A girl? Came out of that thing?'

'Mmm. Yes. Celeste, she said her name was. Kept asking if I'd seen any orbs about the place. Don't know what all that was about. As I say, oddish girl, but quite nice in her way.'

'Orbs?' demanded the owl suddenly. 'Orbs like metal balls with wings on? Orbs like metal balls with wings on that fly like Big Red Himself was after 'em and don't think twice about dumping a humble well-meaning owl on his head in the depths of Blue Dragon Forest?'

The Green Man shrugged—he was a living tree, so it was a complicated, impressive, rather noisy business. 'Orbs was all she said.'

Harper came out of hiding and fluttered his wings. 'D'you know what this means?' he almost yelled.

'Not a clue, old chap. Seems to be that sort of day.'

'Means I haven't gone bonkers after all. For some reason, this *Celeste -*' He almost spat the name. '-has sent the orb ahead. First the orb. Then the teacup. Now the lightning and the sky full of monsters. For some reason, *you* can't see the monsters—s'probably camouflage. Yes, that's it—camouflage, like caterpillars that look like leaves. But I...for some reason, I'm immune to the camouflage. S'probably my highly developed brain, to be fair. I mean, I speak as I find, and you know I think you're an excellent fellow, one of the finest, but after all, when all's said and done, you're a tree.'

The Green Man pursed his lips, but said nothing.

'D'you know what else this means?' asked Harper, almost whispering, in case anyone except the Green Man was listening.

'That you owe Skoros an apology?'

'No,' said Harper, fixing the Green Man with an enormous owlish gaze. 'It means the Garden—*my* Garden—is being invaded.'

6

'Of all the useless-' CLANG.

'Stupid-' CLANG.

'Waste of rivet-' CLANG.

'Creations.' THUNK.

Skoros paused, realizing his sledgehammer had gone through the bronze plating of the Horse 2.0's chest. He nodded, sniffed. 'No more than you deserve, you wretched disappointment-engine.'

He had only decided to try the Horse out so that he could intimidate the Green Man and whoever or whatever owned the teacup. Instead he had ended up humiliated in front of that walking tree and what looked like a twelve-year-old girl with violet eyes.

She'll pay, he promised himself. *One day soon, she'll pay for my embarrassment.*

Her not being intimidated had been bad enough, but the backward-facing journey home on the unstoppable Horse 2.0 had been not only shaming, but painful, too. What was more, the thing had stopped a mile from the castle with steam coming out of its head and oil leaking from a service hatch underneath its tail, and he'd had to drag it up the final stretch of the hill.

She's so *going to pay*, he promised.

'Raark,' said Razor, flying into the stable and landing on a workbench that had long ago replaced the feeding trough in the stable. 'How'd it go, O Dark Lord Of All You Survey?' he asked. 'Strike fear in his old wooden heart, did you? Take the teacup by storm? Grind the noses of the lesser creatures into the dirt, eh? Raaark.'

Skoros scowled at the raven. Did Razor know? Had he seen his humiliation?

'I am considering my actions,' he said, daring the bird to react.

Razor fixed him with piercing eyes. He blinked. 'Raaark,' he muttered, in a tone that said 'I'm saying absolutely nothing about that. Nothing at all.'

Skoros nodded. 'The teacup had an occupant,' he explained. 'A *girl*.'

Razor clamped his silver beak tightly shut.

'She's not from around here,' Skoros explained. 'She's from a whole civilization of people like me. Can you imagine that?'

Razor's beak was, if anything, even more closed than it had been before.

'She said she hadn't seen something like this in hundreds of years,' he mused, throwing a look of accusation at the Horse 2.0. 'Just imagine what I could do with a mind like that.'

Razor's beak opened—and then closed again.

'I went about it the wrong way,' Skoros admitted, pretty much forgetting Razor was there at all. 'Trying to intimidate her with *this*.' He kicked the Horse 2.0 hard in the fetlock, and it fell forward in a clanking pile of metal. 'I need to impress her. To be her *friend*.'

'Raaark,' said Razor, with his head tilted to the side. 'What if she doesn't wanna be your friend, O Dark Lord Of All You Survey?'

Skoros stared at him like a gravestone. 'Then the castle has plenty of dungeons,' he said, quietly. 'What in the name of-?'

Something had caught his eye through the open stable door. He rushed past Razor to look out. There in the sky were what looked like lightning bolts, moving slowly down towards the ground. Skoros narrowed his eyes at them.

'This'll be *her* work, I'm sure of it,' he muttered, watching the streaks of energy move. He stood in the stable doorway for a moment, then rubbed the place where his beard should have been, thinking.

Anyone who could interfere with the Horse 2.0 is either cleverer or more powerful than anyone else on this planet, he thought. *Like me. Now this…*

He made a decision. 'Razor, go—prime the machine. I'll check the wood is available, feed the furnace and channel the power to the central systems. I need a lot of juice, and I need it now. I'll join you soon.'

'Raark. Why, Lord? What do you have in mind?'

Skoros smiled a thin, razor-wire smile. 'I intend to release the CyberBats.'

———————

Celeste looked up at the sky and frowned, concentrating on where the lightning was coming from. She pointed her box at the sky and it beeped and blipped for a few seconds.

'Are you getting this, Alpha?'

There were a few seconds of silence before 'Affirmative' came back to her.

'Speculate on the cause of the phenomenon.'

A shorter pause. 'There are 72, 894, 103 possible causes. Cause one-'

'Narrow parameters to include likelihood of orb involvement.'

'There are twelve possible causes including likelihood-'

'Thought so.' Celeste did her best not to get excited. Still, the orbs must have found something of interest or they wouldn't have done this, not yet. A grin twitched at the edges of her mouth. 'Log bearing and trajectory of orbs on departure,' she told Alpha, 'and send me coordinates for likely seeker-beam drop-points.' She looked at the beams as they split the sky, spreading like giant spider-legs. *Lazy*, she chided herself. She'd been relying on Alpha's calculations too much lately, treating the bio-mech like a glorified calculator. 'Cancel co-ordinate request,' she said, 'I can work it out myself.'

There was a long moment of silence, before Alpha said 'I should think so too.'

Celeste grinned properly at that, did some complicated mathematics in her head, told her bio-mech to still log the departure bearings for the orbs, and set off for the place where she'd worked out the nearest seeker-beam would drop to the ground.

Wish I'd brought my hoverscoot, she thought as she traipsed over the ground of the Garden, keeping the seeker-beams in sight every second.

In the forest, Skoros drew himself up, as though he'd been about to tread in something nasty.

'Witch,' he sneered.

Alditha stopped in her tracks and clicked the heels of her boots together.

'Well, bless my broomstick, if it isn't Lord Skoros himself,' she said, touching the brim of her hat lightly, unaffected by the wizard's sudden appearance.

'What are you doing here?' the wizard demanded sourly.

Alditha ignored the question—everyone in the Garden knew that witches went where they pleased. 'What are *you* doing here?' she replied. 'Didn't you know that cutting down trees at this rate is a crime against the forest?'

'Since it's *my* forest, it would only be a crime if *I* wasn't the one doing it,' he spat back. 'Crime against the forest, indeed—what do you think? Are the trees going to put me on trial?' he scoffed.

Alditha said nothing.

'Gunkin, get this lot fed into the furnace immediately, then come back and cut down another acre.' Skoros stared at Alditha, daring her to contradict him.

Alditha still said nothing.

Skoros grunted in satisfaction, turned on his heel and hurried back into the castle. Gunkin shrugged at Alditha, picked up a big tree under each arm, and began dragging them after his master.

———————

Left alone with the trees, Alditha pursed her lips. There were battles worth winning, she knew, and battles worth losing. Sometimes, the words you wanted to say would only prolong the argument.

Sometimes it was better to say nothing, and just *do* something. She climbed onto her broomstick and took off, flying up and up, just above the level of the treetops. Then she nodded, her mind made up.

———————

The machine was hissing and whirring, steam escaping from some joints.

'Raark,' said Razor as Skoros strode through the doors. He tended to stride all over the place, rather than just walking about. *Camouflage*, thought Razor, though he'd never have dared say as much. *Trying to make himself look big.* He ruffled his feathers to get rid of such dangerous thoughts. 'All ready, O Dark Lord Of All You, Raark, Survey.'

'I'll operate them myself,' snarled Skoros, pointing his corkscrew wand at a side panel in the bronze-covered desk. It opened, and he yanked out a skullcap, just like the one Razor had worn earlier, only larger. He plugged the cap into the main power circuit, brushed his hair back and snapped the cap's pins into two small holes on either side of his head. Then and only then did he sit down, his hands working as if under the control of some distant programming. 'Activate the mirror,' he droned, his voice lifeless.

Razor muttered and whistled, complaining against his lot, but he hopped onto the mirror's crank handle and curled his brass claws around it. Then he began to flap his wings, harder and harder, till the crank handle swung forward. He stopped, swinging back, then flapped again, repeating the pattern until finally the handle went all the way around, carrying Razor with it. He kept flapping, and the handle went round, and round again, something in the mechanism catching, and the mirror coming to life just as Razor lost his grip and tumbled into the wall with an angry 'skrrrrraaaaaark.'

'CyberBats, run awakening protocol,' Skoros intoned, as in the mirror, a dim scene of dangling bats in a cave flickered into view, and all at once, the bats' eyes flicked open. At the same time, Skoros closed his eyes—they wouldn't be needed for this operation.

'Oh no, don't worry yourself, I'm fine,' squawked Razor from the floor.

On the screen, the bats unhooked their grip on their upside-down world and began flying, soundless and in formation, out of the cave. Skoros pressed a button, and a single bronze and wooden joystick emerged from a panel in the desk. He took it and began to move it slowly, his movements fluid.

'Switch to sonar output,' he said, and the mirror's image switched to a reddish blur. Skoros was directing the bats now, his mind linked with them all at once, the joystick simply a way of focusing his thought patterns to get them to go where he wanted. He drove them upward, to look at the lightning that still streaked across the sky. The bats' sonar readings, converted into data, told him what he already knew—it wasn't ordinary lightning. He had difficulty understanding what he was reading—it had an intelligent matrix. It had been programmed, with a search and locate function. Questions flooded Skoros' mind—who had programmed it? Celeste and her kind? How many of them were here? Might the others be more open to persuasion than she had been? Wait, no, there were more important questions—*what* was the lightning searching for?

He sensed something out there. Several somethings, in fact, flying about but giving off power signatures that weren't organic, weren't alive.

'Intercept,' he said, pushing the joystick forward. The CyberBats flew forward, homing in on the objects Skoros had sensed.

———————

Alditha rarely used her wand in private, it was more for show than anything. Witch magic worked in lots of ways, and most of them were much more subtle than pointing a stick at things and turning them into frogs. Now though, she drew her wand from its holster in her right boot, and began to fly in a broad circle around the remaining trees in Skoros' forest. When she'd made three full circuits of the area, she aimed her wand.

'Life of leaf and life of root,
Hear my plea and grant my suit,
Evil seeks to do you harm,
While you stand so still and calm.
Gather up your life and hear,
You have enemies to fear.
So when this, my charm, is done,
Self-defend, fight back or run,
Be alive as men do live…'

Alditha swallowed, knowing what the last line of her spell should be.

'And Green Man, may my spell forgive.'

From the tip of her wand a fine golden spray seemed to pour, touching every leaf and every tree in the remaining forest. The golden spray glowed strong and yellow, then sank to green, to white, and was absorbed into all the trees.

There was the most remarkable sound Alditha had ever heard. It was like the forest stretching, yawning, and scratching itself as it woke up, rustling leaves and shaking branches. She smiled, though she knew she'd have to face the Green Man later, and that he wouldn't be pleased. She was about to fly down and introduce herself to the trees when a dark shape caught her eye. She squinted. Then she made a mental note to apologise to Harper, too—Skoros *had* got his bats out in daylight after all.

Leave the wizard well alone, she told herself. *You've already animated his forest this morning, and he's not going to be pleased.* She bit her lip. *Leave the wizard well alone, Alditha. Leave the wizard-*

'Oh to heck with it,' she muttered, crouching low over her broom.

'Broom, broom, ride the air,

Stealthy mind, let's not be there.'

There was a shimmer in the air, and Alditha and her broomstick seemed to disappear. As illusions went, it wasn't perfect—they looked like a perfectly innocent patch of sky, but as they moved, they'd look like exactly the *same* patch of perfectly innocent sky, moving about as if it was whistling cheerfully and saying 'nothing to see here, folks.' But if the wizard was able to sense things through his confounded bats, it would give her a better chance of not being noticed than just flying up and saying 'What's all this, then?'

'Please state your destination,' whispered the broom in stealth mode.

'Bats ahead,' she told it. 'Follow and hover a safe distance from the...' She realized she didn't know what a collection of bats was called. 'Bats,' she finished.

'Specify safe distance,' said the broom.

'If they start attacking us, you've gone too far,' Alditha hissed.

There was a silent moment, and Alditha thought the broom was probably sulking. Then slowly, a perfectly innocent patch of sky began to drift towards the dark mass of the bats.

———

'It's *this* thing,' said Harper, waving a beak at the teacup. 'It's those whizzing balls, and this thing, and now the sky. Bet you the invasion's controlled from in there,' he added, hooting involuntarily.

'Invasion of the teacups, Harper old chap? That doesn't sound right, somehow.'

'Y'know what I think?' said Harper. 'I think it's not *really* a teacup. I reckon it just *looks* like a teacup, and inside its probably full of… of…worms, and beetles and things, all just waiting to scuttle out and slither around the place and do their invading…thing.'

'It was full of a young girl,' said the Green Man, his voice level. 'And Alpha, whatever that is.'

'Exactly,' hooted Harper in triumph. 'Whatever that is. S'probably the King of the Beetle-People.'

'Astarians,' the Green Man continued.

'And what does that mean when it's at home, eh? Come to that, where *is* home for these Astarian beetle-creatures? I don't know, do you?'

'Astaria?' The Green Man shrugged. 'What does it matter? People have come to the Garden before without anybody flapping about the place calling it an invasion. Somehow they get on with their lives.' He shrugged. It really was an impressive and complicated gesture for a living tree.

'Not this time,' Harper declared. 'This time it's all metal balls that won't stand still and teacups that probably aren't teacups at all and mysterious *girls*. If she *is* a girl, that is. After all, if her teacup's not a teacup, how do we know she's not a beetle *disguised* as a girl, eh?'

The Green Man scratched his head. 'We don't, I suppose,' he admitted. 'Seems a bit of a silly way to go about invading places though, pretending to be girls—and quite polite ones at that.'

'Lulling us into a false sense of…thingy,' said Harper.

'Girlishness?'

'Exactly, yes,' said the owl, who couldn't quite remember the word he really wanted. 'A false sense of girlishness. Then, when we're all happy and smiley and "Oh, would you like a marshmallow?"— boom.'

'Boom?' asked the Green Man.

'Boom,' insisted Harper. 'Before we know where we are, it'll be scuttly, slithery brain-sucking invasion time.'

The Green Man blinked. 'I really don't think it will, you know,' he said.

'I'll prove it to you, shall I?' demanded the owl. 'I'll go and face all manner of scuttly, slithery brain-sucking death in the belly of the beast, shall I?' He flung an accusing wing at the teacup again.

'Do teacups have bellies?'

'It's not a teacup.'

The Green Man said nothing.

'Right, I'll show you,' said Harper, flapping and not looking at the sky, where he knew all the horrid creatures were still trying to break through into the Garden. He flew to the side of the cup and along it, trying to find the door. ''s'probably beetle-shaped,' he muttered. Then, as if by magic, a slab of darkness opened in the cup, and Harper hooted in alarm.

He swallowed, turned his head to look at the Green Man, who was watching him intently, then landed on the lip of the darkness. 'Right,' he called. 'Here I go then. I'm going inside now. I may be some time.'

Owls have extremely good eyesight. They have particularly good eyesight when it comes to seeing things in the dark. Harper stared into the darkness inside the teacup but saw only blank walls and a patch of floor.

'Course, I may be no time at all if I'm captured and have all manner of scuttly, slithery brain-sucking death inflicted on me,' he said, 'but don't let that bother you.'

The Green Man still said nothing, though he did wave a hand— and several branches, for good measure.

'Right then,' said Harper, turning to face the darkness. He took two steps, and the doorway disappeared, leaving only solid wall behind him. As soon as the door became a wall though, the lights came on—low, purple lights illuminating his way down the corridor. 'Oh yeah,' muttered Harper, 'because that's totally innocent and not at all sinister. No way out and weird lighting. Terrific.' He walked a few paces, then shook himself. 'You're an owl, for goodness' sake,' he said, flapping his wings and flying to the end of the corridor, turning right—the only option he had—and then flying down another featureless corridor. At the end of that second corridor, a tall arched doorway stood in front of him, and Harper pulled up, hovering as best he could.

'Oh well,' he muttered. 'Here goes. That's me for the scuttly, slithery brain-sucking death, then.' He flew up and down outside the door, until it simply disappeared, just as the outer door had done. Harper looked around.

Knew it, he thought.

7

Owls may have extremely good eyesight, but what wizards are best at is concentration. They have to be, with all the spell-learning and incantations and wrist-flicking—if you don't concentrate when you cast spells, one wrong wrist-flick can mean the difference between turning your enemy into a warthog and turning a warthog into your enemy. That may sound like no especially bad thing, but you'd be surprised by the number of otherwise excellent wizards who've been killed by a stampede of surprised and not at all happy warthogs, all because of a simple lapse in concentration.

Skoros was concentrating hard. Separating his focus across all the CyberBats and flying them in a formation was tricky at the best of times. Getting them to hunt down a specific and fast object like an orb was making him sweat through his wizard's robes. But slowly, by grouping the CyberBats together only for short periods of time, swooping in, taking bites and nibbles of the orb's outer casing and then retreating, he seemed to be getting somewhere.

Every time a CyberBat sank its brass fangs into the sphere, Skoros jerked in his seat. Information flared into his mind, like a black and white lightning flash arranged into ten pictures one on top of the other, all at once and bright and brilliant. At first when it had happened, he'd gasped, forgotten how to breathe, and then the image in his mind had faded like hope beneath his heel, and suddenly, desperately, he'd wanted to see it again, to feel that jolt of *knowing* things. Now he was doing it like a boy who catches butterflies in a net— swoop, bite, lurch, and then he'd use his mind to catch the image, see it fully before it faded, and tuck it away somewhere in the back of his brain till it was useful, as he commanded the CyberBats away again. Retreat, swoop, bite, lurch—and catch another stack of images, another set of squiggles that would mean nothing to anyone else in the Garden. They didn't exactly *mean* anything to him yet either, but he was the one person—the one in all the Garden—who understood that they meant something to *someone*. To the people who'd built the sphere. To *Celeste's* people. It had to be them, he knew—there was such a thing as coincidence, but it didn't play this sort of game. He directed CyberBat 16 to swoop—his last attack from CyberBat 4 had driven the orb away from one cluster, only to face another. Swoop, bite. And there was the lurch again, the flash of brilliant, beautiful knowledge. But wait—

He sensed a change in the orb. It began to weave erratically, no longer seeming sure which direction it wanted to go. A sickly thin smile creaked into place on Skoros' beardless face.

CyberBats—feeeeeeed. He commanded, and all at once he felt them swoop, land, bite, sinking brass fangs into delicate layers of metal and wire, diodes panicking, flashing lights flickering frantically as the CyberBats hacked and bit and tore at the orb's electronic innards. And in his chair in the secret chamber, Skoros shuddered and convulsed as though he were on fire—which in a way, he was. The information *burned* in his mind, bright and clear and swirling round and round, like a boxful of jigsaw puzzle pieces sliding over each other, searching for the holes that fit. And piece by piece, he began to see the sense of the sphere. If the data kept coming, he knew, he could understand it all, right there and then.

Keep it coming, he almost begged his CyberBats. *Just a little longer— keep it coming.*

Almost as he formed the thought though, he was thrown forward onto the desk, and back into his chair. He felt the orb go dead, dropping to the ground, and taking the CyberBats with it. The power disappeared. The knowledge tried to follow it, tried to dissolve itself from Skoros' mind before he could reassert his will on it. The plugs that kept him connected to the CyberBats were ripped out of the holes in his head and he lay for a minute, feeling like all he wanted to do was sleep. Sleep and keep the knowledge warm, in the hope it might grow in the nest of his head.

Skoros snapped his eyes open suddenly, gripped the arms of his chair.

'Raaark?' said Razor, somehow making it sound like 'Are you all there, ya great big loony?'

'I've got to find it,' Skoros growled. 'Got to have it.' He stood up, his hat almost falling backwards off his head in the suddenness of the move. 'Razor, come.' He decided the moment was worth an evil chuckle, and he gave one. 'We're about to take over the Garden.'

'Raaark,' said Razor, rolling his eyes and whistling, as if to say 'Yep, he's gone. Absolutely, positively bonkers.' But he hopped up onto his master's shoulder anyway, and had to cling on tight as Skoros broke into a run, out of the castle and onward, while the last memories of where the CyberBats had been hunting stayed with him.

———

Knew it, thought Harper. *Knew this place was no ordinary teacup.*

The room he'd flown into was large and round, with three seats at the far end of the circle. There were large banks of some mirror in front of the seats, with lots of lines and squiggles moving all over them like multi-coloured worms.

Maybe it's the invasion of the Worm-People, he thought, *not the Beetle-*

People after all.

Then there was a noise like nothing he'd ever heard before, like thunderstorms fighting cats for a set of bagpipes. One of the chairs swung around, fast, and Harper knew it wasn't the invasion of the Worm-People. It wasn't the invasion of the Beetle-People, either. It was the invasion of the Things That Were Unspeakably Worse than Either Of Them.

The thing in the chair looked like it could once have been a person—it had the right number of arms and legs, and a head like an upturned egg pretty much where you'd expect a head to be. But the whole thing was skinny and spindly and pale, almost the colour of moonlight on milk. It looked like it hadn't eaten a meal in a year, but yet it seemed, somehow, appallingly strong. It got out of the chair quickly, and Harper noticed its feet didn't touch the floor. It was floating, flying towards him. The head, the horrible upturned egg of a head was pale too, with just two puncture wounds where a nose should be, and a terrible thin slit for a mouth. But the eyes…

The eyes were big black almonds that took up most of its face and had no pupils, so when you looked at them, you felt you might get lost, swallowed up and spat out somewhere unimaginably cold.

It spoke.

'Intruder alert. You are an intruder. You must now leave or I will be forced to initiate security procedures. Intruder alert. You are an intruder…'

Its lips never moved. The sound seemed to come directly from its throat and fill the room, and it took Harper a few seconds to realize what it was saying.

There are moments in life when people are scared, when they have one of two reactions. They decide either to fight or to fly. Harper didn't know what he was dealing with, but he knew that he was almost certain to be more scared of it than it was of him. He chose to fly, turning in a tight arc, and heading back out of the door. The monstrous thing followed, floating steadily after him, repeating its warnings.

'You are an intruder. You must now leave, or I will be forced…'

Harper flapped like he'd never flapped before, flapped till his wings ached, and headed for where he knew the door to the outside world had been. Sure enough, as he got close, the wall dissolved and he shot out into the air of the Garden. He didn't look up at the hideous things in the sky that only he could see, and he didn't look down at the Green Man. He just kept flying, determined to get as far away from the horrible invading *thing* as he could.

'What do you mean, an intruder?' Celeste frowned. This mission was getting unnecessarily complicated and she hadn't even found a single orb yet.

'A plump avian,' Alpha reported. 'Designation: owl.'

'Well, what are you doing letting owls in the ship?' said Celeste, crossly.

'Your analysis is inaccurate. The owl was not "let" on board. It came-'

'Oh never mind,' snapped Celeste. 'I suppose it can't do any harm, can it? An owl?'

'Probability vectors of harm to the mission…insignificant,' admitted Alpha.

'Well then, don't bother me with it,' said Celeste. 'I really should have brought my hoverscoot for this mission. Walking's so…so… dull,' she finished.

'Probability vectors of mission being harmed by *dullness* also insignificant.'

'I'm beginning to think *you're* insignificant,' muttered Celeste, and she walked on, trudging through the Garden's greenery.

On her broomstick, disguised inside her patch of perfectly ordinary sky, Alditha frowned. It wasn't that she liked to frown, but some faces were just extremely good at frowning, and Alditha knew that she had that kind of face. She'd watched the bats attack the orb, nipping in, taking bites, nipping out so the next of them could have a go. That was when her frown had really started, but as she watched the sphere fall out of the sky, the frown had announced its intention to stay for a while and had settled itself into her face as though she were an old armchair. She watched as Skoros and his wretched bird came racing along a pathway, and the wizard stooped to pick up the sphere, examining it with a smirk on his stupid beardless face. And she watched as he marched off again, holding the sphere like it was some precious, jewelled thing.

She'd thought, as she watched all this, about swooping down on him and clonking him on his stupid wizardry nose. But that wasn't, she knew, the right thing to do. Witch-magic wasn't often about pointing a stick at people and turning them into frogs. That was more wizard-magic style, and she knew that Skoros would relish the chance to turn her into something warty.

No. For now, the beardless wonder had a new toy, which would keep him out of mischief for a while, at least. She consoled herself with the idea that he'd probably never be able to get it moving again.

Probably.

Promising herself she'd keep a closer eye on what he did in future, just as Harper had told her to, Alditha pointed her broom towards home.

———

Skoros was back in the castle. Back in his secret room of bronze contraptions. Back with the sphere.

Razor had been on his shoulder when he'd found it, and as he'd carried it home. But now Skoros wanted to be alone with the sphere. He'd made the bird hop off and wait outside the secret chamber, then he'd gone in and locked the door behind him.

He hugged the sphere tightly to his body, like a round, metal teddy bear.

'You're going to make me King of the Garden,' he cooed to it. 'Yes you are. Yes you are. And when Daddy's got you working again, who shall he send you out to get first, eh?' Without a breath, Skoros' voice dropped from cooing to sharp-edged spite. 'That meddling witch, Alditha, that's who.'

But then he caught his breath, and the intricate clockwork of his devious brain twirled and danced. 'No. Nooooonononono, I have a better plan.'

And alone in his secret room, with just the powerless orb for company, Skoros laughed at the audacity of his imagination.

Beyond the Garden, above the Earth, the two original orbs soared into orbit. It took them a few moments to get used to the size of the universe again, then they adjusted, and with a silent pop, they expanded to their normal football size. They began to whistle, a sound that no-one heard, and then the sound dropped lower, and lower, from a whistle to a moan, from a moan to a grumble, from a grumble to that sense of sickness you get on long car journeys, and lower, and lower, far below human hearing. When the noise was low enough, the orbs glowed bright cherry red, and sent out a pulse. It wasn't a pulse you could see or hear. It was a pulse that would ricochet through the universe that was, and bounce off everything it hit. It would bounce sideways, through the cracks between realities, the tiny little winks between dimensions, and it would do it fast.

People will always tell you that the fastest things can travel is at the speed of light.

They're wrong. Light needs action to travel, it pours through the universe, full of fuss and energy, like a white rabbit running late for tea.

The speed of dark is faster. All the dark needs to travel is an absence of anything in its way. The dark is almost everywhere already.

The pulse went off into the rippling dimensions, travelling at the speed of dark.

Almost immediately, a thousand cracks away, in a dimension it called home, the pulse was heard.

On a fleet of unimaginably slick, dark spaceships the size of flattened-out worlds, a billion lights switched silently on.

The fleet of unimaginably slick, now bright spaceships took a moment before reacting, as if to consider the pulse that had turned on the lights and what it meant. And then they silently began to move forward.

8

Time passes.

People always say time passes, as if it just slips silently through the world, unnoticed.

People are silly sometimes.

Time passes, but it brushes everything as it goes. It touches us and we grow taller and older, and we learn new things. We change, and little by little as time passes, we're not quite the same as we used to be.

Time passes through my garden, brushing leaves, and grass, and flowers. It pulls a season behind it, like a rucksack drooping from its back. It touches buds that grow; they ripen and their colours stream out into the world, petals shouting 'Look at me.' Fruits just bursting with their mission, spread seeds, begin again, next phase, next year. It touches leaves and deepens all their greens, bringing sunshine to glisten like butter on everything that lives.

It's near Midsummer in my garden now. Two weeks of time have passed, and touched the world and made it shine.

I've seen that tiny owl again.
He's been busy.

Alditha stirred a big cauldron of thick, bubbling, green and purple goo on her open stove.

She'd been on a mission in the two weeks since the arrival of the teacup.

She'd had to go and explain to the Green Man about Skoros' forest, the effect of her spell, and why its remaining trees were now determined not to be cut down. He listened, his face becoming graver and more still with every word she uttered. When she finished speaking, he didn't say anything for several long seconds. Then, in a sad, quiet voice, he said that he was disappointed in her, and that her interference with the natural order of the forest was essentially wrong. *Some trees were meant to talk and make decisions, while others were not*, he said. Then he asked her to leave. Alditha had tried to argue, tried to make him argue back, but the Green Man wouldn't be drawn into a fight. Alditha wished he had. Eventually, she had to get on her broomstick and fly away from him. They hadn't spoken since.

But the Garden didn't stop needing her witchcraft just because she'd disappointed the Green Man. Sagar had suffered from a terrible stomachache for the last two weeks—when your stomach is full of chemicals that can be set on fire at a moment's notice, you're always going to be vulnerable to indigestion. Alditha had prepared a chalky solution for his heartburn and advised him, as a friend, to give a loud, clear warning any time he had the hiccups or was about to fart. Sagar looked scandalized for a moment, but Alditha grinned at him and he burst out laughing.

Dragons were often solitary creatures, and Alditha knew Sagar complained of aches and pains just so he'd have someone to talk to who wasn't scared that he'd burn them to a crisp as soon as look at them.

Then there was Skoros. Alditha had friends in all the levels of the animal kingdom, and she'd asked them to keep an eye on the wizard's comings and goings since he'd got hold of the orb. The strange thing was that they had nothing to report. Everyone who came to see her said the same thing—Skoros hadn't been seen or heard of outside the castle in two weeks. He was up to something, for sure. In fact, knowing Skoros, she thought he was probably 'Up To Something, bwahahahahaha.' She was fighting the instinct that told her she had no alternative but to fly over there and demand to know exactly what it was.

'Stir the pot and stir it well,

Watch the heat, ignore the smell,' she muttered, stirring the cauldron three times anti-clockwise, as the recipe demanded. People think witchcraft is all about messing about with dark, mysterious forces, but sometimes, it's just a load of recipes with twiddly bits added.

The teacup, when she'd finally seen it for herself, was mystifying. Teacups weren't supposed to just hang there, and the Green Man was quite enthusiastic to tell her all about it, and about this young girl called Celeste who'd come out of it. But she couldn't meet his eye, having had to tell him about Skoros' forest, and so had never got the facts of the teacup entirely straight in her head. Apparently though, according to Flitterwing the blue jay, the teacup had flown off to parts unknown—or at least, unknown to Flitterwing, which was not quite the same thing—not long after she'd left the Green Man's house. The lightning bolts across the sky had disappeared about the same time, said Flitterwing. It was all odd.

Alditha didn't like odd, unexplained things, they made her itchy. She sighed.

Then of course there was Dramm. Alditha couldn't help herself— she chuckled as she stirred the goo, waiting for the green streaks and the purple streaks to disappear. Dramm was proving harder to train than she'd imagined he would be. She was making some progress with him, but she'd realized there was only so much he could learn from a human about being a good and useful spellbook.

Inevitably, she'd started taking him for lessons with Jasper, the old spellbook who lived as a hermit in a shack over Spooky End way. Alditha was the nearest thing Jasper had to a permanent friend. The witch and spellbook had once been an inseparable pair; though many a good year had passed since they'd spoken, due to a disagreement over the correct use of red batwing stew and its associated magical procedure.

Jasper didn't like visitors, and seemed always to be muttering to himself in some strange language that no-one understood. But he had at least answered the door when she'd gone to see him, and by bowing and being respectful of his age and wisdom—and by making an effort to reminisce over the good times they'd shared—she'd gained entry to the shack.

Jasper was mysterious and a little weird—even for a spellbook—and had magical runes on his cover and down his spine. On his front cover, whenever he needed to, he manifested a face with quite a big nose, wide, hang-dog eyes and a pair of thick lips that smacked together as he spoke. He was also, as far as Alditha knew, the only spell book in the Garden to bother wearing clothes. They weren't much—a tartan cloth wrapped around his lower third, just beneath his lips, and a woven straw hat perched and always ready to fall off the top of his spine when he moved.

Alditha thought back to the first time Jasper and Dramm had met…

She had explained in detail about Dramm's bouncy, excitable personality, and Jasper's eyes had grown larger, taking up more of his cover-space as he stared down at the younger book. Dramm had stopped bouncing and had scooted behind Alditha's black skirts, peeping around her legs and darting back out of sight when Jasper's eyes caught him again. Then the old book had nodded, his face moving slowly over his cover. Frowning deeply and continuing his perpetual mumbling, his yellowed, musty-smelling pages had rustled and opened. With a long sigh, he had eagerly sat down and begun to teach the younger spellbook all he knew.

Since then, she'd taken Dramm to see Jasper three more times. The first time, Dramm wailed the cottage down and ran around it twice before Alditha managed to catch him and tie him closed, shoving him into a rough sack for the journey. The second time, he didn't wail but moped and dragged himself across the floor, throwing himself heavily onto the broomstick as though no spellbook in all the history of the world had suffered the way he suffered. The third time, Alditha noticed, he forgot to be miserable about the whole thing, and was his usual affectionate, bouncy self. In fact, the third time, when she called back at Jasper's to pick him up, Dramm seemed reluctant to come away. She smiled. Say what you liked about the old hermit, he knew how to train spell books. Since the third session, Dramm had been showing off the new things he could do—he'd conjured her a bunch of pink roses, he'd started levitating, though he still wobbled if he tried to fly too far, and, which was most exciting to her, he'd said his first few words, in a voice that was squeaky and unpracticed. Admittedly, one of the words was 'Why?', which Alditha knew meant she was in for an exhausting time when he learned to attach it to other words. And he also seemed to be picking up some of Jasper's mumbo-jumbo, and would mumble the gibberish to himself when he thought she was out of earshot. She chuckled again, wondering what Harper would make of the little spell book's progress.

She stopped stirring.

Harper. Oh, Harper. She sighed and her shoulders slumped. He was arrogant sometimes, and silly, but she missed him so much it was like a fist squeezing her heart. That was how it was with a witch and her familiar—it was like having a pet and a best friend all in one. Against her will, she looked over to the dresser and saw the clawmarks of his last landing.

The goo on the stove bubbled fiercely, and Alditha snapped out of her thinking. The green and the purple had come together and turned a rich, shiny black that was climbing up the sides of the cauldron. She took the pot off the heat, and scooped great ladlefuls of the thick, sticky stuff into iron funnels, stuck into a row of clear green bottles. Only when she'd scraped as much of the goo out of the cauldron as she could, and it was trickling like treacle into its bottles, did she look sideways at the dresser again, and sigh.

'Oh, Harper,' she said, biting her bottom lip. 'Where are you, darling bird?'

As she thought more about Harper, and reminisced about his sweet personality and habits, her thoughts gradually wandered towards the Garden itself, and her home within it.

Dimensions were funny things, she decided. They were all over the place, sticking out sideways like morning hair, and stacked one on top of the other like sheets of paper. Whole universes side by side, on top of each other, or sideways if you turned your head just right— and most of the time, you'd never know they were there. But she knew that universes were funny things, too—running like clockwork. The spin of this planet, the orbit of that moon, the streaking path of a comet on a journey that might take thousands of years—it all worked together and looked like a dance.

Like all good witches, Alditha understood that if you had the right sort of ears, you could hear the universe move, and it sounded like fierce music. And as the universe turned, as galaxies collided and planets spun around their suns, and moons danced round their planets, there were times and places when dimensions came close to touching—the barriers between them thin as tissue. She also knew, though without ever quite knowing why, that people celebrated at those times, and in those places.

She considered the Hallowe'ens further, staring out of her kitchen window at the flowing summer countryside, as if in a trance…

The folk that lived in the Garden celebrated their Midsummer and Midwinter Hallowe'ens—those times when the dimensions came close—at Stone Hedge, a mysterious carved stone hedge that was almost, but not quite, in the centre of the Garden. No-one in the Garden knew quite who'd built it, or carved it in the first place, but they all felt the pull of the Hedge, and at the right times, they gathered there. They put up a big tent, they brought food and drink, and there was singing and dancing and poetry and music and wonderful gossip, and everyone was free to raise any issues with their neighbours that hadn't been sorted out during the course of the last half-year. It was a time to come together and enjoy your friends, and then, as the night grew old, the chatter would die down to a low hum, and all eyes would turn to the Hedge for the Ceremony of the Eternal Pruning—one of the local beggars would be elected, given a costume and a few coins, and told to play the role of Ven Tao, the Great Gardener. They would prance about, pretending to snip bits off the Hedge and rousing the crowd's expectation. And then, when the dimensions did their thing, Stone Hedge would be struck, suddenly, by sunlight from Somewhere Else, and it would shimmer and glow, its dull grey stone turning white, and pink, and purple and green and yellow and all the colours of a Garden rainbow, and a few more from Elsewheres that could only be imagined. The Hedge would seem to dance, and stretch, and sway to the sounds of an Elsewhere music that only it could hear, and the people of the Garden would all be hypnotized by its dance, drawn to it for reasons they didn't know, pulled to watch the Hedge dance. And as the Hallowe'en ended and the dimensions moved on, the Hedge would release all those colours into the Garden air, to float away like soap bubbles while it stopped moving, and turned grey and cold and still again. When the Hedge stopped moving, everyone in the Garden knew the day was done.

But all that only happened at the Hallowe'ens. Between those days, the high points of the Summer and the Winter, Stone Hedge was just what it looked like—a dullish, blueish, greyish, almost square-cut block of stone. Between the Hallowe'ens, people used it as a meeting place, a place to sit, and chat, and watch the world go by. If people agreed to meet, but never mentioned where, it was taken as read that they'd see each other by Stone Hedge.

'What a strange world we live in,' Alditha said to herself quietly, biting her top lip this time. 'Oh Harper, I do hope you are safe, dear bird.'

ALIENS IN MY GARDEN

Harper had, in fact, been busy in the two weeks since giant teacups full of monsters and flying balls with wings had come into his life. Indeed, since leaving Alditha, he had been making plans—plans to save the Garden from the invasion.

He'd already achieved Step 1—Protect Myself From Seeing The Monsters. It'd taken him several nights to weave himself a visor out of bright green leaves, which he now wore everywhere—the leaves stopped him getting distracted by the horrors that still plagued him every time he looked up, the beetles and worms and other unspeakable giant creatures trying to burrow down to him and eat the world alive.

Now it was time for Step 2—Tell Everybody About The Monsters.

He landed on Stone Hedge with his usual accuracy, bounced, squawked and fell off it again with an 'Oof.' Shaking himself and pushing his visor of leaves back into place, he flapped carefully, rising up into the air just enough to feel the Hedge's rough stone surface underneath his feet, then he stopped flapping. He strutted up and down on the Hedge a little, as if to say, to anyone who'd seen him, that his falling off had been on purpose, and that was how owls in the know were landing these days.

He gazed around the crossroads that served the Middle Garden as a village green, a few shops and rows of posher houses lining each leg of the cross. There weren't many people about, but as he looked around, Harper began to worry for the first time that he wouldn't be able to do what he had to do. He was only a little owl, how could he save the Garden from the monsters? He suddenly felt hot and stupid. He stood on one leg, then the other, trying to relieve the feeling of pins and needles that was reaching down to his claws, but it didn't seem to work. He'd thought about what he'd say, thought about it long into the night before, but now, as a couple of people nodded in his direction, he felt his throat tighten, and his tongue dry up.

'People-' he said, but it came out in a high-pitched squeak. He swallowed hard and tried again. 'People,' he called, louder, and in something a little closer to his normal voice. He cleared his throat. *It's now or never*, he told himself firmly.

'People of the Garden,' he started, and more people turned his way. Harper could feel their eyes all over him. *Don't think about it. Don't stop.* 'I have something to tell you.'

People started wandering over to him.

He swallowed again. 'The Garden is in danger,' he almost yelled, going squeaky again.

'Oh aye?' said an older man who, to his surprise, Harper didn't recognize.

'Err, aye. I mean yes,' said Harper, flinging a wing out. He'd meant to do that when he'd said the thing about the Garden being in danger. It didn't have quite the same dramatic effect now. 'From monsters.'

'Monsters?' demanded Moria P'diddle, the baker—a woman who'd been treating bread dough like it was her worst enemy in the Garden for years, and who had forearms like a wrestler to show for it. She crossed those arms and Harper gulped. 'Monsters like what? I mean, we've got a dragon rules the biggest chunk of forest round these parts, how much more monstrous can ya get? Or d'you mean Big Red?' Big Red was technically a demon, but everybody knew he only used his powers for evil when he had no other option—most of the time he was as peaceful as a pussycat. 'Brave,' sniffed Moria. 'Not sure I'd call Big Red a monster. Not if there was a chance of it getting back to him, anyhow.'

'Nah,' said a voice from the crowd, and Harper saw it came out of Old Tom. 'Oi reckon 'e means the trolls over at Gravel Ridge.' Old Tom stuck a finger in his ear and wiggled it around, then pulled it out and stared at what was stuck on the finger, as though he had no idea where it might have come from. He shrugged, sucked his finger and then pronounced ''s'fair enough. Never trust a troll, that's what oi say.'

Harper blinked his big owl eyes. He'd never had a problem with the trolls at Gravel Ridge. He'd never had anything to *do* with the trolls at Gravel Ridge. For one horrifying moment, he wondered what the trolls at Gravel Ridge might do to *him* if they heard he was calling them monsters. 'No, no,' he stuttered. 'Definitely not the trolls.'

'Told you,' said Moria. 'Must be Sagar. I mean, fair's fair, who ever heard of a dragon ownin' a forest. 'tain't natural.'

There were murmurs of agreement from a few anonymous people in the crowd.

'I don't mean Sagar,' Harper squeaked, having had quite a complicated vision of the Blue Dragon eating him alive. 'Look, listen-'

'Ohhhh,' said Mellifluous Turnipflower, the milkmaid from Daisychain Dairy Farm. 'I know who he means. Means the beardless wizard, don' 'e? Tha' one's a prop'r monster, I reckon.'

Moria nodded, her muscular arms flexing and tightening. 'Always been a couple of dinner rolls short of a dozen, that one.'

'No, look, the monsters are-'

'What's 'e been up to this time?' snorted the baker.

'Well, Jefferson Smallbritches, the blacksmith's boy, stopped in with us yes'erday to take measurement for shoein' the new carthorse,' the milkmaid gossiped, 'an' 'e said there's barely a few acres of forest left up at the castle.'

'Monstrous,' snarled the baker, and a few members of the crowd mumbled in support of her view. Harper could see a few more members of his suddenly gathered crowd were losing interest and starting to drift off.

'But that b'aint the worst of it,' said Mellifluous, almost whispering, but with a glint of excitement in her eye. ''e told our Fandango what calls 'erself the cook but really can't do more'n boil an egg without cuttin' 'erself, 'e told 'er them trees as is still standin' 'as got 'emselves...' She looked around, as if to keep the information to herself. '...*Personalities,*' she whispered. The crowd gasped, hustling around the delighted milkmaid to learn more.

'Ladies?' said Harper. Nobody paid him any attention. 'Ladies?

People?' he tried again, but the moment was lost. Everyone seemed more interested in Skoros and his talking trees, and what the Green Man would say about it, than they were in Harper and his tales of monsters.

Well, almost everyone, anyway. As the crowd dispersed into small clusters, each with their theories about the talking trees, Gunkin the purple goblin sidled up to Harper.

'You're not good at this sort of thing, are you, chief?' he said bluntly, watching the crowd dissolved.

'No,' said Harper miserably. 'I don't think I am. But I have to be. There really are monsters. I've seen them.'

'Have ya now?' said Gunkin, rubbing his chin. 'Have ya now indeed? Well, I tell you what, chief—how about you stand me the price of a hazelnut coffee and a sardine sandwich, and then you tell me all about it? Reckon I might be able to help you get your message across.'

Harper blinked, seeing the last remnants of his crowd had gone back to their business. 'Alright then,' he agreed, flapping his wings and heading to Ma McPumplewick's Eatery. Whistling to himself, Gunkin followed close behind, the possibility of a short-term money-making scheme already forming in his mind.

───────────

Witches and wizards are similar in many ways, but they're not by any means the same. Witches have a tendency to live alone with their familiar animals, and have no need to prove their witchiness, or see who's the witchiest of them all. In fact, witches usually only get together in covens in the event of dire emergency, juicy gossip, the death of another witch, or mischief. Mischief is a big thing among witches—it is a truth whispered by the survivors of many an apparently natural disaster that there is nothing more dangerous than a bored witch.

Wizards, on the other hand, love to get together with other wizards. They love to boast of their new spells, show off their new robes, add diamonds and emeralds and rubies to their wizarding hats, compare the length of their beards, and slyly make out that they've picked up new and amazing spell books that they can't possibly share.

And while witches don't have a hierarchy so much as a lot of hard stares and raised eyebrows, wizards love nothing more than knowing where they stand in the order of things. Especially when it turns out that other wizards stand lower than they do. It's the sort of thing that makes witches raise their eyebrows and mutter about 'stupid wizards.'

The easy way to advance your position in the wizarding world is to read more and practice more than any other wizard. That usually means that simply by having had more time on their hands, the older a wizard is, the higher up the rankings he (or she—the requirement to have a beard becomes less of an impediment to female wizards as time goes on) is likely to be. There are regular degrees of advancement too—from a one-star novice all the way up to a Grand High Universal Wrangler of the Infinite. Each time a wizard goes up a level, they're allowed to sew on a new badge, showing their new rank and status, with whole different classes of robe at regular intervals along the way. It keeps them keen, and it keeps them reading, and wizards, by their nature, want to get higher than their fellow wizards, so for the most part, they keep at it.

Above the rank of Grand High Wrangler of the Infinite though, there is a whole other class of wizardry, only ever reached by the brightest, the best, the most dedicated or the most devious of wizards.

The mages.

And in the Garden, at the top of the wizarding tree, there was Odiz. Odiz the mage. Odiz the magnificent. Odiz the eater of huge lunches and dinners, and just at this moment, Odiz the snorer of loud snores. He'd had a big lunch, and it was afternoon nap time.

Odiz was an old man, and though no-one would call him fat exactly, his dedication to big dinners in recent years had led one or two of the other, braver mages, to nickname him Odiz the Chunky. No-one could quite remember what had happened to the mages who had started that nickname—no-one thought it was *wise* to quite remember. His beard was long and grey and he'd long ago grown tired of tripping over it when it tangled around his feet, so Odiz had permanently enchanted it—now it almost had a life of its own, and would move out of the way of his feet whenever he walked anywhere. While he slept, his beard would twitch and curl in the air, wandering about and getting into mischief without its owner's knowledge.

The beard stopped curling. It quivered, as though it had heard or felt something on the air. There was a disturbance in the house, a voice, a distant scream. Odiz had a large house, as was fitting for a mage of the highest standing, and he slept high up in a turret—something about the career of wizardry leads those who practice it to build towers and turrets on their houses, which is another thing that makes witches raise their eyebrows and mutter.

Odiz kept snoring, safe in the knowledge that his house had more magical charms and alarms and traps on it than any other in the Garden—assassination was not unknown as a pathway to advancement in the world of wizards in the Garden, but it had a couple of catches. The first catch was that you didn't simply take the place of the wizard you'd killed—you had to write an essay about how you'd done it, and demonstrate the method in front of a panel of leading wizards. The second catch was that you had to be inventive about it—no wizard would get on if they simply conjured a troll out of the air and clubbed their superior to a pulp. Any wizard who tried that would find themselves on the wrong end of a disapproving panel.

The disapproval of wizards tends to involve fireballs and being rather deader than you thought you were.

There was a knock on Odiz's bedroom door. He didn't hear it under the noise of his snoring. The beard stood up straight though, then formed itself into a hairy question-mark in the air. Odiz snored, long and deep and snotty. The beard formed a point and snaked back, to prod him in the shoulder.

Prod, prod, prod.

Odiz snored again, snorting. 'Mmmmsausages…' he muttered, then turned onto his side.

The end of the beard softened to a brush-point and tickled Odiz under the nose. He sneezed, rubbed his moustache, breathed —and then began to snore again.

The beard-tip sagged, then shot straight up his nose. Odiz woke up sharply, coughing and snarling and scrabbling at his face.

'Eh, what, what, eh?' demanded the mage. 'Confound ya, ya wretched hairy blighter. Can't a feller get a decent afternoon's kip around these parts anymore?'

The knock came again, and Odiz leapt out of bed, spellcasting hands at the ready. He might be old and a little chunky, but you didn't get to be the world's greatest mage without a healthy set of instincts.

He twiddled his little finger, and the bedroom door shot open, slamming against the wall as if pinned there by a bully. Odiz had lived long enough to know that he who hesitates is lost. In fact, in wizarding circles, he who hesitates often just becomes a greasy smear on the floor. He blasted the unknown intruder with a shot of yellow, crackling energy that should have torn their flesh from their bones.

The orb slid greasily, a little unsteadily into the room. The energy hit it, rippled over its surface, searching for flesh to tear from bones. Eventually, as if embarrassed, the energy fizzled out.

Cunning, thought Odiz. It was the only thought he wasted, blasting a stream of blue-white fire at the sphere with his other hand. The beam was searching for nuts and bolts and things it could unscrew. One or two fell out, and the sphere stopped for a moment in mid-air.

Gotcha, thought Odiz.

The sphere shook off the blue beam though, dodging out of the way. Then it fired a soft red spray-like beam of its own, and the old mage was caught, paralysed in it.

'Ungrrkf,' he grunted, which would probably have been quite rude if he'd been able to get the whole words out.

Skoros stepped into the doorway. 'Ah, Odiz,' he said, smiling a thin smile. 'Lost for words?' The thin smile thickened. 'Don't blame you. I must admit, I'm rather impressed myself. Paralysis beam. Perfectly harmless—unless I decide it shouldn't be.'

The old mage's eyes were trying to widen in fury and indignation, but his muscles simply wouldn't allow it.

'Don't panic, old man, I'm not here to kill you. If I were, believe me, I'd have thought of something far more creative. Oh, sorry about your housekeeper, incidentally—she would keep on. *Her*, I had to kill. As I say, apologies. I know how you appreciated her dinners.'

Odiz tried to moan, but his throat wasn't obeying his commands.

'I need your help, Odiz. I need your knowledge. As long as you continue to be useful to me, you continue to live. Do you understand?'

Odiz tried to say that not only did he understand but that one day he'd tear Skoros a new nose, but none of the words would come out. 'Nnnnnyyymmmmmmnnnnnnsss,' was as much as he managed.

'Splendid,' said Skoros. 'Oh I know what you're thinking, by the way.' He stepped closer to the mage, to look deep into his old, ice blue eyes. 'You're thinking "But how has this happened? All my traps, my alarms, should have stopped any magical attack," aren't you? Yes, I know you are. But you see, you've overlooked one beautiful thing, o magiest of mages.' Skoros was snarling now, the spit flying from his lip and hitting Odiz in the face. 'I've got something *better* than magic now.'

'Raaark. Oh, Skoros? Lord Skoros?' said Razor from the doorway.

Skoros couldn't hear his bird, he was enjoying himself far too much.

'Oi. Dark Lord Of All You Piggin' Survey.'

Skoros smiled, turned to look at Razor. 'Yes?' he said, sweetly.

Razor gulped. 'Might be time we were off?' he said, nudging his head towards the rest of the house.

Skoros thought about it for a moment. He could kill the bird right here and now for his continuing insolence. He hitched his smile wider. *No. No, not yet.* 'You're right, of course. Not going to be terribly dignified, this bit,' he said to the mage, pulling out his wand and aiming it at the sphere.

'Walk,' he commanded.

Against his will, Odiz' legs began to move, and the old man was led down the grand staircase of his home, still in his sleeping-robe, past the dead and bleeding body of Mistress Fazackerly the house-keeper, and out into the sun-drenched afternoon.

9

'So,' said Gunkin, chewing his sardine sandwich with a mouthful of teeth that looked almost guaranteed to one day cut his face off, 'monsters, eh?'

Harper was mesmerized by the sight of the goblin's teeth—they had a hypnotic awfulness to them that was almost worse than the thing he'd seen in the teacup.

'Hmm?' he said, snapping out of it. 'Yes. Monsters.'

'Shhh,' said Gunkin, spraying tiny bits of minced fish in the owl's direction. 'Don't want to panic everybody, now do we?'

'Yes,' said Harper urgently. 'I do. I want people to panic, because there's something to panic *about* and nobody's paying the blindest bit of notice.'

Gunkin swallowed and looked at Harper keenly. 'Well, let me ask you this,' he said, 'do you want them to *just* panic, which involves lots of running around and screaming, or d'you want them to panic and *do* something about the monsters?'

Harper blinked, thinking about it. 'The second thing?' he asked, not entirely sure.

Gunkin smiled, in that disconcerting way he had. In this case, the effect was made even more awful by the bits of sardine between his teeth. 'Yes, the second thing,' he agreed. 'That means we don't let them just overhear the danger they're in. We don't fly about the streets, shouting about monsters, because when people panic, that's when other people start finding their houses and their barns and their fields on fire. Right?'

'If you say so,' said Harper, who was no longer sure he knew what was happening in this conversation.

'We have a message,' explained Gunkin. 'We want them to hear the message and act on it. That, my feathered friend, requires *presentation*. It requires *packaging*.'

'What?' said Harper. 'Like a Midsummer Hallowe'en present? Like a box, and ribbons and that sort of thing.'

Gunkin flashed the horrible smile again. 'Exactly.'

'This is getting ridiculous,' said Celeste.

'Analysis...confirmed.'

Celeste had been tramping all over the Garden for weeks now, moving the scout ship every now and again when she needed a rest cycle. The seeker-beams had activated, which meant the orbs were here, and had found *something* that interested them. But since then—nothing. She'd put out homing beacons for the orbs, she'd done scans for Astarian technology—there was plenty of that here, she knew now, and some of it was ancient—but as far as actually *locating* any of it was concerned, she had drawn blank after blank. It was almost as if the orbs were *hiding* from her. Which was...

'Just ridiculous,' she said, frowning, wondering if it really was.

Although she'd been following procedure when she'd introduced herself to the Green Man and that rude man on the metal horse, since the seeker-beams had split the sky and she'd confirmed that the orbs had found something, she'd thought it best to keep contact with the locals to a minimum. She'd turned on the ship's visual shielding, and she, too, had gone cloaked while she tried to find the orbs, or— she held her breath even as she thought it—what the orbs might have found. But this planet was hot and she was bored of tracking orb activity by hand. She assessed her options and swept her rectangular instrument around again.

It beeped. In fact it beeped and went 'squeeeeee.' For the first time in two weeks, it beeped and went 'squeeeeee.' Celeste frowned at it, sweeping the scanner around again more slowly. The 'squeeeeee' sound grew in pitch and volume as she aimed it at the cottage up ahead. Celeste frowned at the cottage. 'Have picked up a trace of orb activity in a nearby dwelling,' she reported. 'Am deactivating cloak at this time, and going to engage the occupants.'

'Proposed course of action directly contradicts previous search methods,' Alpha chided, Celeste's headband flashing in time with his words.

'Yes, well look where they got us,' she snapped. 'I've been walking around this world getting absolutely nowhere but hot, and tired, and I *really* wish I'd brought my hoverscoot, did I mention that? I'm chang-ing the search methods. Bio-mech Alpha, do you wish to further question my judgement at this time?'

A handful of seconds passed in silence, as the bio-mech seemed to be considering the question.

'Your actions and reasoning will be duly noted in the ship's log,' he said.

'That is not an answer,' said Celeste.

'Confirmed,' said Alpha.

Celeste huffed. 'Disengaging cloak—now.'

Alditha dripped a layer of candle wax into all the bottles of horrid black goo, and pushed a cork into the neck of one bottle, two bottle–

She straightened up. She felt a prickle at the back of her neck. 'Well, come in if you're coming, whoever you are,' she said.

The door of the cottage disappeared, all at once. A young girl stood in the doorway, dressed in an odd outfit and waving a rectangular, beeping box around.

'Hello,' said the girl. 'My name is Celeste. Have you seen an orb around here lately?'

'Stop.'

They had kept to the outskirts and the disused paths on the way from Odiz' house to the border of Skoros' family's land. Now, at the wizard's word and a button-press on his wand, the orb made Odiz stop walking.

Skoros stepped in front of him. 'I'm going to have to do something a little unpleasant now,' he warned the mage, as though killing his housekeeper and kidnapping him in the middle of his afternoon nap had been nothing but jolly playtime fun. 'You may find you panic. In fact,' he said, grinning just a little, 'it's almost a medical certainty that you'll panic. The paralysis ray has levels, you see. I'm sure mages are made of stubborn stuff, and I need you to be unconscious. Rather pointless leading you by the hand to where I'm going to, shall we say, entertain you, only to have you remember the way and tediously try to escape, no?'

Skoros chuckled, and Razor threw in a half-hearted squawk. 'That's where the paralysis ray comes in handy. With a press of a button, I can turn it up, from general paralysis which allows you to walk, to a rather more *compelling* level. I'm going to stop your lungs from moving, Odiz. Stop the blood flowing to your brain for just a little while. It will feel like you're suffocating, like you can't get your breath. Because of course you won't be able to. I advise you to go with it— the faster I can get you where you're going, the sooner I can wake you up.'

Skoros pressed a button on his wand, the corkscrew end turned, and the thick red beam of colour coming from the orb deepened. Odiz' eyes bulged and stayed wide open, even when he fell to the ground.

Skoros' family estate was huge, as was fitting for a family led traditionally by a line of evil wizards. It hadn't started out huge, but along the way, various ancestors had turned up at people's doors and explained to them, either in polite voices or with the visual aid of burning torches, that they didn't live there anymore. And that the inclusion of the word 'there' in that sentence was conditional on them running away.

The Maze had been the brainchild of Salu-Valek The Merciless when he'd run out of conventional dungeon space—there were, after all, only so many hours in any given day that could be dedicated to torturing prisoners to death, and he'd found himself in need of a holding area, a space where his victims could be brought while he worked out his disagreements with his more immediate prisoners. Salu-Valek had many, many disagreements with people. He tended to disagree that they should be breathing.

Skoros walked up to the outside wall of the Maze. It looked horrible, a tangled mass of black and blood-red vines and thorns that slithered over one another as you looked at them. It hissed and made the air taste of metal.

Odiz was laying on his back on precisely nothing at all, the orb's deep red misty beam joined by a pale blue light that bathed him and kept him suspended, pulling him along in the orb's wake.

'Open up, it's me,' Skoros snapped, and the hissing of the vines intensified as they snaked apart to form a hole large enough to let them all through.

'Raark. Ermm, if it's all the same to you, boss, I'll stay out here. This place gives me the right heebie-jeebies,' said Razor.

'What do you have to fear, little one?' Skoros oozed. 'After all, you're a bird. You could fly away at any time.'

'Raark. Pull the other one, O Lord of All You Survey. I know what this stuff is, don't I? Wasn't hatched yesterday,' muttered the bird.

Skoros smirked. 'Come,' he commanded.

'All right,' whispered Razor to himself, 'but if one o'them things comes near me, they'll get a pecking they won't forget in a hurry, that's all I know…'

Slowly, but following Skoros' purposeful stride, Razor went into the Maze.

'Welcome to my cottage, friend Celeste,' said Alditha, stalling for time. 'My name's Alditha. You'll be putting my door back, of course. Only manners.'

Celeste blinked. 'Oh. Yes, of course. Apologies, Alldeet-ha.' She stepped indoors, waved her little bleeping box at the doorway, and nodded with satisfaction when the door reappeared on its hinges.

'It's pronounced Al-dith-a,' said the witch. 'I'm much obliged to you, Celeste. The Green Man told me about you. You're from the teacup, yes?'

Celeste's young face looked blank, and when she spoke, it wasn't to Alditha. 'Query teacup.'

Her headband glowed, then from the ends just above her ears, two beams of soft blue light emerged, forming an image of a teacup.

'Oh,' she said, waving her hand through the image to disperse it. 'The scout ship, yes. It's not really a…teacup, it just has a system that chooses a local object, and then disguises the ship as that object, whatever it is. Helps to not upset the locals.'

A smile twitched at the corners of Alditha's mouth as she recalled Harper's terrified reaction. 'And that works, does it? Usually, I mean?'

'Yes,' said Celeste, 'usually. So—orbs?'

'Metal balls with wings that fly about the place,' Alditha said, nodding once. 'Found one. Heard tell of another. What's it to you?'

'I'm looking for them, because either they shouldn't be here, or they should. Either way, I need to find them to know why they're *still* here.'

It was Alditha's turn to blink. 'No, sorry, you're going to have to do a bit better than that,' she said, sniffing. 'You can come in, by the way, sit yourself down.' She gestured to the kitchen table, and one of its simple carved wooden chairs slid out, revealing a red and white checked cushion.

Celeste smiled. 'Thank you. I've been walking for-' She paused, and her headband pulsed, then a voice said 'Seven hours, local time.' '-Seven hours,' she finished, as though nothing had interrupted her.

'Handy, your little oojamaflip,' said Alditha, nodding at her headband, which glowed almost immediately.

'No known translation for oojamaflip.'

'Means thingummybob. Or whatchamacallit. Or doofer,' said Alditha, watching the rapid pulsing of the headband that followed.

'No known translation for thingummy-'

'Doesn't know everything though. Good. I don't like things that think they know everything,' said Alditha. 'People neither.' She smiled suddenly. 'So, about these orbs of yours?'

'Standard reconnaissance orbs-'

'Come again?'

Celeste's headband glowed. 'Reconnaissance—the finding out of…stuff,' said Alpha.

'So, standard finding out of stuff orbs,' Celeste continued, raising both eyebrows.

Alditha nodded.

'The most recent ones were sent ahead of me to search for any evidence of Astarian technology on the worlds in this sector.'

'Asswhatian?'

'Astarian. *People like me*. People say the Astarian homeworld itself was lost hundreds of thousands of years ago, but no-one really knows anymore. It seems likely our people destroyed or polluted their world to the point where it became uninhabitable. Though others believe that our sun and planetary system was captured by a massive passing star and pulled into a new orbit. Either way, whatever happened, the Astarian fleet has been roaming the galaxy ever since.'

'Not big on history, you Astarians, are you?'

'Not anymore,' agreed Celeste. 'Records were kept originally, but what with even three-dimensional space being the size it is, the chances of finding out what really happened seemed so absurdly remote, we've more or less just decided to go forward with our lives.'

'More or less, is it?'

Alditha snapped her fingers, and on her working surface, a knife cut bread, another slathered it with homemade sheep's butter, and a spoon glooped into some of Old Ma Hazelbrook's plum jam, which was spread on the bread. A plate flew out of a neat rack and scooped up the bread and jam like a passenger, then it slid through the air and across the table to Celeste, who looked at Alditha, curious as to what had just happened.

'Food,' explained the witch. 'Eat,' she said. 'You do eat, I take it?'

Celeste reached into one of her invisible pockets, and pulled out a sleek metal rectangle, which she pressed to produce a small, thin white brick. 'Nutrition pills,' she explained, offering one to Alditha. The witch took it, narrowing her eyes at it along the line of her nose. Then she shrugged and popped it in her mouth. It tasted of absolutely nothing, like a long Sunday afternoon with nothing to do and nobody to do it with.

'Nutrition ain't what it used to be,' she judged, nodding at the girl to try her bread and jam.

Celeste picked it up, turned it round, as if trying to decide on the best way to tackle the unfamiliar object. Then she bit off a corner and chewed. Her eyes went wide.

'Oh…' she said. 'Oh, my…'

Her headband flashed like an alarm. 'Chemical ingestion index violation—complex carbohydrate, animal fat, fructose-'

'Shut up, Alpha,' said Celeste simply, and the voice cut off. 'This is amazing. This is just-' She bit and chewed some more, hardly seeming to breathe between mouthfuls. Bread and jam tasted so much better than strawberry marshmallows.

Alditha smiled again, a tiny triumph glinting in her eyes. She snapped her fingers again, and the process began to repeat itself on her working surface.

'So, if you've given up on history, what are your finding out stuff orbs trying to find out?'

'Mmmeepers,' said Celeste through a sticky, buttery mouthful. As she spoke, her bright blonde hair pulsed pink, then purple, then stood up stiff on end. She swallowed. 'Sleepers,' she said again.

'Ah,' said Alditha. 'And who are they when they're at home?'

'Mmmmnotatome,' said the girl through another bite of bread and jam. 'Lost. There was an expedition, long ago. Thousands of years ago.'

Her headband flashed, slowly, almost as though it was sulking. '6.8 thousand years ago, Galactic Standard Time.'

Celeste licked some jam off her thumb. 'Exactly—6.8 thousand years ago. No-one's entirely sure where they were headed, but they sent a report back to say they'd found a planet that would be ideal for the fleet to colonize. A new home,' she said, sounding wistful. 'But something went wrong. The data compression-' She looked at Alditha, who raised one eyebrow. 'The message with directions to where they were?' she tried, and Alditha nodded. 'It never came through. Only that they were going to come back and lead us there, because there were dimensional anomalies.'

Alditha's eyebrow began to rise again.

'It was odd,' said Celeste. 'Somehow there were complications, and the message got garbled every time they tried to send it. Then-' Her face clouded beneath her purple-pulsing, sticky-up hair. 'Then things got worse,' she said. 'They couldn't make orbit, they said, couldn't get away. A major problem…an unforeseen accident involving the scout ship. So they went into their cryo-chambers-' She didn't even bother to look at Alditha this time. 'They went to sleep. A sleep that kept them alive for a long time. But since then, we've heard nothing from them.'

'Been lookin' for 'em all that time, have you, these Sleepers of yours?'

Celeste fixed her with a quizzical look. 'Space is big,' she said, as if talking to a child. 'Really, really big. But actually, no. We sent out probes for a while—a thousand years or so—but nobody found anything. It's only recently that we've-' Again, she paused, the cloud passing over her face. 'We've needed to look for them.'

'So what are you doing here? Never heard tell of any snoring Astarians in the Garden. Sort of thing somebody would have noticed, a bunch of lazy beggars not pulling their weight.'

'Because some of the recent orbs reported back, obviously,' Celeste explained. 'Alditha, you don't understand…the orbs found something—*here*, in the Garden.'

———————

'Wakey, wakey.'

Odiz gasped for breath, and finding suddenly that he could take one, he gasped for another. He was sitting upright, but something was wrong.

'Back with us? Good, I'd hate to have killed you by accident.'

Odiz said nothing, he was concentrating on getting breath back into his body. His head was pounding, and his eyes felt like fried eggs, still sizzling around the edges. When his body got used to the fact that it was all still there, he noticed something.

Young idiot's got me bound. Normally, even the impertinence of such a thing would have been enough to secure Skoros a special, no-expense-spared trip underground in a wooden box, but Odiz was noticing a few other things.

Damned Blackheart Bindweed. Nasty stuff. Best hear the fool out. Ach, confound it—he discovered that even his head was encased in a skull-cap of intertwining thorny, hissing vines.

Skoros smiled at him. 'Yes, it's Blackheart Bindweed. And you know what that means. You try to escape, you'll be full of blood-drinking thorns before you take two steps. You try to do magic, the Maze will tear your arms off before you can cast so much as a love spell. I advise you to take that seriously; you probably can't feel it yet, but there are already thorns embedded in your skull, Odiz. If you even *think* your incantation, they will know.' He hiked the smile up further. 'It would be such a shame to lose all that learning, don't you think?'

'What is it you want, you odious, beardless little tyke?' Odiz barked.

'Shhhhh, I really wouldn't get the Maze excited if I were you,' Skoros whispered. 'Not when what I want is so simple. I want information, Odiz. That's all. Not your big house or your fancy housekeeper with the fabulous recipe for shepherd's pie. Not your books, not your skills, not any of that. Just information.'

'Ever thought of just askin', ya rat bag?'

Skoros scythed through the space between them, to spit in the mage's face. 'This *is* me just asking,' he hissed.

Odiz snapped his teeth together, and Skoros yelped back in surprise.

'Poke your filthy nose near my choppers again, sunshine, and I'll bite it off,' snarled the mage.

Skoros recovered his sneer, pointed his wand at Odiz' face.

'Raaark, easy boss. Information, remember? If you kill 'im, he can tell you the square root of beggar all.'

Skoros grunted, stepped back, and pressed a button on his wand. The corkscrew tip whirred, and a bluish light shone out of the end. The light clung together, forming itself into a holographic image. A dark red star, with wings on either side of it.

'What,' said Skoros, through teeth clenched tight, 'is this?'

10

Witches move in all the usual ways that most people do. But witches, being witches, have a whole extra set of ways of moving too—ways which would seem silly or dramatic if anyone else tried to use them. They're like witchy cheat modes.

No-one—but no-one, stalks like a witch. When a witch decides to stalk instead of walking, it's almost as though the universe—walls, trees, people, dragons—decides to get out of their way, without necessarily knowing why they're doing it. All it knows is that it's a really, really good idea.

Alditha stalked through the cottage, a curious Celeste following a little behind and to the side of her, in case she was actually powered by spaceship fuel. She went from the kitchen to the hallway, to the bedroom, to a bookcase, then she waved a hand and kept going— *through* the bookcase, down another corridor that, according to Celeste's bleeping box, didn't really exist, and through yet another door which she didn't bother to open eithert. Celeste hopped through after her, before whatever effect Alditha was creating stopped happening.

The two found themselves in a round, wooden room, like being inside the trunk of a tree. It had more bookcases stuck to its round walls, well-stuffed, cushion-covered sofas, and a handful of tables with large pots or bits of odd equipment on them. Alditha stalked her way over to a bookcase, opened a small, unremarkable box and took out a type of spinning top made of rough twigs held together with silver twine. It was only when she turned around to stalk back in the other direction that she realized Celeste was still with her.

'Oh, *you're* here, are you?'

Celeste smiled.

'Well, good, I suppose.' She showed her the crude, wooden spinning top. 'Not just you that has-' she shrugged. '- oojamaflips.'

She walked to a point on the floor, then licked a finger and stuck it in the air. She frowned at it and took two quick steps to the left. 'Come stand by me,' she said, and Celeste did, obeying the command in her voice. 'I'm going to count to three,' said Alditha. 'Then you and me together are going to spin around and stamp once, with our left foot. Can you do that?'

Celeste frowned and nodded.

'You're sure?'

She nodded again.

'Alright then,' said Alditha, pulling her hat firmly onto her head. 'One. Two. You're *absolutely* sure?'

Celeste sighed. 'On three, we spin and stamp, yes.'

'Which foot?'

'The left.'

'Hmm. Good. Just checking. I don't tend to let people see me do this, you know. It's a bit...'

'Over-complicated?' suggested Celeste. 'Exasperating?'

Alditha sniffed. 'I was going to say "magical," but please yourself. Right then—One. Twooooo. *Three.*'

Alditha threw the spinning top into the air. They both spun around, stamped their left foot on the ground, and Celeste's violet eyes grew wide with astonishment. The spinning top was turning slowly in mid-air, but a tiny dancing shoot had sprouted out of its uppermost twig, and pale, waxy white roots were growing quickly out of the bottom. As she watched, the roots reached down to the floor, and shoots and leaves zipped out at greater and greater speed. Soon it didn't look like one plant at all, but lots, all around them, circling them, *building* something. The twigs of the spinning top glowed golden.

Alditha smirked a little. 'Magical,' she said again as whatever it was that was being built was built. 'Oh, hang on-

Past and present, future dark,

Sing to me through root and bark.

Bring the stars, come joy or pain,

Build my Tarot Wheel again.'

Celeste giggled. She couldn't help herself. 'What was *that*?'

'*That* was the spell. Got to give it a spell, so it knows what to make. What shape you want it to take.'

'You really don't,' said Celeste. 'You just have to direct the sigma energy field with the focus of your mind.'

Alditha folded her arms. 'Oh you do, do you? That's all you have to do, is it? And what would you know about magic, missy?'

'It's not magic,' explained Celeste. 'Don't you know what you have here?'

'It's magic if I say it is,' said Alditha firmly. 'And I do. So it is. Are we clear on that?'

'I say it's an oojamaflip.' Celeste grinned up at the witch. 'But we can call it magic if it makes you feel better.'

'It does,' said Alditha, 'yes.'

Celeste giggled again, then looked at the thing that the spinning top had built around them. It seemed to just be a circle of wood with twelve branches sticking up at even points all around the circle. 'Erm,' she said. 'Impressive, this magic of yours.'

'Oh, you ain't seen nothing yet,' said Alditha. 'I haven't done the best bit yet.'

'The best bit?'

'This.' Alditha snapped her fingers sharply, and all the lights in the room went out. It was suddenly pitch black, but all around them in the circle there were stars. Stars and star systems, multi-coloured planets like balls of ruby and emerald and pearl. A comet shot past Celeste's left ear, and she gasped.

'This is my Tarot Wheel,' explained Alditha, and her voice sounded huge, like she could take dust and make a world of it just for fun if she wanted to.

'This is the twelve-dimensional mapping interface from an interstellar starship, that's what this is, but I will admit one thing,' said Celeste. 'It certainly is the best bit.'

'Still not the best bit,' said Alditha. '*This* is the best bit. See, every spoke of the zodiac corresponds to a sign, and every sign corresponds to suits or players. Cups, wands, pentacles, the fool, the hanged man, the tower, all that.'

Celeste blinked.

Alditha rolled her eyes. 'Everything that can be known, you can find out through the tarot. You just have to do-' She tapped a star and it flared, tapped another and dragged it to another part of the circle, where it formed a bright red line of connection. She pinched two stars between her thumb and forefinger and pushed them apart, so they formed a triangle with a third. Then she sent the whole universe of stars spinning around them anticlockwise. '-this,' she said. 'How long do you reckon those Sleepers of yours have been missing?'

'6.8 thousand years,' said Celeste as she watched the stars spin by.

Alditha sighed and gave them another kick of speed, then slowed them, adjusted, peered at the stars that were in front of her then. 'By the will of Ven Tao, the Great Gardener, show me,' she commanded, and the universe around them changed perspective, flooded with light and colour. There were tall men and women in close-fitting suits that seemed like they had been made for comfort—they had a puffy, quilted look. The people had long hair in a range of colours— browns and reds and golds and whites. There were six of them, and as Alditha and Celeste watched, they seemed to be in a panic, running back to a large, round, shiny metal disc with a dome in the middle of it—a thing Alditha didn't recognise.

A thing Celeste knew as the lost scout ship of the Sleepers.

———————

'Oh, that,' said Odiz, managing a grin beneath his beard. 'Oh, I know what *that* is.'

'Goooood,' said Skoros. He waited. 'Well?'

'Well what?'

'Well *what is it then?*'

'Are you daft, man? 's'a star with wings on.'

'I *know* it's a star with wings on,' spluttered Skoros. 'What does it *mean?*'

'What does it *meeeean?*' asked Odiz, imitating the young wizard. 'Well, who knows what it *meeeeeans?* Maybe it's a phoenix too dim to take its eggshell off. Maybe it's a fireball that thinks it's a butterfly. Maybe it's a beautiful red sun that likes to swan about the skies making all the yellow suns feel jealous, how should I know?'

'Ohhhh you know, old man. I can sense the knowledge in you. What's more, *I've* seen it before. Somewhere in the back of my head, I've seen it before. I just can't get it out. Can't remember. So do you know what I did? I read every book in my family's house. Every single one. You know my family?'

'Mmm,' said Odiz, darkly. 'Stark, raving bonkers, most of 'em. They'd be proud to see you carrying on the family tradition.'

'We go back a long way,' said Skoros, ignoring the insult. 'We have *a lot* of books.'

'Bet there are none on how to grow beards.'

'And not one of them—not a single one—has this symbol in it. But it's in my head, somewhere, just forever out of reach. I knew it the moment I first saw it, but...but I...'

Odiz made a face. 'Where've you seen it?' he asked, like he was coaxing a bird off a branch. 'Recently, I mean? What made you start thinking of it in the first place, old chap?'

'Ha,' Skoros snapped himself back together. 'You won't get round me like that. I know you know. I mean, if I know what it is, somewhere in the back of my head, then you must know too, because you're Odiz, and you're the most powerful mage in the Garden.'

'And what good is that to you when I'm trussed up here in Blackheart Bindweed?'

'Ahahaha—I'll *make* you remember what it means, and you can tell me.'

Odiz coughed politely. 'I highly doubt that, young man. You can't even make *yourself* remember it, and you already want to help me? How do you propose to make someone *else* remember it if you can't make yourself? Especially when you go about it by killing their housekeeper and draggin' them off in the middle of a perfectly good afternoon kip and sticking Blackheart Bindweed in their hair? I mean, it's hardly conducive to the memory, is it, all this? You've not really thought this through, have you lad? Are you sure this evil wizarding's really the game for you? Maybe you'd be better suited to quantity surveying. Or dentistry. Not tried it myself, but they tell me dentistry's all the rage.'

'Shut up,' yelled Skoros. 'You know what it means. I know you do.'

Odiz sniffed. 'Might do. Thing is though, the more you try and make me remember and tell you, the more I'm going to try and forget.'

'Why?' Skoros asked, his patience failing.

'Because,' said Odiz. 'Just because of all the shepherd's pies I'll never get to eat, thanks to your horrible bully boy tactics.'

'But you have to. You have to tell me,' Skoros sneered. Then, moving close to the mage, added, 'I'm being patient with you Odiz. Just remember, I can make you *suffer*.'

Odiz' beard formed itself into a point and cleaned out one of his ears. 'Yes,' said Odiz, 'but that's about *all* you can do to me. Well, that and kill me, I suppose, but then you'd never know if I know what you want to know. Would you?'

Skoros turned on his heel and fumed. The light-image abruptly died on the end of his wand.

'Of course, one thing you haven't considered,' said Odiz, making Skoros spin back to face him again, 'is that maybe it's not human knowledge you need after all. Maybe it's demon knowledge. Try getting Big Red in here with your little ball of doohickeys, see what he has to say about being tangled up in Blackheart Bindweed. I'd enjoy watching you try and explain that one—briefly. Maybe it's *dragon* knowledge you need—go threaten Sagar with your ball of pretty lights, see how singed you get. Maybe it's witch knowledge. Pay Alditha a visit, see if she calls you a wet blanket again, eh?'

Skoros' patience snapped. 'Bindweed. Hear your master. Tighten your grip every half an hour till I return. Pull this old fool's arms and legs off, inch by inch. We'll see who's a wet blanket then.'

One of the other things Skoros had never been terribly good at was his evil laugh. It was pretty much part of the entrance requirement to his family to have a big, terrifying evil laugh. It was like the family birthmark. Skoros had only ever been able to conjure a watery, nasal snicker, but some moments in the life of an evil wizard absolutely demanded a big evil laugh, and this was one of them. He took a deep breath and tried his best.

'Wahhheeehaaaahhhhheeeurrgh.'

Then he coughed and spluttered and spat out snot.

'Dear oh dear, are you coming down with something?' asked Odiz as the bindweed slithered tight around his wrists.

Skoros stomped away, followed by his orb.

Razor stayed behind. He coughed. 'Erm. Sorry about him,' said the raven. 'He gets a bit...well, y'know?'

'Barking mad at times?' suggested Odiz. 'Yes, I know.' He rolled his eyes. 'Run along little bird, before the Maze decides it's peckish.'

Razor nodded and flew off after his furious master.

———

Alditha and Celeste watched as the Sleepers silently ran about, bringing samples from different directions to load into the ship.

Celeste frowned. 'Why can't we hear what they're saying?'

Alditha rolled her eyes. 'It's magical, isn't? Mystical. *Visionary*. No sound, ever.'

Celeste looked at her, then rubbed the end of her nose. 'Sound,' she said, loud and firm. A green bar appeared in the corner of their vision.

'Volume, up thirty percent,' said Celeste, and as though it were water pouring into a paper bag, the sound of the scene pushed softly into their ears.

Alditha ground her teeth.

'You never turned the sound on,' said Celeste simply, as though to say that anyone could have made the same mistake. There was a note in her voice though that seemed to add that anyone who did would be a bit dim.

'Bit of a witch yourself, aren't you? On the quiet?' said Alditha, through teeth that were still pretty gritted.

Celeste smiled up at her. 'If you think that was good, this is going to blow your magic socks off,' she said, then added 'Change aspect ratio to full immersive.'

The scene spun around them, and Alditha nearly lost her footing as somebody ran past her. She blinked to see the size of the scout ship up ahead—it was about the size of...

She tried to think of a space as big as the ship, and decided it was as about as big as the main crossroads in the Garden, the one with Stone Hedge in it.

'Peridot,' said a boy with hair the colour of conkers, 'where's Ven? Quarka says we have only about thirty slipaways before the gate opens. I swear, that brother of yours is going to get us all killed.'

A slightly taller girl with a pronounced nose and a bob of hair like Celeste's, only green as summer grass and with eyes to match, smiled at him. 'Don't worry. You know what he's like, "Oh, there's plenty of time yet, and look at this, and that, and the other thing." He's still collecting flora samples to take home.'

'The idea is that this is supposed to *be* home. Tell him to leave it all and get to his pruning, or I'll use his shears myself.'

Peridot sighed, put down the box of mineral deposits she was carrying and strode off behind the ship.

'POV Character-Peridot,' said Celeste out loud, and the world spun around them again.

'Will you cut that out, ya meddling child,' demanded Alditha, making sure her hat was still on. Without moving, they seemed to have gone *into* Peridot, to be seeing what she saw as she walked around the ship and into the dense trees.

Peridot found him easily—it unnerved Alditha to suddenly know that she'd always found it easy to find her little brother.

'What's going on?' demanded the witch. ''s'like she's inside my head. I don't allow anyone to go barging in there without wiping their feet. How do I know what she's thinking?'

'It's actually more like you're inside *her* head,' explained Celeste. 'I'm getting it, too—it's nothing but a sense memory. She always used to win at games of hide and find—but you know that, too.'

'Yes,' said Alditha, her lip twitching as she received the memory. 'I do. This is a...*witchy* way of doing things.'

'Then you should be happy, shouldn't you?'

Alditha opened her mouth to say 'But *you're* doing it, and that's not at all the same thing as *me* doing it. In fact, that means it's getting done and I'm *not* doing it, which is worse than it not being done in the first place.' She looked across at Celeste, remembering her joy when she'd discovered bread and jam. Then Alditha closed her mouth, defeated, and watched the scene in front of her. She couldn't be cruel to the girl.

There was a boy who looked younger, and if anything blonder than Celeste, his hair more unruly, his robe-like uniform covered in smears of mud and green and grey and white. He had a tear in his uniform across his right knee.

'Zirca is getting anxious about you,' said Peridot to the boy—and in the room, Alditha and Celeste both said it too. 'What have you found now?'

The boy looked up, and his concentration broke into a gleaming smile at his sister.

'Worms,' he said warmly. 'It's quite hypnotic to watch them, Peri. Look how they move.'

He pointed to a dip he'd made in the earth, where pinkish-brown earthworms scurried to burrow back into the dark.

'Interesting,' Peridot, Alditha and Celeste agreed, 'but not interesting enough to risk the wrath of the mission commander, little brother. Everything in its due proportion.'

The boy rolled his almond-shaped, amethyst-coloured eyes at his sister.

'I don't know why you people go anywhere,' he chuckled. 'As soon as you get there, all you want to do is turn right round and go straight home.'

'Fifty years is hardly turning right round, Ven,' said Peridot, joining in with the banter, despite her brother's impatience.

'Feels like it,' he said. 'I think I could watch these worms for fifty years and never get bored.'

'Ha. You get bored more easily than anyone else I know,' said Peridot, swooping down suddenly to tickle him. 'Look up, little brother, there are birds you haven't seen yet. Look over there, a clump of mushrooms. Ooh look, a new tree.'

She was mocking him, but only with the special license that sisters have. And besides, it came with a tickle, and Ven had always been helpless against the power of tickling.

He fought to get his breath between laughs. 'Alright, alright, enough.'

She let him be, and he looked back at his wriggling hollow of worms. 'I'm just going to miss everything, that's all. How do you not miss everything, Peri?'

'You keep it all,' she said. 'Up in your mind, so you can watch it again, any time you like. That means you have to take good mind-pictures. The shades, the smells, the *everything* of things. You'll get used to it,' she assured him, getting up and offering him her hand. 'Besides, you'll be coming back, won't you? But only if you get your disgraceful self into the engine room and stop annoying Zirca. You're not the only Gardener in the fleet, you know.'

Ven chuckled again, taking her hand and letting her pull him up. 'No, but I'm the best,' he told her, grinning. 'I doubt Zirca would have even been able to *see* the leaf-growth that led us here, let alone make it flower.'

'Maybe not, but he's still the commander. I've no doubt you're a genius in your mind, Venny, and maybe you are in the real world too, but a little humility would serve you better than throwing your genius in his face and flouting all the rules, all the time. Look at you now, keeping him waiting, to look at *worms*.'

'Worms are more interesting than Zirca,' muttered Ven, and, leaving his sister scandalized and shaking her head, he strode forward, calling out 'I'm here, fans. Don't panic, life can go on.' as he marched up the ramp and into the ship.

'Switch to POV Character-Ven,' said Celeste. 'Forward, speed by six.'

'Wait,' gasped Alditha, but the world didn't—it marched them through corridors on the ship and into an indoor jungle. Plants, pools, a miniature forest, a compost heap. Creepers and vines and an explosion of colour and green. They marched with Ven's confidence down one leg of the pathway through the jungle, to a central point, where sat…

'Wait, what?' Alditha demanded.

'Hello again,' said Ven, stroking the rock-like fronds of a large, square stone hedge.

11

To anyone watching, it wouldn't have been quite clear whether Odiz was asleep or dead. He slumped in his harness of black binding weed and thorns. Skoros hadn't been lying—the Blackheart Bindweed had punctured the mage's skull, dug thorns deep down, to know if he was even *thinking* magical thoughts. But Odiz was neither asleep nor dead. He was somewhere in between, in a state of meditation. To a mage, his most important weapon wasn't in his fingers or in his books, but in his mind, and Odiz, in an effort to keep as much of his mind as safe as possible, had rolled his eyes back in his head, packed up his mind in the equivalent of a small suitcase, and gone on a mental vacation, to think about the situation he found himself in, without actually *thinking* about it. Right now, while his body was sagging in its harness of black binding weed and thorns, Odiz' mind was laying on a sun-lounger somewhere by the sea, with a mug of mead in one hand and a sausage sandwich in the other.

Sadly, the moment you enchant something, you lose some control over what it does. Odiz' mind might be off having a fine time, but his beard was among the least happy beards in the history of magic. It crept slowly sideways, investigating the bindweed that was keeping the mage's right hand bound and spread, unable to form the finger-movements needed to fire anything beyond a level three fireball. The beard tickled his fingers, but there was no reaction. It curled like wisps of smoke between his chubby thumb and the stringy, rubbery bindweed-strands.

Odiz' beard wasn't stupid—it had been attached to the greatest mage in the Garden for too long. It knew it had made a mistake whole seconds before the trap was sprung. It felt the vibration in its hairs, felt the shift in the bindweed.

It didn't see the vines of the Maze twist together behind it.

Suddenly, the bindweed holding Odiz snapped taut, a trunk-like intertwine of vines forming in front of the unconscious mage. It yanked, and his arms were pulled painfully wide. Odiz' mind packed up its sun-lounger in a hurry, and his eyes shot open, staring into something that wasn't a face. It was the sort of thing that black, slick, sticky evil-minded vines would make if they were trying to *make* a face, but it wasn't enough of a face to warrant the word. The vines parted, and a sticky, black stamen waggled, like a tongue in a decrepit man's mouth. It oozed a black, tar-like nectar, dripping down the vines, and extended towards Odiz' face.

'This is a fine mess you've got us into,' muttered the mage. 'You're more trouble than you're worth, you enchanted hairball.'

'Hold.'

The voice, sharp with its importance, was unmistakable—Skoros had returned. The bindweed slowly, almost reluctantly, shrank back out of Odiz' face.

'And what have we here?' Skoros sneered. 'Trying to escape? Oh Odiz, I'm really quite disappointed in you.'

'Blow it out your beard-hole,' growled Odiz, still annoyed at having had his meditation interrupted.

Skoros smiled at the insult.

Oh, that's not good, thought Odiz.

'And there was I, coming to tell you about my day. Coming to offer you your freedom, for just a little information. Tut tut.'

'Were you dropped on your head as a child?' asked Odiz.

'No,' said Skoros, still sneering.

'Want to give it a try sometime?'

'Funny man,' Skoros replied. 'But I wanted you to know that you gave me an idea. Big Red? I captured him not long after I left you. Sagar will take more orbs, I should think, but soon, I'll *have* more. Tonight I take care of Alditha. Join me, Odiz. Join the winning side, be a part of my bright future.'

'Big words for a beardless boy with a lot to do.'

'Foolish words for an old man who likes breathing.'

'Raaark. Err, boss. Really? Is this, y'know, wise? In any way?'

'Just tell me what I want to know, Odiz. That's all I ask—not much for your freedom, surely? Tell me what the symbol means.'

Odiz sighed. 'And then you'll "let me go," will you?' He made small twitchy speech marks in the air with his fingers, and the bindweed hissed at him.

'Yes.'

'Let me go as in release me, let me go home and get on with my life, or let me go as in kill me because I'm no further use to you? Sorry, don't mean to sound suspicious, but you're not the first megalomaniac I've encountered. I knew your father, for one.'

'Help me, and you'll be free to walk out of the Maze, if you can find the way,' said Skoros, fixing Odiz with a dark stare.

'Aha. So that's how it's going to be. Okay, I can work with that,' said the elder man. He sucked his teeth, seeming to consider. ' Well, far as I know, the red star with wings is the mark of the *EngineSeers.*'

Skoros frowned and nervously rubbed his chin.

'Okay...' he said slowly, with the faintest hint of understanding. 'And who *are* the EngineSeers, pray tell? Come on, mage. I have to know.'

'Ancient magicians. Highest magicians. Higher than any mage who ever lived. None of 'em left now of course, though your orb thingy looks like it might have been made by 'em, I'll give you that. They combined blacksmithery and magic. Metal and nature—brought 'em together for the ultimate power. You know the local legends about Ven Whatsisface, the Great Gardener?'

Skoros nodded. The legends went back further than anyone could remember. There had always been Hallowe'ens in the Garden, and the ritual of Ven Tao had been performed, as far as anyone knew, back to the first of them.

The girl. The girl was an EngineSeer, like Ven Tao? Like the most powerful magicians in the whole of history? Like a god?

But what was he if not a new EngineSeer? He'd made his wand, hadn't he, combining blacksmith-work and magic. He'd made the orb work, when his CyberBats had dismantled it. He had the understanding, he had the skill.

He'd been right—the girl was crucial. He smiled, a thin, sudden, brittle smile with barbs on.

'Thank you,' he purred. Then something occurred to him and he frowned again. 'How do you know this? I've seen the ritual of Ven Tao performed many times—the symbol was never a part of it.'

'There's a book,' said Odiz, breathing heavily against the tightness of the bindweed. 'Legend says the Manual of the EngineSeers holds all the secrets of their arts and how to work 'em. Good luck looking for it, though. It's eluded even the most insane of mages for thousands of years.'

Skoros stared into the distance, his mind working overtime, then grinned. 'But of course it has. That makes perfect sense. It's been keeping itself hidden. Secret. Waiting for its natural owner. The one who will bring their secrets back to the Garden.'

'Annnnd that would be you, would it?'

Skoros kept his grin in place. 'Me. Yes.'

'Ohhh, brother. Is this the part where you do another stupid laugh and "set me free" then?'

'No laughing, Odiz. Not this time.' He put his thumb and forefinger in his mouth and gave a sharp, whiplash whistle.

'Knew it. Y'know, for a would-be EngineSeer, you're not imaginative, Skoros.'

Skoros flashed him a smile, then turned and began to walk away.

The bindweed round Odiz' wrists tightened, sliding into thin strands, razor-sharp and thorn-toothed. They twitched, and Odiz groaned and screamed as both his hands were severed. He fell forward onto his knees, his beard quickly forming itself into a pillow to protect his head as he fell.

Skoros paused, grinned. 'Imagination's overrated,' he said to himself, then kept on walking.

'He's got a Stone Hedge,' Alditha pointed out. 'What's he got a Stone Hedge for?'

'Pause,' said Celeste, and the world stopped. 'It's not a Stone Hedge,' she explained. 'It's a primitive dimension drive.'

'Ah,' said Alditha matter-of-factly. 'And that would be?'

'A dimension drive. Back in the early days, Astarian explorers used things like this to find the cracks in dimensions, and slide through them.'

Alditha blinked. 'Is that what they did? Really?' She sniffed. 'So glad I asked.'

'It's a tree,' said Celeste, 'only it's a special tree.'

'I know, yes—certain times of year, it lights up and dances and everybody goes all gooey,' Alditha agreed, nodding.

'They go gooey?' Celeste frowned. 'Never used to have that effect on matter when we used them.'

'No, I mean they—oh, don't worry about it.'

'Most of the time, it's inert.' Celeste looked over at the witch. 'It does nothing,' she simplified. 'But it's sensitive to points of dimensional contact. When dimensions come close it-'

'Does a happy dance, right?'

'-reacts to that closeness. If you have the right tools, you can prune it at those times, and get it to extend its branches into other dimensions nearby. And it can pull you with it. Fascinating technology, really. Ancient now, of course—we've been using a holographic quantum matter version for thousands of years.'

Alditha looked at her. 'You do know that people only understand about half a teaspoon of what you say, don't you?'

Celeste smiled at her sweetly. 'Play,' she said, and the world started moving again.

Ven felt a few stone fronds, examining them carefully. It felt strange to Alditha to suddenly know that he was checking the quantum harmonics of leaf-growth.

'Delta Six, confirm nutrient levels,' said Ven, frowning. 'Jazper 5-9 —to me, please.' A book was thrown across the engine-room by an unseen operative and Ven caught it in one hand. It was a well-used book, with a faded symbol on its cover, though Celeste and Alditha were unable to see it clearly. As the book reached his hand, Ven closed his eyes and colour began to pulse, through the dimension drive, through the book, and through Ven himself, as though the three were connected.

An area of space that had looked for all the world like a patch of shadow in the jungle resolved into a spindly figure with a bulbous head like an upside-down egg and large, black eyes. It stepped out of the shadows.

'Checking,' it said, in a voice that was half robotic, half something else, something more like Ven's. 'Nutrient levels at twelve percent of optimum,' it reported.

'What?' Ven ran a hand through his spiky hair. 'Why so low? We'll never achieve transference with levels like that.'

'Analysis shows unanticipated nutrient leak through root system. Additional: root system has become entrenched in planetary bedrock. Postulate nutrient leak into local environment.'

'Not good, Delta. Not—not even *close* to good. I'm never going to hear the last of this from Zirca.' He took a communicator from a holster on his belt. 'Gamma Thirteen, initiate…'

He stopped, watching as the dimension drive, glowing with a hundred rainbows, began to unstiffen, to melt, to bridge the gaps between dimensions.

'Please complete instruction, Gardener Ven Tao,' said the bio-mechanoid on the bridge. Ven swallowed, knowing what his instruction would mean. 'Initiate hibernation protocol. Inform Commander Zirca the dimension drive has suffered a major nutrient leak, and cannot achieve dimensional branching at this time. All crew and bio-mechs should report to their assigned cryo-pods. Fleet Command are to be informed immediately. Oh, and personal note to Mineralogist Peridot. Sorry, Peridot. Look after my worms for me.'

'Acknowledged,' said the bio-mech, but Ven wasn't listening anymore. He put down the communicator and pulled his Probability Shears off his belt. Normally, this would have been the highlight of the trip for him, his moment to shine, to look at the dancing dimension drive, to feel its rhythms and its growth, and to prune it precisely so it reached into the right dimension and pulled the ship with it, to start them on their journey home. Now though...

He swallowed again, knowing what he had to do. If the hedge branched now, it would rip the ship apart trying to push through to its home dimension, and fail, and maybe take the planet with it. He had to prune it more savagely than he'd ever done before, stop it stretching out its branches till everyone was safe in their pods. And he had to give them a chance, a way of using it when they finally came out of their sleep chambers.

Alditha and Celeste both felt it at the same moment—the punch in the heart of knowing what that meant.

I'm going to die here.

Now.

On the outskirts of his attention, Ven knew his faithful engine room bio-mechs were moving, heading to their assigned pods, where he should be. With a moan of desperation, he threw the small manual he was holding as far away as he could from the vicinity of the hedge. It landed on the edge of a nearby crevice, then slipped down its side and was lost.

Now he had both hands free to finish the job.

He switched on the Probability Shears and made his first cut. The hedge screamed, a noise of electricity and pain. It flared blue and pink and angry red. He lopped another branch, as he heard machinery doing what it had to do—punching holes into the earth, burying the cryo-capsules like weird triangular seeds. The hedge flared purple and turquoise, writhing and lashing out at his hands as it had never done before. A branch caught him, and the pain shot up his arm as he felt the flesh burn cold. He heard machinery shutting down beyond the whining screech of the hedge.

One more, then, the final cut.

He reached towards the centre of the hedge, plunged both his hands into its golden glowing heart, felt the agony of its fightback, and forced the blades of the shears closer together.

Alditha and Celeste felt the screaming pain, felt the roar of his agony and his need as it shot up his throat like vomit.

'POV EXTERNAL,' said Celeste through the pain—just in time to see the scout ship vapourise in a blinding flash of white, flattening everything around it for a mile. Ven's worms, caught in the blast, would have been atomized in an instant. Celeste fell to her knees, crying, and Alditha, too, felt a weakness in her legs, but she gritted her teeth and stayed standing.

The Sleepers were buried. Ven Tao, the Great Gardener, had died, saving them. And there, horribly recognizable in the middle of their field of vision, was the same Stone Hedge Alditha had always known, had played on as a girl, and watched every Hallowe'en.

It was cold, and grey, and motionless. It looked like it was waiting. It looked like a killer.

12

Skoros felt the call of Destiny.

He was skipping down the corridor of the ancestors, with Razor and the orb in tow.

'Blast it,' he ordered, and the orb shot a bolt of angry orange energy at the portrait of Radzack The First And Only, leaving only a smoking black hole where his face had been.

'Melt it,' he instructed, and the orb sent a beam of heat towards the portrait of Salu-Valek The Merciless, till the paint bubbled like cheese on a pizza, making Skoros giggle. It was the sound of someone who'd never been entirely happy to play well with others, finally slipping free of convention, and society, and everybody else's expectations. It sounded liberating, but not sane.

Quite a long way from sane, in fact.

He moved on down the line. Malcontent The Peaceful had been his oddest ancestor, but as a young boy, Skoros had liked the old duffer. He had seemed to have not a care in the world, and despite being locked away in the topmost tower of the castle by his son, he was placid and happy with his lot. When Skoros had been allowed to go up and see him, Malcontent had called bluebirds from the forest in through his turret window to land on his arms, and squirrels to play and peep through his beard at the boy.

'Just…' Skoros paused. 'Just the eyes. Melt the eyes, so the old fool's not *looking* at me all the time.'

The orb sent out its beam, and Malcontent's eyes melted to dribbling tears of hot paint that ran down his face. Skoros moved on.

'And then there's you,' he grunted, staring at his father with a defiance he'd never managed when the man had been alive.

Subracken The Broody sneered down at his son from dark, clouded eyes above a beard like a Blackheart Bindweed hedge.

'You require the personal touch, I think.' He chuckled. 'Though not touch, of course. Never that.' He pointed his wand at a ceremonial two-headed battleaxe that hung on the wall down the far end of the corridor, and it rattled. Then with a scraaaach, it tore itself off the wall and hurtled end over end towards Skoros, who laughed a loud genuine laugh.

'Skrraaaak. Err, boss? Boss. Axey thing, heading our way, fast. Might be best to-'

Razor hid his eyes under his wings and held his breath, then shuddered when he heard a hard thud, rather than the dull whumpf of axe hitting flesh. He peeked.

The axe had taken a last-second detour. It was embedded in the wall, having split the portrait of Subracken, right along the line of his stern, disapproving mouth.

Skoros sighed in satisfaction. 'Now, to the workshop. I need more orbs if I'm to subdue Sagar.'

'Skraaak. Err, really? Thought you were all fired up. Y'know, destiny and all that? Might be wise to find the book, maybe? In case, y'-know, someone else has a destiny too?'

Skoros considered, then gave a tiny head-shake. 'The book is waiting. Waiting for *me*. You heard what the old fool said—it has hidden itself from mages for thousands of years. It knows I am coming for it. No, first I need more orbs. Then we silence Sagar. And then tonight…' He gave the kind of smile usually smiled by people whose idea of fun is to put frogs on a griddle and watch them pop. 'Tonight, we deal with that meddling witch.'

'Easy, child,' Alditha said as Celeste sobbed and held her tight.

''m'notachil',' sobbed the alien girl who looked like a child.

'Nono,' said Alditha, 'course you're not.' She didn't take her eyes off the image of Stone Hedge. Something about what she'd seen bothered her. Something beyond the death of the Gardener, but she couldn't work out what it was. It was like having a raspberry seed stuck in your gums. It would come when it was ready, not before.

She held Celeste, soothed her, then, as Celeste's sobs softened to snot and sniffing, she reached out to what she'd always thought of as her Tarot Wheel, flicked her wrist, and found the tiny seedling that generated the images. It vibrated, buzzing softly between her fingers.

'Wheel of all that's seen and known,

Teller of what seeds are sown,

Blessed are we by what you've shown.

Rest now while new life is grown.'

Slowly, quietly, the world disappeared around them, until just the network of white roots and green shoots remained. Then, returning and condensing, they, too, became just a single fading point of golden light in the twig spinning top.

'I knew someone had probably died—it's just that knowing it and feeling it are different things,' said Celeste in a small voice, clearing her throat. 'Though I guess I should be relieved it wasn't all of them.'

Alditha nodded, and Celeste finally let her go. She straightened her uniform and watched as the last dim light faded from Alditha's magic spinning top. Suddenly, it stopped turning and glided to the floor.

'At least I know the Sleepers are actually just sleeping. They made it in time. Now all I need to do is find where they are.'

'Oh, I know that,' muttered Alditha, picking up the crudely-built circle of twigs.

'Really? Is it far? Could you take me there?'

'Could. Will. But not yet. You and I need to have a conversation. Preferably one I can understand.'

'But, I need to-'

'Stone Hedge has been there a long time. It'll still be there in the morning. Come back to the cottage. I need to know what I'm dealing with here.'

'Yes, but-'

'There'll be more bread and jam.'

Celeste closed her mouth. She shrugged. 'All right. What is it you need to know?'

Skoros smiled.

He hadn't thought it could be this easy, but when you have several broken orbs, and one that works, it turned out you could get the working one to repair the first broken one, then the two working ones could repair two more, and so on.

If only I could get a blueprint, he thought, *I could fill the world with orbs.*

As it was, six would have to do. It would be enough.

'Let's go dragon-hunting,' he commanded, and the orbs filed out in mid-air, followed by their master and his reluctant bird.

Celeste was eating again. Alditha had set her kitchen into a repeating pattern of bread buttering and jam-spreading, and for the moment, was happy to feed the girl until she didn't want any more. Her hair was flowing with colour and sticking up again.

'So, you Astarians were looking for a new planet, 6.8 thousand years ago?' asked the witch.

Celeste nodded, licking a little jam off the corner of her lip.

'Still looking for one now, are you?'

Celeste frowned, and Alditha was struck again by her eyes. Their violet colour was arresting enough, but they were also mature, wise eyes, set in a young and childlike face.

'Yes,' said Celeste. 'And no. 's'difficult to explain in terms you'd understand.'

'Try,' Alditha insisted.

'Well, we don't *have* a home, as such. Not anymore. The fleet pretty much *is* home. So yes, there are people who want to find a planet again—the oldies, you know? But I'm not sure most of us would know what to do with a planet if we had one. Feels a bit…small?'

'Small?'

Celeste swallowed a lump of chewed jammy bread. 'Well, imagine all you'd ever known was this cottage. Imagine you were born here, raised here, that you spent every day here, and didn't know there was anything outside. You'd be content with that, because it would be all you knew. But then imagine one day, someone came and opened your front door, and encouraged you to go out and see the rest of the Garden. You'd be wary at first, but then you'd go and you'd see everything, wouldn't you?'

Alditha considered it, sniffed. 'Maybe,' she allowed, not entirely sure the girl wasn't insulting her cottage.

'Then imagine whoever it was that had opened the door came back and pushed you back inside, and told you, you could never go outside again. You were happy indoors before, but now all you'd want would be to go outside, because you'd know it was there.'

'Mmm,' said the witch.

'Cottage, planet,' said Celeste, 'same thing. As I say, I think the oldies still want to feel a planet beneath their feet though.'

'The oldies? How old are your oldies?'

'Old,' said Celeste.

'Well, how old are you?'

'Not old,' said Celeste.

Alditha knitted her eyebrows together in frustration, and Celeste giggled.

'It's a meaningless question. If you don't mind my saying so, it's the sort of question only someone with a planet's interested in. How "old" you are depends on how many times your planet goes round your sun. If you don't have a planet and you don't have a sun, you stop counting pretty quickly.'

'Humph,' said Alditha. 'So if you're not still looking for a planet, what are you doing here?'

'Told you, looking for the Sleepers. Or are you in the habit of putting your ancestors in the ground and just leaving them there for thousands of years.'

'Well, yes,' said Alditha. 'Sort of. Usually, we make sure they're dead first though.'

Celeste blinked. 'And if they're not?'

'Then we dig 'em up and say sorry. A lot.'

'Quite. I'm part of the dig 'em up and say sorry a lot expedition. Sort of. Actually, I'm part of the dig 'em up and take 'em home to the fleet expedition, so that someone else can do the sorry-saying.'

'Hmm,' said Alditha again. 'So what about your orbs?'

'Very odd behavior. They were supposed to do scans beneath the surface of the planet. Easier and faster to get the orbs to do that, because they have a lot of capabilities, and they get about quite fast.'

'Yes,' said Alditha. 'I noticed that.'

'Well, they found something, but not what I was hoping for. They found more orbs.'

'Original orbs, I'm guessing, from the Sleepers' expedition?'

'Must be,' agreed Celeste, taking a bite of a new slice of bread and jam that had slid onto the table in front of her. 'What I don't understand,' she said, chewing, her hair dancing, 'is why they then disobeyed the recall signal.' She swallowed. 'Rather unnerving, really.'

Alditha sighed, disgruntled. She'd loved the potential of the orb she'd seen, but she hated the thought of several of them flying about the Garden, disobeying orders. Or obeying someone *else's* orders. She shivered as uncomfortable thoughts dribbled down her spine. 'Do they have weapons, these orbs of yours? No wait, never mind, I know they can break enchantments, that's more of a weapon than most people round these parts will have seen in their lives.'

'Living in a sigma field like this, you're probably right,' muttered Celeste.

'Here we go again.' Alditha laughed, shaking her head.

'Sigma,' said Celeste. 'Sigma energy—what you call "magic,"' she explained, with a faint smile on her lips.

'I call it magic because it *is* magic,' Alditha chuckled. 'If you call it something else, that's your affair, right?'

'All right,' agreed Celeste, clearly barely suppressing a giggle.

Alditha fumed quietly. *Infuriating girl.* Coming here with her orbs and her dimension drives and her damned Sleepers, turning everything on its head. Maybe Harper's been right, and they should have chased the teacup off the minute it had arrived.

She sighed. Even as the thought occurred to her, calmer thoughts washed over it. The girl was here to do a job, to pick up her great, great, great, great uncles and aunts and suchlike and take them home. That was all. The chaos she brought into the tidy, understandable, magical world of the Garden wasn't her fault, it was just like her shadow, following her everywhere she went.

That thought made Alditha frown again. Those *things* on the Sleepers' ship—what were they called? Bio-mechs? Had they made it to the sleeping pods or whatever they were called?

'Those bio-mechs—are they dangerous?'

Celeste giggled. 'Would you like to meet one?'

'That depends—*are* they dangerous?'

'Mine's going to try and scold me to death, if that's what you mean.' Celeste pressed the side of her headband and it lit up, glowing briefly and making a low musical noise. A second passed, then it chimed and jangled incessantly. 'He's been trying to get hold of me,' she explained. 'Really quite a lot,' she added, frowning. 'Alpha, come in.'

'Danger. Danger. Danger,' said Alpha. 'Significant orb activity since comms link was *deactivated*. Orbs have acted with aggressive intent against indigenous life-forms.'

'*What?* Alpha, set the scout ship in stealth mode then join me at this location.'

'Acknowledged.'

The uncomfortable thoughts shivered down Alditha's spine again. 'Aggressive intent?'

'They've attacked people.' Celeste squealed. 'They're not supposed to *attack* people.'

'I have a nasty feeling I know why they might have.'

'Why?'

'Could be wrong,' said Alditha, standing up and reaching out for her broomstick, 'but I reckon that Skoros is behind this. I bet he's manipulated the orbs somehow.'

'Skoros?' Celeste frowned. 'Skoros, Skoros, Sko- Oh. Rude man, shouts a lot, has a metal horse with not enough plating?'

'Sounds like him, yes.' Alditha walked around her kitchen with a purposeful stride, collecting a woven cloth bag and picking up bits and pieces to put into it.

'But why would he do that?'

'About those weapons the orbs carry…' Alditha picked up a shiny red apple and dropped it into the bag.

'They're not even really weapons. Just tools to let the-'

'They can be *used* as weapons though, yes?'

'Well, I suppose so, but really, why?'

Alditha growled to herself as she examined a small blue globe of stars. 'Do you not *have* power-hungry leaders where you come from?'

'A few,' snapped Celeste. 'How many planets have you visited recently?'

'Power is what Skoros wants. Always has been. He's a bully. Now imagine a bully with orbs.'

'That's not a good thought.'

'*Exactly.*'

'Alpha will be here soon.'

'That good, is it?' Alditha grabbed a bunch of dull green herbs off a hook by the door.

'Oh yes. He'll be able to stop the orbs.'

'You reckon?' The witch sighed, opened a cupboard and picked up a bottle of the black goo she had distilled the day Harper had left her. She weighed it in her hand, then pushed it firmly into the bag and tied up the straps.

'Absolutely. He's linked into the main systems of the scout ship. He can act as a main control node.'

'A *what?*'

'A big off-switch.'

'Right,' said Alditha. 'Then I think we've got just three things to worry about.' She took off her hat quickly, slung the bag over her shoulder and replaced the hat firmly, as if daring Celeste to mention that it had ever been off her head.

'What three things?'

Alditha huffed. 'Firstly, Skoros is a *clever* bully. Secondly, Alpha's coming here, and he's linked into the systems of your ship, which I'm guessing is just full to the brim of oojamaflips and whatchamacallits, the likes of which a clever bully might quite like to get his greedy little hands on. And thirdly...'

'Yes?'

'Well,' said Alditha, licking her bottom lip, 'thirdly, you think he can act as an off-switch for orbs that didn't obey your recall signal.'

Celeste's almond-shaped eyed widened. 'Oh.'

'You don't have to-,' called Alditha, too late, as her front door disappeared again, the tall, spindly-legged, bulbous-headed figure of Alpha taking up the space. 'Really,' she said, 'knocking's not a big thing with you Astarians, is it? You do have doors, yes?'

Celeste didn't answer her—she was lost in thought.

'Well come in, bio-mech Alpha, and replace the bloomin' door while you're about it.'

'How are you aware of my designation?' demanded Alpha. 'You

are an indigenous primitive.'

'And you're not good at making friends, are you?' snapped Alditha. 'I can see why you sent Blondie in first. I'd advise you to keep a civil tongue in your big eggy head, because for your information, I know where your precious Sleepers are.'

'You will share all information regarding the location of the Sleepers,' said Alpha, moving forward smoothly, towering over the witch.

'You will watch your step unless you want a clip round the ear, Mr. Alpha. Always assuming you have ears, that is.'

Alpha reached out and grabbed Alditha by the arms, lifting her up with no evidence of effort, so his big dark eyes could stare into her face. 'I will initiate brain scan,' he said.

'Alpha, no,' Celeste commanded.

'You keep out of this, Missy,' Alditha rasped, making eyes at the bio-mech. 'Manners have to be learned, they can't be enforced.' Her voice had gone terribly, horribly quiet. 'You do your worst, Mr. Alpha.'

Small red points of light flared in the wide dark eyes of the bio-mechanoid, sending thin red beams into Alditha's eyes.

But Alditha didn't put up barriers to her mind; Alpha knew how to break down or break through mental barriers to get at the truth. Instead, her mind welcomed him in, and then he found himself reading the recipe for plum pudding, for cough mixture, for the cure for Athlete's Foot, found himself discovering the story of young Evangeline Beswick down in Fern Bottom, who was no better than she should be, and Old Mother Fenugreek and her 'arrangement' with the Cremini family, and a whole host of other things that were anything but what he was looking for. And just at the point where his sensors were filling up with data that was useless to him, Alditha sharpened her eyes, and Alpha found *his* mind, *his* processors, investigated. Alditha discovered his capabilities, his mission, his recharge cycle, and though she didn't ask for this information, the precise balance of biological and mechanical technologies that made up all his systems. Alpha was unable to stop the information flowing out of his data core, the barriers he threw up were too weak and too late, and their protocols failed even as he tried to establish them. That was the difference between wizards and witches—wizards learned things. Witches learned *people*.

'Put me down now, please, Mr. Alpha,' said Alditha calmly.

Alpha did as he was told.

'Do we understand one another, you and I?' she asked, flicking her eyes up to his again, half as a peace offering, half as a threat.

'Aff-aff-aff-affirmative,' he said.

'I should think so too,' she muttered.

'Orbs approaching,' said Alpha, still sounding slightly scrambled.

'Skoros.' Alditha straightened her hat, grabbed her broom again, and marched them to the front door. 'Will one of you do your twiddly zapping thing, or shall we be old-fashioned about it?' Neither of the aliens moved, so she turned the handle on the door, opened it and went outside, leading her new alien friends to meet the wizard.

As it happened, they didn't have to go far. He was marching towards them, three orbs flying alongside him, Razor, as ever, perched on his shoulder like a pirate's parrot.

'Skoros, how *do* you do,' Alditha said, nodding about as far as a mouse would stumble over a crumb of bread.

'Alditha, my *dear* witch,' Skoros acknowledged. 'I've come to make friends,' he added, smiling a sickly smile.

''s'that right?' Alditha couldn't stop the beginnings of a smirk from creeping over her lips. 'Think you know Miss Celeste, here. Wouldn't suggest you get on the wrong side of her again, you might find yourself walking backwards to the castle. And this here's Mr. Alpha, who I don't think you've met. I'm betting you have no idea what he can do, do you?'

'Impress me,' said Skoros.

Alpha attuned his brain to the orbs, absorbing the altered rhythms of their programming. 'Shut down motive power and initiate standby mode,' he commanded, in that strange combination of a robotic and a human voice. He raised both his arms and sent the shutdown signal. All three orbs went suddenly dark with a disappointing electronic blip, and fell to the ground.

'Impressed yet?'

'What?' cried Skoros. 'No.' He pulled out his wand, but Alditha was ready for him. She snapped her fingers, loud and clear, and the wand shot out of his grasp, tumbled end over end in the air, and slid into her hand.

'Boys and their wands—honestly, it's an obsession,' she muttered. 'That all you came for, was it? Bit of a threaty, stompy moment, show us your orbs, wave your wand about and play the big wizard? Cos if that's all, I think we're done, aren't we?'

The metal wand sparked in Alditha's hand, giving her a shock and sparking blue energy into her arm. 'Yaaargh,' she yelped, dropping it. It didn't fall to the ground, but shot straight back to its master's hand.

'Nobody waves my wand around but me,' he snarled.

'You're not kidding,' muttered Alditha, rubbing her arm.

Skoros aimed the wand at the fallen orbs, and a crackle of yellow energy shot from its corkscrew end, touching each of them in turn. They gave an optimistic electronic whine and bobbed back up into the air. Alditha grabbed her broom and swept air at them. From nowhere, a wind whipped up that blew the orbs and Skoros backward, the wizard tumbling, his red slippers bending back, almost as if they would kick him in the head. The wind was unfocused, but Alditha jumped on the broom and rode it round and round, directing the air into a cyclone that caught the orbs and swirled them like bubbles in a plughole. Alpha pressed his palms together, rebooting his control matrix and aiming the termination signal at the cyclone.

'No response,' he reported. 'Orbs have received a replacement primary command structure.'

'Oh, they have, have they?' Celeste demanded. 'If I can get my hands on them, we'll see about that. I'll rebuild the wretched things from the primary elements up if I have to. Alpha, there is Astarian technology in the hands of an indigenous primitive. Retrieve the orbs.'

Alpha turned his big egghead to look at her. Her almond eyes didn't flinch at his gaze.

'Acknowledged.' He waved a palm at Alditha's cyclone, then made a quick series of chirping, beeping noises. 'Increasing density to compensate for atmospheric...disturbance.'

Nothing visible happened to his body, but he stepped into Alditha's cyclone and kept his feet planted on the ground. His large black eyes observed the swirling of the orbs and, with the precision of a crossbow, he stuck out a hand and batted one of the metal balls to the ground, where it landed heavily at Celeste's feet. She picked it up in both hands, searching with her fingers for the access hatch that would let her turn off the main power distribution links.

Skoros, blown off his feet but now out of the main path of the cyclone, raised his wand, watching Alditha go round and round, a blur of black on the cyclone's edge. His father's frequent angry words came back to him, accompanied by the memories of slaps and punches. 'A wizard lives or dies on his instincts, you idiotic boy.' *Slap.* 'You've got the instincts of a pig-handler.' *Punch.* 'Where are your wizard's instincts?'

Skoros stood up, pointed his wand and closed his eyes. *You want instincts*, he thought, *I'll give you instincts.* He sensed the movement of the wind, feeling it on his face, hearing the rhythm of its whip and whoosh. Felt the button underneath his thumb. Felt the moving of the stars and the turn of the world and the beat of his heart and found the still moment underneath it all, in it all, because of it all. Everything came together.

He pressed the button.

There was an 'Urrrrrgh' noise, and the sudden death of the cyclone. He opened his eyes and saw Alditha, unconscious on the ground, a deep cut in her forehead oozing blood, and her lip split.

Alpha reached down and picked up the two remaining orbs, one in each of his twig-like alien hands.

'Now,' yelled Skoros, his voice hoarse and his eyes shining.

All three orbs sparked and crackled, a yellow lightning crawling over their surface. With a short squeak from Celeste, and a long moan from Alpha as the lightning crawled up both his arms to dance over his head, both of the aliens slumped to the ground.

I've done it, thought Skoros. *I've actually done it.*

And there were no voices raised to tell him any different. Skoros stood alone and unopposed. He was the King of the Garden.

13

The sun set, and the sun rose.

Having taken care of Odiz and Alditha, it was at least reasonably accurate to say Skoros now ruled the Garden, forcing it under the yoke of evil magic and machinery.

Faced with the threat of Skoros' strange, new mechanical toys, Big Red and Sagar had put up little resistance to the wizard's plans, having begrudgingly agreed to take up residence in the general vicinity of Skoros Castle—albeit in the deepest, darkest corner of the Maze. Being both shrewd and intelligent creatures, the prospect of being permanently silenced by the wizard's new-found power had swayed their decision not to immediately go on the defensive. However, considering that demons and dragons did not normally crave a life of captivity, this was unlikely to be a long-lasting arrangement.

The Garden didn't have a King or Queen, it simply had people, and things that were also-people, just getting on with the business of being alive. There were other wizards, other witches, there were trolls and goblins, but there was no particular system in place for one lot of people to rule another. There was just power, and having removed the most powerful people from their places, Skoros technically had the most power left in the Garden.

That said, much of the Garden still hadn't heard that it was now being ruled under the yoke of evil magic and machinery, and so it carried on pretty much as normal. That's why evil dictators tend to go in for big, spectacular, 'Now you all die' plans—if they don't, the 'little people' have an irritating tendency not to notice they've been ground underfoot, and nothing is more calculated to get up an evil dictator's nose than the idea that they're being ignored.

As the sun rose on the first day of Skoros' rule, four small flocks of birds were taking off, one from each corner of the Garden. Each bird carried a satchel appropriate to its size, and as they flew, they dipped their beaks into the satchels, pulled out some sheets of paper and sent them fluttering down on the land below, like colourful rectangular snow.

At the head of the largest flock, noble and resolute, flew Harper.

The Committee of Concerned Folk Against Alien Invasions—The CoCoFoAgAlInv—which was how Harper thought of it, for all Gunkin begged that he call it something snappier, had taken some time and planning to put together, and as the birds flew, Harper felt proud. The leaflets all said the same thing, and it had taken some of Gunkin's goblin friends the best part of a day to write and draw them. There was a picture of the alien he'd seen in the teacup-ship, only Gunkin's friends had made it look even scarier than it was, with big sharp teeth and pointed claws, dripping blood. 'ALIENS' was written, all jagged and scary, across the top of the leaflet. Then, in smaller words, it went on to explain that there were aliens in the Garden and that they were big and scary and were there to invade. They would take food out of the mouths of ordinary Gardenfolk, it said—that had been a line of Gunkin's. Harper was more concerned about ordinary Gardenfolk *being* the food of aliens, but Gunkin had said people weren't frightened of being eaten until it was a real and immediate possibility, because they'd never been eaten before, and part of them wasn't sure it was as bad as everyone made out. 'Whereas hunger, chief…hunger they know about. Hunger they can relate to. Hunger while some other beggar eats, *that* they can be frightened of today, even when they're not hungry. That they can get *angry* about, even without having seen a single alien themselves. And fear, Chief— that's how you move people.' He had smiled that disconcerting goblin smile again, and Harper had felt a little queasy looking at it. 'Trust me,' Gunkin said. 'Fear's like a goblin magic.'

So that was what the leaflets were full of—fear. Fear that people could understand, according to Gunkin. Fear of hunger while other people ate. Fear of being turned out of their homes while aliens used their favourite chairs to park their alien backsides. Fear of change, which Gunkin said, nine times out of ten, people knew was likely to be change for the worse. Fear of all those things, and then a plan to band together and stand up against the aliens, so their fears never came true. A plan to march on the teacup, and wave banners, and tell the aliens politely but firmly to go away and leave the Garden unin- vaded, thankyouverymuch. Gunkin had sniffed at that, said it 'needed more fire and pitchforks, but whatever you say, chief.' Gunkin had drawn the line at adding the bit about the worms and beetles in the sky though. 'I believe you, chief, course I do—you tell me there's great big worms and beetles dangling down from the sky, I say righto, there's great big worms and beetles. Ooh. Scary stuff. All I'm sayin' is, people are gonna look up, and they ain't gonna see great big worms and beetles. At which point, they crumple up our leaflet, chuck it on their fires and get on with their lives, missing our crucial message about the *aliens*. One step at a time, sort of thing, yeah? One *fear* at a time.'

So, reluctantly, Harper had agreed to leave out the part about the giant worms and beetles and centipedes threatening to come down from the sky and eat everyone. For now.

He pecked out another beakful of leaflets and let them drop. It would all be decided by lunchtime. The last thing on the leaflet was what Gunkin said was a 'call to action.' It was an instruction as far as

Harper understood it—'If you want to stand up against the aliens,' it said, 'meet our brave leader, Harper the Owl, at Stone Hedge at midday.' He flung the last of his leaflets from his satchel and watched them go, spreading their message.

Soon, he thought. *Soon I'll know if one owl can stop an alien invasion.*

He flapped his wings, fast and fretful. If today went as badly as his last attempt, the aliens had nothing to fear. He gulped. *I need to talk to the Green Man*, he told himself, and wheeled his flight around to head to his friend's house.

Ow.

Witches think clearly most of the time, and the pain was the first thing to cross Alditha's mind when she woke up. She pressed her tongue to her lip, felt where it had split and blood had crusted.

I am going to slap that beardless wonder into next week.

Witches think clearly most of the time. Alditha heard hissing, smelled something that was like sap, but also almost like blood. She felt the presence of a consciousness pressing on her mind, like a snake waiting for her to move, waiting for her to make a mistake.

Blackheart Bindweed, she decided. *Not good.* She dared to open her eyes, realized she couldn't move, that her witchbag, broom, and even her hat were nowhere to be seen.

Witches think clearly most of the time. Many of them are in a simmering state of bad temper most of the time too, but rarely does a witch give way to full-on, out-and-out rage. But then, people don't tend to go around stealing witches' hats often, not for the most part wanting to be turned into frogs and the like. Alditha gritted her teeth, wondering whether she could find it in herself to get *really* angry.

She counted to five, then decided it was worth a good rummage.

Alditha rummaged big time, took as deep a breath as she could, and yelled some dark, inventive, fury-flaming words.

'But which are you? A living creature or a machine?'

'Question does not compute. Which are you? Flesh or blood?'

Skoros sighed out his irritation. The bulbous-headed alien was either being deliberately difficult, which didn't seem possible if it were a machine, or it simply didn't understand what he was asking it. Could it be? Flesh and circuitry, bone and steel, united at some fundamental level?

'Al…ditha.'

Astarians didn't sleep much—there was too much to see and do—and when they woke, they usually went from full sleep to fully awake in the opening of an eye. But unconsciousness was not quite the same thing, and Celeste took a moment to rouse herself. She instinctively tried to sit bolt upright and found she couldn't. She was strapped to a metal board, with cuffs around her wrists and ankles.

'Indigenous primitives,' she muttered to herself.

'Ah, you're awake,' said Skoros. 'I was beginning to fear you were dead.'

Celeste chuckled to herself, then looked sideways to where Alpha was strapped to an identical but much larger table. She flexed her arm muscles just a little, then smiled again.

'Something funny?'

'Alpha, increase tensile strength by…oh, I should think a factor of three would be sufficient. Increase external energy capacitance by a factor of eight and await further instructions.'

'Acknowledged.'

'Wait,' said Skoros, 'what? What was that? What's all that capacitance talk?'

'Capacitance in this case means the amount of energy that can be absorbed by a surface,' said Celeste. 'I'm going to need cover in a moment, you see? When I escape from here.'

Skoros stalked round to look Celeste in the eye. 'Big talk for a *child*. You know, I had to dig this torture-table out especially for you. Evil as my family were, it's been a long while since we had to torture a teenager in the Maze.'

Celeste chuckled again, this time right in his face.

'What's so *funny*, girl?' yelled Skoros. He drew his hand back to slap her across the face. Celeste brought her hand up sharply to grip his wrist, the shackle falling pointlessly off her skin.

'The funny thing,' she said as he goggled at her, 'is how keen you all are around here to judge by appearances. Just because you think I look like one of your *teenagers*, you assume I'm the same as them.' She flexed some more muscles and swung her legs off the table, pulling her other hand free without a second thought. She twisted his arm and he followed it down so she could look him in the face. 'I'm really not,' she assured him. 'Alpha, now.'

Without even his usual acknowledgement, Alpha swung up, snapping the shackles that held him to the table. Celeste flung Skoros across the room by his arm, then walked behind Alpha as he approached the watching orbs. The orbs shot Alpha, time and time again, while Celeste kept herself hidden, then as they all discharged their weapons at once, she ducked through his legs and scrambled out into the corridors of Skoros Castle, dodging this way and that as Alpha followed her, and the orbs flew after them both. Suddenly, Celeste heard the sound of major fire, and Alpha fell forward, landing heavily.

'Alpha. Increase capacitance to maximum.'

'Acknowledged,' he groaned. 'Escape indigenous entanglements and affect primary mission objective. Retrieve the Sleepers.'

She nodded, took one last look at him laying on the floor as the orbs advanced, then ran. The orbs sped up now that the corridor was free of Alpha-shaped obstructions, and when they could lock on to her, they blasted plasma bolts and paralysis rays. Celeste ducked, weaved, jumped and even somersaulted, knowing the way the orbs were programmed to run pursuit patterns. A large wooden door studded with iron bolts and a round iron ring stood in the wall in an open area at the end of one corridor, and she ran to it with every ounce of strength in her legs and lungs, twisting the ring up and slipping through the narrowest gap in the door, then pulling it tight after her.

She assessed her situation. Outdoors. Late morning, judging from the position of the sun in the sky. Her options were limited. Going back for Alpha was impossible with the orbs on their way—they'd blast away the door in less than a minute. There were outbuildings she could hide in, but the orbs would simply activate a life-form scan programme and track her quickly. Probably that would be followed by an incineration blast and quite apart from everything else, she didn't want to give Skoros the satisfaction of killing her.

There was a forest.

Forest. She decided. It would confuse any life-form scan, because if there was one thing you could guarantee in a forest it was that it would be full of life, most of it running away from anything that looked and behaved like the orbs. She took off, running towards the treeline. She reached it just as the sound of a big wooden door being blown off its hinges echoed behind her, and she darted past the first few trees she encountered. Then—something went wrong. She was still running, but she was no longer getting anywhere. A branch had snagged the back of her collar and lifted her up. Suddenly she saw it —the bark of the tree frowned at her. It had a face.

'Now then, Little Missy—where might you be running to in such an 'urry?'

Despite her haste, Celeste remembered her training. 'Hail, noble tree-oid,' she said. 'I'm running away from some-'—she thought about trying to explain the orbs full of sensors, self-defensive weaponry and various scanning technologies from a distant civilization, and decided she simply didn't have the breath. '-balls of death,' she said.

'Aye, that's as mebbe,' said the tree, 'but where d'you stand on choppin'?'

'Chopping?'

'Choppin' down of defenceless trees.'

'Oh,' said Celeste, catching on fast. 'I'm against it. Absolutely against it.'

'Mm-hmm,' said the tree. 'What about Skoros? Local lad, lives round these parts.'

'He's the one sending the balls of death after me,' she told it. There was an audible gasp, and not just from the tree doing the talking.

'Right,' it said. 'You leave this to us, Missy. Front ranks—balls of death, approaching. Prepare for war. In the rear, listen up. This here's an enemy of both Skoros and choppin'. That's good enough for me. I say get her through safe, all right?'

A bizarre, haunting rustle of leaves and a clatter of twig on branch sounded through the forest. Then, before she knew what was happening, Celeste found herself being hauled from tree to tree, like a package in a post office.

'Whooooooah,' she said as she was bundled upside-down and downside-up and caught moments before she hit the ground, and swung on and on. It seemed to take only minutes before she reached the other side of the forest, from which she could see the route to what was surely the centre of the nearest village.

'Thank you, noble tree-oids,' she gasped, then looked back into the forest. Among all the greens and browns and mud-mix in between colours she expected to see, there was an ominous grey, and a frightening orange. A second more and the smell hit her. Wood smoke.

'Wait,' she said. 'You'll all be killed.'

'Run, girl,' said one of the last trees to have handled her. 'It were always gonna come down to him or us. Might as well be today. Run.'

'But I-' said Celeste. 'I can't let you-'

'Beggin' your pardon, Miss, but how many talkin' trees have ya come across in your life?'

'Erm…' Actually in her travels in the fleet, she'd come across quite a few.

'That daft beggar with the balls of death thinks it's up to him what we do and what we don't do. When we fight and when we die. Don't be makin' the same mistake, and thinking you get to choose how we spend our lives, eh? Worry about your own, and get you gone.'

The smoke was billowing closer. But it wasn't the smoke that made Celeste's eyes water.

She turned and ran, leaving Alpha, the orbs, and the talking trees behind her.

This time it was different.

The crowd was early, and curious, and before Harper had even said a word, they wanted to know about the threat these 'aliens' posed. Gunkin and a couple of his friends had made a banner, which they held over Stone Hedge. 'The Garden For Gardenfolk,' it said, and some people had already been nodding at it, talking about it with their neighbours.

Harper had received a shock that morning, when the Green Man had told him he wouldn't be coming to the meeting. Harper was wrong, he'd said, and Celeste, the girl from the teacup, had been perfectly charming. Harper had rehearsed all the arguments in the leaflet. The food, taken out of their mouths. The houses. The…the…the *change.* Probably, he'd said, when the aliens invaded, there would be *no strawberry marshmallows* left for honest, decent Gardenfolk who liked them. The Green Man had simply folded his branches, told him he was talking rot, and that he, the Green Man, would never support such fearmongering.

'Well, I'm sorry you feel like that,' said Harper. 'Sorry you're so keen to be a *traitor* to your friends and neighbours, that's all. You remember this when they invade. When they turn you out of your house. Don't come crying to me then, that's all. Just…just don't.' And Harper had flown off, wondering if everybody would feel the same, and whether he was just a silly owl who was making a fuss over nothing.

Seeing so many people turn up to the meeting did him a power of good. Seeing them curious, and asking questions, and nudging each other and nodding at his banner made him feel like he was among friends. Like he wasn't silly after all. Like he was right, and clever, and the only one strong enough to take a stand against the coming danger. Harper puffed out his chest and plumped his plumage. 'I'll make a start then, shall I?' he asked Gunkin.

'Hold on, chief. Never go in front of a new crowd cold, right? Let me go out there first and warm 'em up a bit for you. Give 'em the idea, right? Then you come out and knock 'em dead.'

'Dead?' asked Harper, hooting nervously.

'They'll love you by the time you say your first words,' said Gunkin. 'By the time you're finished, you'll have 'em eating out of your hand.'

'Ah,' said Harper. 'I see.' He wasn't sure he did, but Gunkin hadn't steered him wrong so far. Except possibly about not including the worms and beetles on the poster, but that was an argument for another day.

Gunkin went out in front of the crowd. He stood behind Stone Hedge, looking out at them all, taking in their faces, meeting their eyes. To look at, he was a strange creature. Purple, and with a head that curved up into two points, like horns on a bull. And then of course there were his teeth. But he went out in front of the crowd, and just stood there, looking entirely comfortable.

The crowd, which had been talking amongst itself, grew quiet, just watching Gunkin do nothing, say nothing. The hush grew hypnotic, vibrating with an electric expectancy, and still Gunkin was silent.

Suddenly, however, the goblin came to life, and the crowd were not disappointed. His voice was clear, his delivery intense and animated.

'Gardenfolk,' he said, 'you've worked hard for everything you have. I know it ain't much, but you've worked for it. Earned it. You deserve everything you have, and you deserve more. There's no folk like Gardenfolk, and we wear that fact like a badge of pride,' he said, reaching out a hand to them, as if to touch each and every one. 'Garden pride. We know who we are, and we all work together. Doesn't matter what species we are, what colour we are, whether we're 'animal,'—he pointed at some humans—'vegetable,'—he opened up an inviting palm to Old Tom the potato—'mineral,'—his hand swooped to take in a couple of Gravel Ridge trolls—'fungi'—he pointed at Alberto Cremini, the Mushroom Don who had bought himself a lift in Old Tom's wheelbarrow to attend the meeting. 'Doesn't matter if we're witches, wizards, dragons or trees. Even a humble goblin like myself is accepted here. We are all Gardenfolk. And we are all proud.'

There was a loud murmur of approval at his words. They were Gardenfolk, they said to themselves. And they were proud.

'But Gardenfolk, I am here to tell you, there's other folk out there. Folk who are *not like us*. Not proud. Not prepared to work for what they want, but who think they can just come in and take what we have,' he added, his voice growing in pace and volume.

The murmur turned sharp and sour, a wave of growling growing in the crowd.

'Aliens,' he said, letting the word hang there above their heads. 'Yes, aliens. Outsiders, from Who-Knows-Where, coming to do Who-Knows-What in our Garden. The Garden you live in. The Garden you love. The Garden you're proud of. Coming, to take food out of your babies' mouths. Jobs from honest working Gardenfolk, so they can't support their families. Houses, even—your house. Your house, where your youngest son was born. Your house, where your little girl plays. Your house where you hoped to see 'em married from, raising young 'uns of their own, like proper, decent Gardenfolk. Your house full of weird, outsider, alienfolk, doing weird, outsider, alien things.'

The crowd was roaring now, folk were yelling at him that the things he was describing wouldn't happen, not while they had anything to say about it.

'Is that what you want?' he demanded—the wave of 'Nooooooo' hit him even before he'd finished asking the question.

'That's not what I want,' he assured them. 'So how do we stop 'em?' He didn't let them think about it. 'Harper.'

The crowd fell oddly quiet for a moment. *Harper?*

'You all know Harper the owl,' he told them. It was true, most of them did. Most of them thought he was a bit of a silly flibbertigib-bet. 'He's an owl of rare brain. An owl of wit and cunning, and an owl of conviction. A strong leader.'

There was an odd murmur in the crowd. *Really? Harper?*

Gunkin gave a nod, and a handful of his friends in the crowd roared their support, as though Harper was the perfect choice to lead them in this time of crisis.

'Harper has *seen* these aliens,' Gunkin insisted. 'He's fought them, single-handed.'

His friends roared their approval again, and this time a few of the crowd joined in.

'He's been inside the aliens' *spaceship*, and fought them, with all the fierce pride you'd expect of your fellow Gardenfolk.'

More roaring of support came, though now it came from more and more of the crowd. Gunkin grinned to himself—he'd got them, and he knew it.

'Harper's the leader we need right now, to say no.'

'Nooooo,' said the crowd, echoing his words.

'To say go.'

'Goooooooo.'

'To stand up and say the Garden is for Gardenfolk, and we don't want no aliens here.'

Gunkin winced—the line was too long, and the crowd tripped over itself trying to parrot it back to him.

'Harper,' he said.

'Harper,' they repeated.

'Harper,' he yelled, throwing a purple fist in the air.

'Harper,' they cried back, fists everywhere raising.

'Harper,' he roared, pointing sideways with both hands, and usher-ing Harper himself onto Stone Hedge.

'Harper. Harper. Harper. Harper. Harper,' chanted the crowd, and

Harper followed Gunkin's example, waiting a moment till he could be heard.

'The aliens are here,' he said. 'The aliens are dangerous. It's down to us to tell them to…to…' He blinked. Blinked his big eyes, looking out at all the faces expecting him to lead them. Then he remembered what he'd been told to say. 'To go back where they came from, and leave us alone.'

The crowd roared its support.

'The Garden for Gardenfolk,' he said, because it had seemed to go down well when Gunkin said it. It worked now too, and the crowd cheered. Gunkin's friends raised the banner high and waved it a little.

'Wait,' said a female voice in among the hubbub. 'Please, someone listen to me.'

In all the yelling and chanting, no-one had heard Celeste running down the road to the centre of the square. She saw the dimension drive, but for the moment, it wasn't her prime concern. 'Skoros is coming,' she yelled. 'Skoros and the orbs. He's got Alditha, somewhere. He's taken her prisoner.'

Most of the crowd had no chance of hearing her, but owls have extremely sharp hearing, and Harper had heard three important words. Skoros, orbs, and Alditha. He hopped across the Hedge and called to Celeste. 'What? Did you say the wizard's got Alditha? And those orb things?'

Celeste, glad that at least someone had taken notice of her, fought her way over to him. 'Yes,' she confirmed. 'He took her somewhere, I don't know where. I've just escaped from him myself.' She put her hand on the Hedge to steady herself after pushing through the crowd.

The Hedge began to pulse. It melted out of its stone form, began to thrum with green and purple, red and blue, pink, orange and violet colours pushing their way through its leaves and fronds. There was a heavy 'worp' sound, pulsing like a dragon's heartbeat through the Hedge, and within the crowd, which grew very quiet very quickly, a look of horror on every face. Then they felt it—the tremor in the earth. The ground beneath their feet began to shake, to shudder, to split apart. The crowd began to scream.

Suddenly, with a grumble and a groan and a sigh of resolution, P'diddle's the baker's shop disappeared in a cloud of rubble. Ma McPumplewick's Eatery followed it into oblivion. The townhouse of Major Sprout fell in on itself. At six separate spots in a rough circle around the still-glowing Stone Hedge, buildings collapsed as though they'd never been there. But when the dust cleared, something had replaced every one of them. It was as though the earth had been pushed up from underneath and just wiped the buildings off the face of the Garden, replacing them with six smooth-sided, one-story pyramids.

'What the heck have you *done*?' yelled Harper, who had got off the Hedge pretty rapidly when it started doing its rainbow dance.

'Erm…' said Celeste. 'I know it might not *look* especially good to you now, but I've just raised the Sleepers.'

The multiverse is a strange place.

There are people who think the whole multiverse is made of dimensions, all tangled together like a ball of unruly string. And that's true—if you happen to have a drive that can extend between dimensions, you can travel between what people call 'realities' with the blink of an eye and a careful calculation.

But what people forget is that any given reality has plenty of dimensions, all of its own. Height is a dimension. Depth is a dimension. Space is a dimension. Time is a dimension.

On a fleet of enormous ships like flattened out, brightly-lit planets, they knew all about dimensions. The ships had leapt their way across unimaginable distances since the signal had reached them, from the dimension of There and Then to the dimension of Here and Now. They were getting closer. Closer. On board the ships, drives synchronized once more, branches of causality extending, touching, forming an elaborate invisible lattice connecting every ship. With a sound like roots growing, the ships slipped suddenly through space, like one enormous suit of shining armour.

The fleet emerged in a vacant patch of blackness and lit it up. Far in the distance, the star could be seen. It registered on scanners on every one of the ships, pale, and small, and yellow. The planet was too small to be seen yet, but the drives shut down. The people on the ships knew they were close now—they wouldn't need to jump across the dimensions of space again. The lattice that connected them dissolved, and they began to advance, pushing space behind them like swimmers in dark water, heading for that star and its tiny, promising little blue-green planet and its Garden World.

14

I love this time of year in my garden. It's nearly midsummer, and the sun, when it shines, seems to give everything new colours—colours I never see at any other time.

Sometimes I wonder about my garden. Whether I should go and do the Thing, see what that tiny owl is up to, maybe ask him why I see him sometimes, and not others.

And then I wonder whether there are things up there, beyond what I can see, who sometimes look down and see me, going about my business. I wonder how I'd feel if they arrived, to see what I was up to.

I'm not sure I'd be grateful. Would you?

Odiz groaned, and found himself face down in the rich dark earth of the Maze, felt the Blackheart Bindweed slithering over his body. He sent out a thought to prod around, but found no thorns in his mind anymore. The physical pain of having both his hands severed was intense to the point of madness; though he quickly bypassed this by shutting off the parts of his brain and nervous system that screamed blue murder at him.

Foolish boy thinks I'm dead, he thought, and the beginnings of a smirk formed on his lips. *Course, not having hands is going to be an inconvenience.* It would mean some of the higher level spells were beyond him just at the moment. *Still*, he thought, *'s not like we need anything complicated.* He did a quick run-down in his head, found a spell he liked, and allowed the smirk on his lips to grow all the way. *Aloric's Lamp should do nicely*, he thought, then he closed his eyes, focused on the words of the spell.

Aloric had been a mage in the Garden two hundred years before. He'd had something of a dry sense of humour, and a gift for understatement. As Odiz recited the spell in his head, a bright orange light burst into flame around him, and the Blackheart Bindweed that covered his body recoiled, screeching as the heat caught it, burned it, set it on fire. Odiz tightened the focus of his concentration, and the flame went from orange to red, then from red to white, and finally from white to blue, while all around him, the bindweed burst into flames and writhed in agony. Odiz slammed his arms together, and a large part of Skoros' Maze exploded.

Odiz nodded as he saw the devastation around him, the bindweed which formed the walls of the Maze burning, screaming, retreating from him in pain and fear.

'That's better,' he muttered. 'Now then...'

His superior mage body had automatically stopped him from bleeding to death, but Odiz desperately needed a new pair of hands. Utilizing the full power of his mind—and so opening all pain centres once again—he recited the words of Moloch's Helper in his head, and winced as his arms began to throb, growing longer, growing fleshy pointed stubs at the end. He grunted against the pain, as the stubs grew more and more defined, became blobs, and grew bones. He thought seriously about swearing as the bones extended into five points, with joints bending into fingers and thumbs. When his new hands had grown, he waggled his new fingers to make sure they worked.

Wouldn't like to have to do that every day, he thought. *But needs must. Now, the fool said he had the rest of them here somewhere.* Hekalion's Party Finder was a little unorthodox, as spells went —it was technically a bit of mischief used by junior wizards to find other wizards with a mind to do the same sort of thing as them: when they wanted to go and party, it was an easy way for the would-be revelers to find each other. But right now, Odiz was willing to bet the Maze was dotted with people with a similar intention to him—to escape the Maze, to find Skoros, and to have some really rather strong words with him. Sure enough, when he cast the spell, it located five other people. A spinning blue gyroscope appeared in the air in front of him, then zipped ahead, pointing forward.

'Lead on,' said Odiz, following the gyroscope, and setting fire to more and more of the Maze as he went.

———

Magic is an odd thing. It gets inside those who use it, and it changes them. Odiz' original hands, when the bindweed had severed them, hadn't hung around to be eaten by the evil plants. They had run away, using their fingers for legs, dragging the stumps of his wrists behind them.

Alditha felt something crawl up her leg. She refused to shudder. Witches didn't *do* shuddering, it wasn't in their nature. The thing, whatever it was, crawled up the front of her, and put a finger across her lips.

A finger. All right then. Her eyes drew in to focus on the hand that pressed itself against her face. Then the hand scuttled up to the top of her head. The bindweed hissed, seeming to sense its presence for the first time. The hand snapped its finger with a loud clicking noise, and Alditha felt her wrists suddenly drop free. Something wet slithered down behind her ears, and when she moved her arms, Alditha found the bindweed had fallen off her. It had turned to wet, black spaghetti. The hand tapped her on the shoulder, and made a gesture for her to creep away quietly. She shook her head briefly. Witches didn't do creeping away quietly either.

'I'm not going anywhere without my hat,' she said aloud to the bindweed. She reached out and grabbed a sticky, slick thorny strand of the stuff and it tried to wrap itself round her wrists. 'Without a hat, a witch is just a bad mood trying to happen,' she told the weed, grabbing it between her two fists and yanking it tight. Before the weed knew what was happening, Alditha had wrapped it round her head and tied its thorny ends together. Like a snake obeying the instinct to bite, the bindweed sank thorns into her head. 'And there's no wizard alive-' she snarled, sticking out her tongue to fight the bindweed's influence on her mind, 'more in tune with plants than any witch born.' When the weed had first got hold of her, she'd been unconscious, stunned by the orb. But now she was in control of her thoughts, and as she pushed back against the bindweed, she smiled, tasting victory.

'Fetch,' she told it, and like a flock of birds coming together to fly south for the winter, the bindweed she'd tied round her head hissed to another strand, and another, which wound around her head, and built itself up, and up, reaching to a thorny point. A witch's hat made out of living, interwoven bindweed, connected directly to Alditha's mind. 'That's better,' she said, 'now, who do you belong to, hand?' The hand pointed a forefinger to show her the way, and with a determined stride, Alditha began to follow it. *If only I had a ring made of black cherries for good measure*, she thought to herself.

———————

'You're having a laugh, aren't you?'

Odiz faced another impenetrable hedge of bindweed. The spinning blue gyroscope spun faster, insisting the way ahead was through the hedge. Odiz turned his back on the hedge and began to retrace his steps. There was a slick, slithering, hissing sound, and he saw another wall of the Maze unweave itself, then reform in front of him.

'Oh I see. Like that, is it? Whichever way I go, you're going to stop me?' He sniffed. 'Cunning,' he granted. He held up the spinning gyroscope again. 'Well, fireballs to this then.'

Odiz blasted three fireballs at the wall of thorns, leaving a human-shaped hole in the bindweed, which fizzed and bubbled and squealed.

'Never could see the point in a piggin' maze,' he muttered to himself. 'S'just getting lost, for fun.'

He stepped through the hole he'd made and followed the gyroscope forward.

'You've done what?' said Harper.

'I've raised the Sleepers,' said Celeste.

'You've demolished our shops and houses, that's what you've done.'

Celeste looked at the pyramids that had replaced some of the key buildings around the square. 'Not sure how long the revival process took in the old days,' she said to herself. 'Probably not long, though. Given the local timeframe, maybe an hour.'

'What's your name?' asked Harper suddenly, widening his large eyes towards her.

'Hmm? Oh, my name is Celeste,' said Celeste. 'What's yours?'

'Teacup-girl,' he said. 'You're the teacup-girl. You're an alien. HELP. I'VE GOT ALIENS IN MY GARDEN.'

'And you're a talking owl,' said Celeste, calmly, 'but we have bigger things to concentrate on at the moment. Two bigger things. We have a local wizard who frankly seems a little unstable, and who's got his hands on some Astarian technology, heading this way.' She threw a nervous look at the nearest pyramid. 'And then we've got these.'

'Alien,' squawked Harper again. The word, yelled by their fearless leader, caught the crowd's attention. It caught Gunkin's too, cowering in his hiding place behind the Hedge.

Gunkin saw his hopes of creating an army with Harper as its figurehead dissolving in front of his eyes. If the Gardenfolk got the idea that this *girl* was the terrifying alien who was going to come and steal the food out of their mouths, it was probably a lost cause. It was always the way—once you could put a face to the danger, and they turned out to be just like you, fear tended to die.

Celeste walked up to the cryo-pod, pulled her oblong scanner out of her pocket and waved it at the smooth, metallic pyramid. She was probably in trouble, she knew. She wasn't supposed to initiate the revival process, she was only supposed to find them and report back. This would be where things got…complicated. She knew enough of the story and Astarian design to understand that the pyramid, the bit they could see, was like the tip of an iceberg—there would be more still beneath the surface, and the Astarians themselves would be at the bottom. The bio-mechs would be the first things to come back online.

They might already be awake for all I know, she acknowledged, thumping her scanner. It was useless. Either the pyramid was shielding its occupants from her scans, or the scanner was just having one of 'those' days and refusing to tell her anything.

'Alien,' yelled Harper, flinging a dramatic wing in her direction. Gunkin grabbed him, shoving a determined goblin hand over his beak. 'No need to worry, chief,' he smarmed. 'These nice people don't need to be suspicious of a little girl, do they, no matter how she dresses or what colour her eyes are? Not when their homes and shops and belongings have been flattened by these pyramid-things?'

'Bufft theirrrallientooo,' squawked Harper round the goblin's fingers.

'Are they now?' asked Gunkin, thoughtfully. 'Alien pyramids just popping up out of the ground? Today's just got "one of them days" written all over it, hasn't it?'

'He's right, if that matters to you,' Celeste called from the nearest pyramid. 'This *is* alien technology.'

Gunkin brightened. 'So the aliens are not happy just to invade, brothers, sisters, Gardenfolk,' he called out. 'They wanna drop great big pyramids of doom on our heads, on our homes.'

'Oh do be quiet, you infuriating little creature,' snapped Celeste. 'They didn't drop from anywhere, they were here long before your-' She stopped. 'Talking owl.'

She blinked. Astarians didn't blink often, because their eyes didn't need to stay moist. But Celeste did it every now and then, when she was thinking too hard. She turned to face the crowd. Walking rock-like creatures looked back at her. Vegetables turned eyes in her direction. Mushrooms inclined their caps to her.

There had been no intelligent life on the planet when the original survey team had come to look. That was what had made it such a promising option for the Astarian fleet. But now there was sentient life *everywhere* here. She'd known something was odd the moment she'd landed in the Garden, for Astarian craft didn't take on the form of local objects without reason. But where had all the intelligent life come from in such a short space of time? Celeste realized she'd been avoiding this question since arriving in the Garden.

'And you have a legend of the Gardener,' she continued uneasily. 'Don't you? Ven Tao, the Gardener, you know who that was, and you know what he did?'

There was a murmur of agreement from some of the crowd, who were shushed by others, who weren't sure they were allowed to talk to the alien.

'How?' said Celeste. 'How do you have a legend from before there was any intelligent life here? Who *told* you the legend?'

The crowd was uncomfortable. ''s just always been,' said a man with a dark brown beard spilling down over a big body. 'Ven Tao did the thing with the Shears of Destiny and the Secateurs of Fate, and, and…and then it was Midsummer Hallowe'en.'

'Always is a very long time,' said Celeste. 'Believe me. I'm assuming you tell the story to your children, and your children tell it to their children and so on. The question is who told it to the *first* children capable of passing it on. How did that happen?'

'Well, I dunno, do I?' said Brown-Beard. 'S'pose someone saw it, and told it on.'

'Except they didn't,' said Celeste firmly. 'No-one saw it and lived. Of course, it's recorded in the mapping database. In the Astarian...' She shook her head. It was too incredible a thought, and she didn't want to jump to conclusions. 'When's the next one? The next Midsummer Whateveryousaid?'

'You daft or some'ing? 's tomorrow night, innit?'

'Of course it is,' Celeste muttered. 'Because there's nothing like a little extra pressure. The drive must be priming itself already, trying to find new dimensions, that's why it woke up when I touched it. Err, and yes, incidentally, I have a feeling I *am* daft. Or some people like me were daft. What nobody ever tells you is that daftness can have *consequences.*'

'Consequences like having pyramids dropped on your house? Oh, I'm sorry, like having pyramids burrow up from *underneath* your house?' asked Gunkin, half-sarcastically.

But *only* half, Celeste realized. Part of him was much cleverer than most of these people. Part of him really wanted to know what was going on.

'Well-' she said, but then the pyramid went ping.

Pyramids rarely go ping anywhere in the universe, so it drew everyone's attention. As they watched, the tips of each of the pyramids seemed to separate themselves, forming a mathematically perfect miniature pyramid of their own. Then the mini-pyramids began to pulse with colours: pinks and greens and blues, and some that only Celeste's eyes could see.

'It's begun then,' she said. 'Final thawing and revival.'

'Revival of what?' said a voice like cat-claws down an eyeball. People had been so busy getting on with their public meetings and raising the Sleepers, they hadn't seen Skoros and his orbs approaching. But the kind of people who become evil dictators *really* hated to be ignored. He waited until everyone was looking at him before gesturing to the three orbs he'd brought with him.

'Skoros,' yelled Harper. 'And he's in league with the aliens, look.'

'He *really* isn't,' said Celeste. 'Although I think he has Alditha held hostage somewhere.'

'But the balls,' said Harper. 'The balls of whizziness-'

'Stolen, yes. And yes, you all should know, they're dangerous as long as they're under his control.'

'Really, Celeste?' said Skoros. 'Well here's some news for you. I am the King of the Garden now. My will is law. That makes you a dangerous alien outlaw if I say so. Any questions?'

Brown-Beard—whose real name was Timmoluk Van Der Buck—shuffled and humphed. 'Yeah, who died and made you king?' he grumped, making some of his friends chuckle.

Skoros snapped his fingers. The orb to his right floated forward and spat a beam of deep, harsh red light at Timmoluk. He turned red, and white and grey as the light hit him, then turned into a small whiff of ash.

'Any *further* questions?' asked Skoros.

'Yours, I believe,' said Alditha, dangling Odiz' severed hands from one of hers like a pair of odd, fleshy gloves.

'Nice hat,' Odiz huffed. The mage grinned at the witch, who gave the brim of her new thorny hat the barest of touches in acknowledgement. Odiz' hands leapt the gap between them and clambered up his body, like eager kittens, to sit on his shoulders. His beard split into two strands and stroked the hands.

'Complicated life you lead,' sniffed Alditha. 'See you're using *spells* to find your way through.' The faintest hint of a smirk caught in her voice, as though using anything as brash as spells was beneath her.

'We must hurry,' said the mage. 'Seems like Big Red's tied up somewhere in the Maze, and there's a faint reading for Sagar, too. I doubt either of them are happy with our friend Skoros.'

'Skoros,' Alditha spat. 'When I find that beardless wretch, I'm going to-'

'Steady,' Odiz cautioned, frowning. 'Don't let the *hat* do your thinking for you.'

'Oh, it isn't, I promise you.' Alditha felt the rage of the bindweed in her veins, felt its fury. 'Though your warning is a good one,' she acknowledged.

'Big Red then?'

Alditha nodded and they set off together.

'No?' sneered Skoros. 'Then answer mine. Who or what is *unthawing* in these pyramids?'

'Reinforcements,' said Celeste, wishing she was altogether taller.

'Really?' There was a manic quality to the twitch in Skoros' grin, like the ominous cracking sound you hear on frozen ponds when you're far too far out on them suddenly.

'Really,' she assured him. 'Reinforcements who've been asleep for a long time, and who might, just possibly, be a little bit cranky at being woken up. How's your arm?' she added, as if to twist the knife.

He held up his wand. 'Fine, thank you. Amazing what one can do with magic.'

Celeste snorted. 'Magic. Honestly, you people. It's a simple sigma field.'

'Still useful though.'

'Just proves you have no idea of the potential of the orbs. One of those could have put it right for you in half a heartbeat. You killed the trees of course.' It wasn't a question, it was a statement. Of course he'd killed them. People like him always did.

'*My* trees,' he corrected her. 'Just as these are my people.' He paused, read the banner and the few placards that were around the square. 'Very distinctly my people. Look, they don't seem to care much for *aliens* around here, do they?'

'They've been misinformed.'

'Sure of that, are you?' He sniffed. 'Their alien looks rather like your Alpha.'

'I mentioned the reinforcements, yes? Keep talking, Skoros, and you might just see how dangerous we aliens can be.'

'Condemned out of your mouth. My people, see how the alien child boasts. See how she threatens.'

The crowd no longer knew how to play their part in this confrontation at all. They had gathered to learn about the evil aliens, but no-one had signed on to support Skoros. Now Skoros had killed one of them, using alien technology, but was claiming it was the alien girl who was the baddie. In their heart of hearts, most of them wanted to just shuffle off and not be there, and some of them wanted to mourn Timmoluk, who'd been a really good bloke who'd always stand you a drink if you needed one. What they'd all have agreed on, if anyone had asked them, was that they didn't want to be stuck in the middle between an alien girl and the mad wizard who was declaring himself King of the Garden.

'Let them go, Skoros. Let them go, and don't make the mistake of trying to torture me again, and we can talk. I'll even introduce you to the Sleepers if you want.'

'As opposed to what, exactly? Me killing you here and now, or holding you hostage for the good behaviour and knowledge of your "Sleepers"? Assuming of course you're even remotely important to them.'

'Hostage? Really? You didn't learn from your last attempt?'

Skoros pointed his wand at the orb on his left, and a green beam shot out of it, surrounding Celeste and taking her breath away. 'Only to be more persuasive,' he told her. He angled his wand, and the orb flew higher, far above the heads of the tallest trolls in the crowd. Celeste was pulled silently into the air, bobbing behind the orb, supported on a string of energy. 'Take her back to the castle and hold her there,' he told the orb, and it moved off, dragging Celeste behind it.

'Friends, subjects, Gardenfolk, we have vanquished the alien threat that…erm…threatened us. Go from this place and be…jolly, or whatever it is you people do. Spread the good news across the King-dom of the Garden. No-one is to come within the square for the span of one night and day, but then we invite you as our honoured guests to attend us here for my coronation…erm…my inaugura-tion…or should I say, my *crowning*, as your rightful king, on the night of Midsummer Hallowe'en.'

The crowd looked at each other, unsure what was happening.

'Cheer,' said Skoros, motioning for another orb to buzz in front of them. A loose and ragged wave of cheering went up. 'That's better,' said Skoros. 'Now, leave us.'

The crowd dispersed. Gunkin and Harper were keen to disperse with them, but found their efforts blocked by orbs.

'Not you two,' said Skoros. 'I'd like a word.'

'Thank you, thank *you*,' said Big Red simply, as Alditha and Odiz freed him from his temporary prison of Blackheart Bindweed. 'I don't think I could have taken much more of that.' He rubbed him-self down, shedding several patches of leathery red skin that had be-come entangled with the bindweed. 'So, what do we do now?'

'Depends what that maniac's up to,' muttered Alditha. 'I mean, other than settling scores and showing off, what does he *gain* from keeping us here?'

'Power,' said Odiz, blasting away at the remaining bindweed that threatened to hamper their escape. 'Damned orb thing—impressive bit of kit. Together, we could stand up to them. Maybe that's why he took us out. Surprised he didn't have a few of 'em guarding Big Red, unless he's saving the rest for-'

'I wouldn't be that impressed,' Alditha cut in. 'He didn't build the orbs. Just cannibalized one and made the others do what he wanted.'

'He didn't build them?' Big Red remarked.

'I've met the real owner,' said Alditha. 'Assuming we survive this, I'll introduce you. And sorry, but I'm not buying your theory. Clearly, we were all knocked out by the orb. So was the real owner. Not convinced we'd have done any better if we'd all joined forces, and frankly how likely would that be?'

'Mayyybe,' said Big Red, 'mayyybe it's something only *we've* got. Wizards, witches, demons?'

'Knowledge,' said Odiz bluntly. 'Sorry, being an idiot. Been a trying day. Damned fool boy was asking about the symbol of the EngineSeers.'

'The what?' said Alditha and Big Red together.

Odiz rolled his eyes. 'See what ya miss if you're just messin' about with plants or faffing with the elemental wossnames. The Engine-Seers were a bunch of ultimate mages. Mixed blacksmithing and magic together for the ultimate power.'

'You mean like Skoros has been trying to do since he was knee-high to a mole?'

'Well, quite. Got to give the lad credit—can't have been easy to grow up in that family with about as much native magical talent as a lentil casserole. Still, he's found his niche.'

'A niche for taking people prisoner and growing Blackheart Bindweed,' Big Red pointed out.

'Y'know I really wish you hadn't said "growing,"' said Alditha. 'Hadn't occurred to me that he grew all this. Like a dark garden, all of his own.'

'Didn't,' sniffed Odiz. 'Was old Salu-Valek who started the Maze. Used to be stories about it, but hadn't heard anything of it since young Skoros was born. Till today, obviously.'

'Still here, though,' said Alditha. 'He's been cultivating it. That sounds a bit too much like practice for being a Gardener for my liking.'

'Crikey,' said Odiz. 'He's trying to get his hands on the Manual of the EngineSeers. If he's been practicing to be a Gardener too, that could be astonishingly dangerous.'

'Oh, you think?' snapped Alditha.

'What's the Manual of the-' asked Big Red.

'Oh, there'll be a book,' sighed Alditha, exasperated. 'One thing you can always guarantee with wizards is there's a book at the heart of everything.'

'There is,' agreed Odiz, either missing or ignoring the sarcasm. 'The Manual of the EngineSeers. Tells you how to be one, apparently. How to do the ultimate magic.' Odiz scratched his moustache. 'Not called that, o' course. It's called The Somethin' NIB-IRU somethin' Codex. Foreign lingo, y'know how it is. But that's what he's after. Kept on about the symbol o' the EngineSeers, and where to find it and all that guff.'

Something went 'click' in Alditha's mind.

'This symbol. Red star, wings?'

'Good grief. That's privileged mage knowledge, y'know.'

'As I say, if we survive this, I'll introduce you to a girl who'll privilege your brains out. *So, the Astarians became the EngineSeers in our legends,*' she mused to herself.

'The who?'

Alditha smirked just a little. 'The EngineSeers. They're not from round here. They're from another planet altogether. They really like bread and jam.'

'Aliens? The EngineSeers are-'

'Like I say, I'll introduce you if you really like. There's one swanning about the place right now. We really need to find her.'

'Blimey. Can you imagine how much Skoros would want a word with her?'

Alditha frowned, her eyebrows knitting together. 'Did I mention we *really* need to find her?'

'Sagar, first,' said Big Red. It was that way with demons—sometimes they were chatty, sometimes they didn't say anything for weeks and you had to poke them with sticks to make sure they were still alive.

'Hmm?' Alditha blinked. 'Mm, yes. When we catch up with Skoros, couldn't hurt to have a dragon on our side. Alright, but Sagar, then Celeste, yes?'

'Celeste would be the-?'

'The EngineSeer, yes.'

'Be dashed useful to have *her* on our side as well, then.'

Alditha sighed. *Wizards.* 'You've got a big book at home, where it says you should always state the obvious in stressful situations, haven't you?' she muttered, setting off again through the slithering, hissing Maze.

———————

Razor hadn't said a word for hours. Not through the business with Celeste and Alpha, not through the horrible business with the trees, though he doubted he'd ever get the smell of smoke out of his wing feathers. Not through the grandstanding with the crowd and the killing of Timmoluk. He didn't particularly want to say anything now, either, as the tips of the pyramids began to flash faster and faster.

It was a strange life, being a magic-user's familiar. You were bound to do what they told you, bound to do what they wanted, even before they told you what it was.

And yet…

And yet you don't have to like it, he thought, sighing heavily through his beak-holes. *Then again, maybe you don't even have to do it.* Seeing Harper, alone up there, without Alditha, had been weird. Wrong, somehow, but he'd still done it—and all to protect the world from what he thought was a threat. Razor sighed again, watching his master punch the goblin.

'Thought you could run away from me, did you?' Skoros landed a blow on Gunkin's jaw. It didn't have much force—he'd never been much good when it came to hitting people—but still, it looked like it stung.

Gunkin turned his eyes on Skoros, and there was nothing in them but a spiderweb of mockery. 'Feel better now, do you? Like a good dose of punchin' someone smaller than yourself, I expect. Mind you, don't suppose you get to do it all that often.'

Gunkin stopped as another punch smashed into his mouth. He rooted around with his tongue, then spat a sharp tooth back at Skoros. 'You wanna watch yourself, *my lord*. Many a numpty's come unstuck by waving something they wanted to keep near a goblin's mouth.' He flashed his disconcerting smile in the dark lord's face. 'Fists included.'

'Would you prefer me to break your legs?' demanded Skoros. 'Hey, where do you think *you're* going, owl?'

Harper had been edging ever further out of Skoros' reach. 'What are you going to do, *wizard?* You can't beat up an owl,' he remonstrated. 'Quite apart from the fact that there are treaties and such, you haven't got enough scars to convince me you've ever punched an owl. We're all talons and beak, don't you know.'

Skoros chuckled. 'You're right of course. I can't punch an owl, even one in a stupid visor.'

'I should think not.'

'Much better to roast you on a spit,' spat the wizard.

Skoros paused. When you've lived with someone most of your life, you get accustomed to the way they think, the way they speak. You begin to leave pauses in your speech for them to have their moment. Now, he fully expected Razor to butt in with a 'Raaark. Err, Boss, maybe not the best thing to do, bringing the witch down on us like a ton of bricks, raaark.' However, this time, there was only silence.

The wizard looked around. Razor was just visible, flying over the trees and houses. *Getting away.*

He looked back at Harper. The owl turned his head deliberately sideways. 'Raaaark?' he demanded.

Skoros snarled, pulled his wand, pointing the corkscrew end right between Harper's eyes, and seemed on the verge of doing something nasty to the bird, when-

-there was a wub-wub-wub-wub-wub sound, followed by a series of bings from the pyramids. Harper straightened his neck without ever taking his eyes off the wand.

Each of the pyramids split open down the middle, the metal walls parting with a smooth shushing sound and a wisp of steam.

Skoros stepped back from Gunkin and Harper and went back to his orbs.

Harper blinked, then shivered. Slowly, each of the six pyramids gave up their treasure. A tall, thin, bulbous-headed grey alien with blank dark eyes stepped out of every one.

And in the sky he tried his best not to look at, the worms and beetles and other scuttling monsters grew sharper, grew larger, grew *closer* to the world, as though the sky was heavy with them, and threatening to burst.

15

'So about that theory of yours,' whispered Alditha.

'What-?' said Odiz aloud before Alditha clapped a hand over his mouth.

'The theory that we were put out of the way because Skoros thought we might be able to deal with the orbs.' She gestured to where Sagar, the Blue Dragon was being held, motionless, in the beams of *three* orbs. 'Skoros obviously considers Sagar to be a bigger risk than us three. Mind you, even for a dragon, he *is* quite big.'

Odiz counted them, noted where each of them were positioned. 'Damn and blast the man,' he whispered.

'That's the plan for later,' Alditha assured him. 'Any plans for now? Believe me when I tell you the odds aren't good. I've already tried the whole "three of them, three of us" technique. Didn't turn out too well.'

Odiz snorted. 'Never knew a witch that could count properly,' he whispered.

Alditha pursed her lips, as if to say 'Take that back old man, or you and I are going to have a falling out.'

'One, two three,' counted Odiz, pointing at each of them in turn. Then his extra left hand waved its fingers. 'Four,' said Odiz. 'Five,' he added when the extra right waved too. 'And, well…' He humphed a sigh that was too heavy for someone engaged on an espionage mission. 'I'm prepared to make it six as long as you two agree never to speak of it to anyone. Agreed?'

Big Red blinked and shrugged. Alditha looked curious, but inclined her head a fraction of a degree.

Odiz closed his eyes tight, held his breath, and went a deeper shade of pink than he always was. All at once, with a loud ripping sound, his beard came free of his face, standing there like a hairy shadow in front of him.

'Yaaaaargh,' yelled the mage, making one of the orbs that was guarding Sagar twitch. It drifted away from the dragon a little and hovered, as though sniffing for a scent. Odiz' disembodied hands each raised three fingers, showing six in total. Alditha turned her eyes up in her head, and the tip of her new bindweed hat unraveled, twitching and slithering down her body, till only the last ring of the foul black weed was around her head. She held up one hand, and two fingers of the other. Seven against three. Eight if they could only distract the orbs long enough to let Sagar himself get a shot at them. Alditha didn't breathe. Breathing during ambush situations, she decided, was vastly overrated. The unraveled weed began to slither softly through the undergrowth, while Odiz' enchanted beard scuttled up a tree trunk. You soon had to already know it was there to be able to follow its progress. Alditha watched it, determined not to look at the now beardless, triple-chinned old man beside her. She understood why he didn't want this spoken of—a mage without his beard was like a witch without her hat. It made you ordinary, and ordinary was dangerous for a witch or a wizard. Ordinary made you desperate.

She felt the ground underneath her, felt the slithering slow progress of the weed. Saw the beard on a branch, preparing its attack. She swallowed.

Then everything was happening at once. The beard leapt, jumping into the air like a flying squirrel, landing on the suspicious orb and quickly shifting its shape, forming a cone of hair that slid down the sphere and jabbed into the hole from which the beam was coming. The beam that was helping keep a huge blue dragon motionless.

The thing about Big Red was…

Well, there were two things about Big Red. First, he was big. And second, he was red. He was also, however much of a pussycat he seemed to people who were nice to him, a demon. All the time they'd been standing, waiting to begin the attack, he'd been sucking up power from the ground itself. Now, in the moment of the orb's confusion, he roared, put down his head, and pointed the tips of both his curved horns at the second orb. Thick waves of deep red energy pulsed off the horns and joined together in mid-air, screaming towards the orb as one firm bolt of power. The orb exploded.

Alditha and Odiz, as one, fired bolts of their magic at the last of the orbs. It dodged and swerved them, keeping its beam of restraining power trained on Sagar.

Alditha concentrated, forming the bindweed that had slithered away from her into a noose with the power of her mind. It leapt and lassoed the third orb, slowing down its ability to dodge the blasts of magic. Slowing it down, but not, sadly, stopping it.

The thing about Sagar was that he was blue. But the other thing about him, the thing that people and orbs forgot at their peril, was that he was also a dragon. While initially willing to be imprisoned by Skoros to save his life, the dragon had grown increasingly angry at being incarcerated in the Maze. Whereas a single orb and the element of surprise had been enough to subdue Odiz and Alditha, it had eventually taken three orbs, constantly covering him with their paralysis beams, to keep Sagar subdued.

As the final orb dodged and weaved out of the way of the blasts of magic, Sagar brought his neck up, opened his mouth, and crunched. The orb crackled and fell to bits, and Sagar spat it out.

'Ugh. Horrible,' he pronounced. 'It's all oily. What that's gonna do to my digestion, I shudder to think.'

The first orb, the one with Odiz' beard stuffed in its beam-nozzle, had bobbed away to the back end of the dragon, away from the jaws of death.

There are many rules about sharing an environment with a dragon. To be fair, the first and most important of those rules is to keep away from the pointy front end where all the teeth and the fiery breath are kept.

Unfortunately for the orb, the second rule is to keep away from the back end, too. The back end leaves you open not only to Hell's flatulence, but the whim of the dragon's extremely sensitive tail. Being hit by an adult dragon's tail, according to Granny Melandra's Almanack of Dragon Keeping, the foremost authority in the Garden on the subject, is 'like bein' hit by a tree-trunk made o' cow.'

Sagar swung his tail, there was the sound of rupturing metal, and the orb fell out of the air, hitting the ground with a spasming crunch. It flickered for a moment, then all its light and life went out. Odiz' beard immediately unfurled itself from the nozzle, and danced a jig of victory on the dead orb's casing.

Odiz whistled, and the beard jumped up, and flew through the air, turning and tumbling as it went. It hit his face and there was the opposite of a loud sucking sound, a kind of *sccccchhhlukk* as hairs sank their roots back into pores, and settled back into their home.

'Yyyyyeeee-arrgh,' yelled the mage. 'Swear it hurts more going in.'

Alditha snapped her fingers, and the bindweed slithered back to her, up her back, and reassembled the hat on her head.

'Care to buy into my theory now?' asked the mage.

Alditha raised one eyebrow.

'You do not compute,' said the alien.

'Do I not?' asked Skoros, fighting the urge to giggle. 'I am the king of this world. You are one of the Sleepers, are you not?'

'Bio-mech Delta-Epsilon-Kappa,' said the bulbous-headed thing. "The Sleepers" does not conform to any description in my databank.'

'You are from somewhere else,' explained Skoros. 'Another star, another world?'

There was a silence, and the alien fixed him with those dark, disturbing eyes. 'Confirmed,' it said eventually. 'You have Astarian survey-orbs, but scans of your biology indicate you are not Astarian. You will explain this dichotomy, or you will be treated as hostile.' It raised a hand towards him. Out of the corner of his eye, Skoros could see the other aliens had done the same.

'Easy,' he cautioned. 'I am not your enemy—I am your friend. I welcome you to the Garden—to *my* Garden...to my world.'

Bio-mech Delta-Epsilon-Kappa ran scans. 'There was no intelligent life on this world when the survey team were forced into cryo-sleep. Internal and external chronometers confirm there has been insufficient time for evolution to produce life forms of your level of intelligence-'

'Thank you,' said Skoros, smiling a sudden, dangerous smile.

Skoros could never have predicted what happened next—it came out of nowhere. The Bio-mechs pointed their hands at the orbs, and power erupted out of them, white-hot and furious. The two orbs dribbled to puddles of melted metal on the floor.

'Technological theft has been rectified,' reported one of the other, as-yet-unnamed aliens.

Skoros blanched. 'Now, wait a minute.'

'Mission parameters were to find an uninhabited world. An uninhabited world was found. Scans confirm this is that world.' Bio-mech Delta reached out and grabbed Skoros by his wizard's robe. 'You are an error,' said the Bio-mech, its dark eyes growing larger in its head. 'You will be corrected.'

The atmosphere in the Red Petunia was subdued. Normally on the night before Midsummer Hallowe'en, the Garden's most popular pub was thrumming with bonhomie and songs. Now there was a tense quiet, as men, women, trolls, goblins, animals and the occasional vegetable and mineral sipped or gulped at their various drinks.

'A king,' said Don Cremini. 'A king of the Garden? It's not right, you know? No-one said "Hey, you with no beard and the stupid red slippers. You be king now."'

'Don't think that's how it works,' muttered Verno Hefterlink, the pea-herder. 'Kinging,' he explained, when everyone looked at him.

'How does it work, then?' asked Mistress Alloban, from behind the bar.

'Works like this,' Verno sulked. 'Some bloke says "I'm king now," and if people don't like it, he cuts their 'eads off or... or...' No-one wanted to think about what had happened to Timmoluk. 'Summink.'

Old Tom sat on the bar, drinking his regular thimbleful of ale. He swallowed. He pulled off his hat, scratched his head, and came to a decision. He put his hat back on and stood up, using his shovel as a prop. ''t'aint right,' he declared. 'I reckon there's badness afoot 'ere. And I don't know 'bout none o' you lot, but I know 'bout me, see? Now I'm only an 'umble spud, right? But I ain't gonna let this badness go. Timmoluk was a good ol' lad, far as I know, and I know Harper's a good lad too. Daft as a brush half the time, but pure-hearted as they come. An' I ain't standin' for it, this 'ere wizard an' 'is badness. I ain't askin' none o' you to come wi' me, and we all know I'll like as not be chipped alive. But there's standin' for summat, and *not* standin' for summat, an' *that's* my path, I reckon.'

Nobody said anything for a long, long moment. Some people sipped their drinks, nervously.

'I'm with ya,' said Verno quietly, gulping down a mouthful of ale as though he couldn't believe what he'd said.

Mistress Alloban sniffed. 'Me an' all. He was always a good lad was Timmoluk. Can't be doin' with this kingin'.'

'Si,' said Don Cremini quickly. 'I too. I pledge the lives of my family to this cause, Signor Tom. I do not care for this so-called wizard-king.'

'I'm in,' said a voice from the corner. Old Tom couldn't see who it belonged to, but soon it didn't matter.

'Right,' said another.

'Yeah, I'm in an' all.'

'Down with Skoros, that's what I say.'

Voices came from all over the room, till there was a chorus of them, all pledging to bring down the so-called king.

The chorus stopped abruptly when there was an intense rapping at the door. Everyone went quiet, as though they had decades of experience at plotting to bring down kings and queens. Mistress Alloban nodded to Verno, who went to the door. He clenched a fist, ready for action, then grabbed the handle and yanked open the door.

Razor was hovering there in mid-air, flapping furiously. No-one said anything, but every eye stared at him.

'Raaark. This the right room for a revolution, is it?' he asked.

'She'll be in the castle,' said Alditha.

'You're sure we need this…this *alien*, are you?' asked Sagar.

'I am, yes,' Alditha said, putting her hand on the dragon's neck. 'She knows how to build those orb things, and who only knows what else. Got a great big grey alien friend an' all, and he's pretty handy in a fight. Don't know how many more of those orbs Skoros has, but she's the one we need.'

'What about the Green Man?' asked Sagar. 'Should we get him involved, do you think?'

Alditha sucked her teeth. She knew they probably should. 'I'm not his favourite person at the moment,' she admitted.

'I'll go and fetch him,' said Big Red. 'He likes me.'

Alditha winced. 'I'm just worried it'll take all of us to rescue Celeste.'

'You, me and the dragon should be enough, surely?' said Odiz.

'Big Red and the Green Man can form a second front, trap the blighter in the middle.'

Alditha boggled.

'Book learnin'', said the mage with a smug smile.

'All right,' muttered Alditha. 'We'll get Celeste, you get the Green Man if you can, meet back at Stone Hedge—Celeste'll want to go there anyway.'

'For the Garden,' said Odiz, shoving his hand out, palm down.

Alditha looked at it dubiously. Then she sniffed and put her hand on top of his. 'For the Garden,' she agreed.

'For the Garden,' said Big Red and Sagar together, putting a clawed red hand and a giant blue foot lightly on the pile.

And here's to not dying in the process, thought Alditha as they nodded at each other, and broke the moment.

In another, secluded part of the Garden, there was another knock on a different door. It was a young knock, an enthusiastic one. It was the kind of knock you had when you were a small spellbook, throwing yourself against a door. Maybe some of Jasper's intense training had caused the little spellbook to become more sensitive to his environment, or maybe he just sensed something different in the air. Either way, Dramm was excited.

Jasper opened the door, and his face appeared on his cover, smiling down at the impetuous little book. It's difficult to nod when your face is two-dimensional, but Jasper did it. And then, where his eyes, nose and mouth had been, they faded to blankness.

Blankness that was replaced with streams of numbers and symbols that ran over his whole cover, chasing each other up from the bottom. Then, suddenly, the numbers and symbols vanished, too.

A red stain grew in the middle of his cover, blooming like a blood spot. A blood spot that formed a perfect red star. Then the star unfurled fiery red wings on either side. Jasper looked up at the sky and

saw changing colours, other dimensions, moving, drawing nearer—
things he had not seen before, but instinctively understood throughout his whole body. Here was something that only spell books—and
maybe a select few—could see and understand. He knew that, like
the coming and going of the seasons, there would soon be an important change in the Garden. He also instinctively knew that he—Jasper
—would soon be no more.

———————

'Delta, hold.'

'Holding,' confirmed the bio-mech, still gripping Skoros by the
front of his robe.

Skoros couldn't see around the alien, but the voice behind it
seemed amused.

'Let go of the creature, Delta, before you sprain something.'

There was a long moment of stand-off, while the bio-mechs large
black eyes seemed to burn into Skoros. Then it let him go. Skoros
rearranged his robe, ran a hand through his hair.

'I apologise,' said the voice, and Skoros moved aside to see who it
belonged to. It was another teenaged-looking girl, this time with
green hair and green eyes. 'Hail, humanoid,' she said.

'Thank you,' said Skoros. 'My name is Skoros, and I am king here.'

'My name is Peridot,' said the girl, 'and this...complicates matters.'

Skoros raised both eyebrows. 'How?'

Peridot frowned. 'Because-'

'Intruders,' called a voice from another of the pyramids. 'Bio-
mechs, sterilize the area.'

'Because of him,' said Peridot, nodding at a boy who was stepping
out of his pyramid. A boy with hair the colour of conkers and a
scowl that said the universe was beneath him. 'Zirca,' she added. 'I
advise you to run.'

'I am a king,' said Skoros, puffing out his chest, 'and the greatest
wizard of the age.'

'Marvellous,' said Peridot. 'If you still want to be all that in about thirty slipaways' time, you need to run.'

Each of the pyramids had contained a bio-mech and an Astarian, and each of the bio-mechs raised both arms, palms out.

'Run,' yelled Peridot. And Skoros, King of the Garden, looked quickly around the square, did some rapid calculations, and ran. Before he'd gone two hundred yards, he heard the sound of buildings collapsing, and felt a prickling heat on the back of his neck. He ran, and ran, expecting every second to be his last, for the heat to catch him up, and burn him, turn him to nothing but bits of surprised ex-wizard. His lungs ached, his muscles cramped, but Skoros kept running, never daring to look back.

When most people have friendly disagreements, they tend to blow over in about a week or two.

When magic-users have friendly disagreements, it can tend to leave continents smouldering and charred.

Alditha and Odiz had engaged in a friendly disagreement about the best tactics for rescuing Celeste from Skoros Castle. Alditha had favoured magical disguises, saying it was traditional for witches to pretend to be ugly old peasants to get into houses.

Looking back, Odiz supposed it was when he'd said 'Pretend?' that the argument had really begun. Alditha had held out her hands and muttered an incantation in which the words 'get your useless bristles to my hand as quick as ya like' had featured strongly. Her broom had shot through the undergrowth from wherever it had been held, up-ended itself and slid into her grip.

'Yes,' she'd said, smugly. 'Pretend.'

The argument had gone on from there. It might be traditional for witches, Odiz argued, but it wasn't for wizards, who were more in-clined to blast the door open. 'All the mystic hoo-ha and being at one with nature is no match for a good fireball,' he maintained.

They hadn't spoken for fifteen minutes, as they rode towards the castle on Sagar's back. They could have each flown independently, Alditha on her broom and Odiz on the air's understanding that he was a bally wizard, and the normal laws of physics didn't apply to him, but when Sagar flapped his big blue wings, the laws of physics had a really good go at applying to them both, buffeting them about the skies.

'Besides,' said Odiz out of nowhere, 'what do you suggest we disguise our blue friend here as? 'm not sure a blimmin' great blue dragon can be disguised as anything other than a blimmin' great blue dragon. Or if he can, it's probably as something even scarier.'

It's difficult to get an air of icy disdain into your voice when you have to yell to be heard against the wind as you fly on the back of a dragon. Alditha though, had not become a witch without knowing a trick or two. 'I'm sure you're right,' she said, in a tone that made it perfectly clear she was sure Odiz was a dribbling idiot. 'Approaching the castle now,' she added with clipped precision.

'Are we...*alright*, then?' asked Odiz.

'We're fine,' said Alditha, which even Odiz knew meant they were anything but fine. 'Let's just do this, shall we?'

And with that, she swung her leg over Sagar's shoulders, shuffled sideways, and dropped like a dignified stone on her broomstick.

'Confound the woman,' muttered Odiz, as Sagar took him round in a wide arc, to face the front of the castle. 'Hate going on rescue missions when there's bad feeling. Not good for morale, y'know?' Sagar didn't answer him, so Odiz patted the dragon's neck. 'You sure you know what to do, old chap?'

'Let me see now,' said the dragon, 'has something to do with breathing *fire*, doesn't it? Y'know, being a *dragon*? Not like I have any experience in that, or anything. Not like it's what I *do* at all.'

'Good grief, can't a fella ask an honest question any more?' Odiz bluffed. 'Right, well then, let's be getting on, I suppose.' He huffed and puffed his thick, meaty leg over the dragon's body, slipped, and tumbled into the air, his spare hands losing their grip on his shoulders and falling to the ground on their own.

16

Alditha dropped through the air. Normally, she would have had all
sorts of fun, letting the slipstream blow her skirts up to her chin as
she fell, or throwing her hair back carelessly in the wind, screaming
'yo losers, out of the way' as she went.

But not today. Today the witch was on a mission.

As she came close to the ground, she swept her broom underneath her feet and her fall slowed, till she put first one booted foot,
then another, on the floor. She sniffed, satisfied that the first part of
the plan had gone well. She was outside the back door of the castle—
witches always went to the back door, because that was where you
usually found penniless serving girls whose lives needed a boost and
also because that was where all the best gossip was. Alditha was in no
sense stupid—she knew there was unlikely to be anyone to fool with
a disguise in the castle. But some things you did because they were
traditional. She bent down and took a pinch of dust off the back
step, sprinkled it over herself, and felt her features change, her skin
grow loose, her nose grow longer, her teeth retreat, leaving just one

visible on the bottom row, and a couple of warts sprout on her chin and her cheek. She felt an ache grow in her back as it stooped. Normally, she'd have changed her clothes to something more ragged and dirty, but she didn't have time.

Now I'm ready, she thought, gripping the handle of the back door and pushing.

———————

Odiz landed in a less dignified heap, his legs flailing in the air and his robe flapping.

'Oof.'

Within seconds, both his spare hands landed by the side of him, and Odiz rolled his old body up onto all fours, nodding his head to the spare hands, which scuttled forward, using their fingers as legs. Odiz stood up, rubbing his new hands together.

'Right then, ya beardless loon,' he muttered. 'Let's be havin' ya.'

———————

Inside the castle, the two orbs Skoros had sent to keep Celeste sedated had manoeuvred her to a slab in the dungeon. They kept their beams fixed on her, meaning she couldn't move.

''Ello,' a croaky old voice called. 'I'm an old washer-woman, come to see if there's anything as needs…erm…washin.''

The orbs ignored the voice. Their master had instructed them to keep the female captive and immobile, and until he gave them further orders or their mission was threatened, that's what they would do.

The voice coughed. 'P'raps you didn't hear what I said?' it called louder. 'I said I'm an old *washer-woman*, lookin' for anything as needs *washin'*—Oh I dunno, no respect for the traditions, some people…'

Then there was the sound of a distant crump, which the orbs analysed immediately. By the relative distance of the sound and the components of its waveform, they judged that someone had exploded the front door, and turned the first three metres of the entrance hall to molten rock. The orbs did a rapid assessment of the need to investigate, but decided the likely threat level was too low to disturb their core mission—the keeping of the Astarian in a state of inactivity. The orbs noted the noise and activated their advanced surveillance sub-routines. But they didn't move.

In a corridor off the dungeons though, the body of a bio-mechanoid lay sprawled out. The bulbous head, face down, didn't move. But it heard the voice of the 'washer-woman' and somewhere in the complex mass of organic matter and circuitry that was its highly advanced brain, it ran a pattern-matching programme. It found a match, which it hadn't expected to do. Power surged and lit up neurons in its brain.

'Al-al-al-al-' it said. Its spindly arms moved, pushing it to its knees, then to its broad, splayed feet. 'Alditha,' said Alpha, moving off silently in the direction of the voice.

Odiz' extra hands skittered down the melted corridor, scouting each turn as they came to it, and giving him a thumbs-up before he followed them. His beard formed itself into a fist, punching at the air, and yanking him along with it.

'Confound ya, lay still,' he told it. The beard ignored him and kept punching.

At the end of the corridor, one of his hands pointed down.

A dungeon? Makes sense. He nodded at it, and it disappeared, leaping down the steps on its fingers like a spider on its legs.

Moments later, the hand came jumping back up, and formed a ball with its fist.

Orbs, thought Odiz. *Gotcha.*

He formed his hands—the hands that were attached to the end of his arms—into a point on the top of his head. The signal was clear— 'Find Alditha.' Both his old hands finger-ran off down the corridor.

Odiz moved forward as quietly as he could, rolled up the sleeves of his robe and stood ready, both his hands in spell-casting positions in case the orbs should venture up the stairs.

I dare ya, thought Odiz. *I double dare ya.*

———————

Alditha hobbled along the corridor, playing the old washer-woman for everything she was worth.

Alpha rounded the corner, fixed her with his big dark eyes then raised his hands.

'Mr. Alpha,' said Alditha. 'I'm glad to see you alive.'

He lowered his hands again. 'Al-al-al-Alditha,' he said.

She nodded, felt a twinge in her back. *Ah, to heck with it—you can take tradition too far*, she thought, and shook her arms. It was as though the old woman fell off her, like dust or sand, and Alditha stood in front of him. She couldn't help herself though, sweeping the dust of her disguise off to the side in a neat pile.

'Why are you here?' asked Alpha. 'This is the fortress of our enemies.'

'I know it is. I'm looking for Celeste. D'you know where she is?'

'She was running,' said Alpha. 'I stayed to stop our enemies. They prevailed. My systems went offline.'

'I know you're a clever person, Mr. Alpha. Can you perhaps use the 'fluence to find her? Can you tell me where she is now?'

'Scanning for Astarian life signs,' he said. 'There is one Astarian within this building.'

'That'll be her.' Alditha nodded her approval. 'Lead on, Mr Alpha.'

'Delta wave signature confirmed,' he reported. 'It *is* Celeste.'

'Well *of course* it is—on ya go.' she said, shooing him forward. 'Wait.' She grabbed one of his thin, pale arms. 'Listen.'

There was a sound coming towards them. A sound like the pitter-patter of tiny feet.

Two hands with no bodies came running round a corner, and before she could stop him, Alpha raised an arm and blasted one of the skittering things with bright blue energy. It stopped in its tracks and flipped over, twitching. The other hand dodged and ran to Alditha for protection.

'Mr. Alpha, it's on our side,' she hissed.

'Ac-ac-ac-accepted. Designation ally accepted.'

The hand formed a tight ball.

'Orbs?' asked Alditha. 'Here?'

The hand gave a thumbs-up.

'How many?'

It showed two fingers.

'I'm going to assume you're not just being rude,' she told it. 'Lead on.'

It began trotting back down the hallway, then stopped, walked over to the other hand, prodded it encouragingly, once, twice. The hand lay dead.

The living hand sagged, then intertwined some fingers and began to pull its dead companion after it.

'Here,' said Alditha quietly, lifting them both up and carrying them. 'You point, I follow, right?' The still living hand gave a slow, sad thumbs-up, and pointed down the hallway.

'What the?' Whispered Odiz when he saw Alpha striding along next to Alditha. She told him with a look that Alpha was one of them, was on their side. Odiz' eyes widened, but he shrugged. His spare hand took its fellow and climbed up the old mage's robe, as if presenting the dead flesh to its owner for repair. Odiz took the dead hand, examined it, and slipped it quietly into one of the big pockets in his robe, then patted his shoulder, inviting the remaining hand up to its perch. It slunk up and held on tight.

Alpha detached his hand silently and offered it to the mage.

Alditha rolled her eyes, and Odiz shook his head. Alpha slipped the hand back on at the wrist and flexed it.

Alditha pointed at Alpha, then waggled a finger between herself and Odiz. The bio-mech inclined his head only slightly, then went down the steps to the dungeon, his legs looking oddly bandy on the stairs, as though he were new to the concept.

Alditha and Odiz followed one after the other. When the bio-mech walked into the dungeon room, there was no pause, no consideration of tactics—the three just went from walking downstairs to full-on battle mode. Alpha walked up to the nearest orb and grabbed it, held it tight between his hands. Code seemed to stream across his black eyes, in shades of bright, luminous yellow, and pour like heat into the orb's casing. It began to shake the same moment that the second orb hit Alpha with its red ray. Still able to keep Celeste in its imprisoning beam, it floated up towards the ceiling of the dungeon, trapping them both. The orb in Alpha's hand popped open at the top, a thin tube jutting out of its casing. He gripped the orb tight in a bear hug, then pulled out the tube. The orb went limp and dropped to the floor, and Alditha and Odiz piled into the room, firing blasts of magic from their hands. The orb weaved, avoided them. Alditha changed her focus, pointed the tip of her bindweed hat at Celeste. The hat unraveled, becoming a sticky black lasso and, with a thought, she flung the loop around Celeste's feet and yanked. The girl was momentarily caught in a tug of war, but the orb fired bolts of hot energy at the magic users, and severed the bindweed. Odiz' beard was singed by another blast and scurried up to hide beneath his chins.

'Damn and blast the thing,' spat the mage.

'I'll damn, you just blast it,' Alditha called back.

Odiz fired a couple of his special favourites at the orb, and they hit it. 'Grab the girl,' he said, and Alditha moved, pulling Celeste towards her. It was hard work for a second, but with the orb stunned, she pulled Celeste out of the beam that was trapping her, and the girl fell into her waiting arms.

'Got her,' Alditha reported.

Odiz advanced on the orb, curious—it was still in the air, its beam still operating, but otherwise it was silent and still. Sperrywaller's Dagnabbit was a spell rarely cast in battle, its effects were angry and mostly unpredictable. Odiz wanted to be sure the orb was no threat anymore. He frowned at it, tiptoeing forward.

'ALERT. ALERT.' The orb's metallic voice came suddenly, making Odiz jump. He was a mage, and he was fond of his dinner, but Alditha had to blink as she saw him zoom past her, running for the stairs.

'Leg it,' Odiz called down to them. 'You've got the girl, what are you-' The rest of his speech was lost as he ran away, and the orb started to remember what its function was.

Alditha clicked her tongue. *Wizards.* Still, on this occasion he was right. 'Leg it, Mr. Alpha. Run.'

Alpha took Celeste from Alditha, nodded, and ran up the stairs after Odiz.

Alditha closed the big wooden door after him, then turned to face the orb.

'That was a mighty fine hat you cost me, orb,' she told it. 'I think it's time you and I came to an understanding.' She rolled up her sleeves.

———————

The Green Man chewed fretfully on a strawberry marshmallow as Big Red filled him in on what had been going on.

'-so we need your help,' the demon finished.

The Green Man said nothing, just kept chewing.

'Skoros has to be stopped,' Big Red added, in case the Green Man hadn't understood him.

The Green Man swallowed, looked sadly at the demon. 'I'll not help spill the blood of any creature in this Garden,' he said. 'And that's what "stopped" means, isn't it? You plan for him not to be alive?'

'Haven't thought that far ahead,' admitted Big Red. 'Too busy worrying about *us* not being alive by the time he's done. You know what he did to his forest?'

The Green Man raised a spindly hand, closed his eyes. The memory of the tree-burning still haunted him. He had felt them die, his brothers and sisters in consciousness.

'Every effect has a cause. Every cause is an effect, and that effect in turn had a cause,' he murmured. 'Skoros is a dangerous being, we all know that now, if we didn't before. But once he was a child, as innocent as any in the Garden. Evil is not born, Big Red, it is *made*. Begging your pardon, of course.' Demons were a bit hazy on the whole good and evil thing.

'That's as may be,' sniffed Big Red, 'but he ain't a child no more. He's a wizard, and he might even be a whatchamacall. An EngineSeer. Or somesuch. Big, powerful herbert, Odiz says.'

The Green Man frowned. It was an impressive frown, rippling across his wooden, lined face. He sighed, like a breeze through branches.

'I'm going to need more marshmallows,' he said, walking over to his dresser and opening the drawer. He saw the bag that Celeste had given him, full of the little round silver balls. 'Hmm,' he said, scooping up the bag. 'You'll give me your word, Big Red, or I will not go on this journey with you. Skoros does not die. Not by our hand.'

The demon grunted. 'Not by mine, nor any I can stop. Good enough?'

The Green Man looked at him. Getting a demon's word on a bargain was traditional. Usually it had to be in writing for it to mean anything, but looking at Big Red, the Green Man relented. The demon was *scared*.

The Green Man put the bag of Celeste's silver balls on a sidesprout on his leg, and paid it no mind as thin branches wove themselves around it, keeping it safe. He straightened his trunk. 'Good enough,' he agreed.

Big Red nodded and led the way outside.

_____

Odiz and Alpha were crouching in the undergrowth outside the castle's blasted door. Crouching wasn't a position that came naturally to Odiz, and he was trying not to moan about it in the presence of his unusual company.

Celeste had come too, and he'd introduced himself to the two of them. Introducing Sagar, flying in circles above them had been… trickier.

'What's keeping her?' demanded Celeste.

'Would you like to mount a secondary rescue plan, Celeste?' asked Alpha.

'Calculate strategies, given known parameters and skill sets,' she said, which appeared to translate as 'yes, please,' in Astarian.

They all heard it more or less at the same moment. The sound of cheerful whistling. It was a smug whistle that seemed pleased with itself.

Then, from out of the doorway came a different noise. The noise of metal rolling on flagstone. An orb rolled out of the door and stopped when it hit grass.

Alditha strolled out after it. _Whistling._

'How the blazes did you-?' blustered Odiz, bursting from his cover.

'Me and the orb, we had a conversation. Came to an understand-ing,' she explained airily. 'It understands quite well now.'

Odiz stared at the orb. Though he couldn't be sure, it appeared to have several dents and marks on its side that it didn't have before. _Badass witch._ He thought to himself.

'Alpha, cancel strategic planning,' said Celeste, popping up from behind the bush she'd been using for cover.

'Acknowledged,' said the bio-mech, as Celeste went to greet Alditha.

'Thank you for the rescue,' the alien girl said, smiling.

'Oh we're not out of the woods yet,' Alditha told her. 'Not by a long way. But it's time we got out of here.' She put two fingers in her mouth and gave the most piercing whistle any of them had ever heard.

The Blue Dragon swept round in a wide arc, lowered and came in to land, his feet scrabbling at the earth for the last few metres.

'All this flying about is giving me the most terrible indigestion,' muttered Sagar. 'Not to mention the stress. But that's just fine, don't worry about me, just climb on my body and expect to be flown wherever you like. Maybe I should start a service. *Blue Dragon Air.* You'd like that, wouldn't you? Riding me around like you own the place.'

'Have you ever paid a witch for your stomach medicine?' asked Alditha reasonably.

'Paying? A witch? The very idea.'

'Then think on and get flapping,' Alditha told him shortly.

'It's exploitation, that's what it is,' muttered the dragon, as he began to flap his wide blue wings.

———————

It took Skoros quite some time to reach the castle. He'd been humiliated. By aliens. Outsiders.

That's not going to happen again, he told himself as he reached the front door.

Or at least where the front door had been. Now there was a gaping hole and the stone around it looked melted and charred.

Tedious.

He didn't waste time on it though, marching straight to the corridor of the ancestors and his secret room. He pointed his wand and watched the cogs and wheels on the wall turn.

Make me run, would you? Me.

When the door opened, he went inside and straight to his desk. He took his headset out of its drawer and pulled it onto his head. Then he cranked the handle and saw his machine grind and groan and steam its way into life. He felt under the desk and plugged the helmet in, feeling the spikes poke through his hairline and connect him to the machine.

Now then...

Zirca smiled, standing in the square. He had bio-mechs stationed at the far edges of each of the legs of the crossroads, to keep the local lifeforms out of what was now Astarian territory. He'd sent a pair of orbs into the atmosphere to scan the cracks in the dimensional eggshell above the planet, and had been surprised to hear a message from Astarian Command. The fleet was close, and in just a couple of slow-slips, or what the bio-mechs said the local life-forms called *hours*, the Hedge would activate, the cracks would align like lenses in a telescope, and the fleet would be able to come through to this dimension without endangering the fabric of them all. His job would finally be done.

Of course, before that, he had to rid the planet of all its irritating sentient life. That was outside his mission parameters, and when they'd found the planet, it hadn't been a problem. He was determined it would not be a problem again by the time the fleet arrived. He hadn't mentioned it when he'd contacted Command, hadn't wanted to tell them there were indigenous lifeforms here now, and that the long Astarian search for a new home planet would have to continue.

That was the trouble with going into prolonged cryo-sleep of course—you never knew what would happen while you were locked away.

That idiot, Ven Tao.

If he hadn't been so busy looking at the local lifeforms, this would never have happened. It was just as well he'd died when the engine had flared. *I'd have had to execute him otherwise.*

Zirca hadn't decided yet quite how he was going to kill all the primitives. He could send the bio-mechs and the orbs to destroy them all of course, but there seemed to be rather a lot of the wretched creatures about the place, and life had developed in unusual ways here—his scans showed him there were intelligent vegetables here, even intelligent fungi and minerals. He clicked his tongue—that was what you got when you went to sleep for 6.8 thousand years. Even the mushrooms started getting ideas above their station.

Zirca squinted down one leg of the crossroads and frowned. There was a darkness in the sky there, moving deliberately towards the square. A cloud? He pointed a scanner at it. No, a *swarm*. A swarm of flying creatures.

'Because the day wasn't complicated enough already,' he murmured to himself. The swarm grew closer, and closer, a formation of black, flapping creatures. He glanced at his scanner again. Bats, apparently. Zirca's lips twitched in a smile. This was a stupid planet, with its talking mushrooms and argumentative potatoes and walking trees and so on. *For all I know, the bats are coming to beg for mercy,* he thought.

But no—suddenly, the swarm dipped, dropped out of his eye line. It took him a moment to adjust his view to see they had fallen out of the sky and were landing on bio-mech Gamma-Omega-Delta. The swarm seemed to be attacking it, but then, after a handful of seconds, the bats detached, flew off and dispersed, flying individually again, not with the same purpose. Gamma simply stood there, seeming unfocused for long seconds as Zirca watched him. Then he turned his bulbous head and swiveled to look at Zirca. Gamma's huge black eyes seemed to grow larger and blacker in his head. And then the bio-mech started to run.

Straight towards Zirca.

Zirca's smile grew broader. *What have we here?*

'Bio-mechs Delta and Lambda, run Astarian defence protocols, apprehend bio-mech Gamma-Omega-Delta.'

'Confirmed,' said two almost identical voices through Zirca's headband. The bio-mechs ran fast from another leg of the crossroads, sthen headed to intercept Gamma.

They always looked odd when they ran, thought Zirca idly. The spindly legs didn't look as though they were built to move at speed, but they did, the organic components being taken over by the mechanical in moments of need and powering them precisely where they were instructed to go. The two loyal bio-mechs stood between Gamma and Zirca. Gamma moved rapidly—almost too rapidly for Zirca to register what happened. The rogue bio-mech tore the head off Lambda before he could even raise its hand. Gamma slipped a leg out, tripped Delta, grabbed him as he fell, and pushed both thin-fingered hands against the sides of Delta's head. Blue electricity sparked from Gamma's fingers, and Delta shook and slumped. Then he got to his feet, and both bio-mechs jogged, calmly and in perfect unison, towards Zirca.

Zirca stuck out his chin as they arrived. 'Bio-mechs Gamma and Delta, you are in contravention of your ord-'

He gasped, as Gamma's long fingers grabbed him by the throat and lifted him up, squeezing gently, but with a perfect judgment that was a message in itself. 'One wrong move,' the grip said, 'one wrong word, and you join Lambda in the Headless Astarians Club.'

'Do I have your attention now?' demanded Gamma, his voice more angry and grating than any bio-mechanoid's in Astarian history. 'As I was saying, I am Skoros, King of the Garden, and you will obey me.'

17

'What in the name of sanity?' murmured Alditha. Unfortunately it did no good to murmur when you were on the back of a dragon, flying high over the Garden, because nobody could hear you. 'I SAID WHAT IN THE NAME OF SANITY?'

'What?' Odiz called back. He was fine with most magic, but whereas witches traditionally flew about on broomsticks, wizards, if at all possible, liked to keep their feet firmly on the ground, so he wasn't looking down any more often than he had to. 'What's going on?'

Alditha looked down. She saw the crowd of Gardenfolk, marching more or less in unison, towards Skoros Castle. They had banners, and signs, and from what she could see, they seemed to be chanting something, occasionally throwing an arm into the air.

'IT'S LIKE A RIOT,' she explained. 'ONLY SLOWER.'

'Eh? What're you-?' Something in Odiz' brain told him this was one of those moments when he had to look. He looked.

'The damn fools,' he said. 'The man's a pointy hat short of a wizard. There's no telling what he'll do to them when they get there.'

Wizards, thought Alditha again. 'OF COURSE THERE'S A TELLING WHAT HE'LL DO TO THEM. HE'LL BLOOMIN' WELL KILL THEM ALL, THAT'S WHAT HE'LL DO TO THEM.'

'You're not wrong,' said Odiz after a moment's consideration.

Alditha raised her eyebrow, but Odiz, behind her, couldn't see it. 'I KNOW,' she told him. 'SAGAR. *LAND.*'

'Oh yes, m'lady, as you say, m'lady. HUMANS,' bellowed the dragon, tilting his wings towards the ground.

———————

Alditha always commanded attention whenever she arrived anywhere. That was part of being a witch. When she thought back though, she didn't think she'd ever commanded so much attention with so little effort as when she landed in front of the crowd of marching Gardenfolk and swung herself off the back of the Blue Dragon, followed by the highest-ranking mage in the world, an alien teenager, and a bio-mechanoid. You commanded *a lot* of attention when you did that.

'Afternoon,' said Alditha, nodding ever so slightly to the crowd. 'Blessings be upon you this Midsummer Hallowe'en. You'll be turning around now, I expect.'

Some of the folk in the front row looked sheepish. It wasn't that witches ruled anything, anywhere, or that people would necessarily let them if they tried. It was just that people who didn't listen to witches' warnings had a history of spending periods of their lives hopping about on lily pads eating flies. Some of them even got turned into frogs first.

'No, madam, we will not,' said a strong voice to Alditha's right.

Some of the folk in the front row winced.

Alditha turned to look at the speaker. He was tall and willowy with long blonde hair and features that seemed designed to minimize wind resistance. 'Brangle the Elf of Recycling Hill, I see you,' she said. It was the witch equivalent of 'You disrespecting me?'

Brangle appeared either not to know what it meant, or not to care. Really speaking, it was a miracle he'd lived as long as he had. 'We intend, madam,'—the crowd winced again—'to present our grievances to the dictator Skoros, and to demand he forfeit his claim to be "king" of the Garden.'

'I see,' said Alditha. 'That's a lot of words for an elf without a head.'

'Are you threatening me?' Brangle demanded, looking down the ski-slope of his nose.

'Certainly not, Mr. Brangle. Witches do not threaten, you should know that. We do *promise* a good deal,' she said, letting the words dangle there. 'But at this time, I'm merely pointing out that Skoros is as nutty as a squirrel's privy, and he'll zap your heads into dust before you get a fine long speech like that out of your mouths.'

'Scuse me, Miss Alditha?' said a small, squeaky voice from somewhere rather nearer ground level. 'But if he zaps our heads off, won't that make it hard to rule us, like? As king and all?'

Brangle sniffed. 'Stupid boy,' he muttered.

Alditha crouched down. 'It's Sprat, isn't it? Sprat of the Pratts of Lower Hedgerow? My, how you've grown since I last saw you. I must get over and visit the pixies more often.' Alditha was being extra-specially friendly to the young pixie, mostly, she admitted to herself, to get right up Brangle's pencil-hole nose. 'The thing is though, there's lots of you here, aren't there?'

'Yes, miss.'

'So he could blow your little head off your shoulders, and Mr. Brangle's, and Old Mr. Ragbag the scarecrow's, who I see hiding behind Mr. Verno Hefterlink there, and still have plenty of noses left to grind into the dust as his slaves, you see?'

'We're doooooomed,' moaned Ragbag, who'd been carried away with the moment in the Red Petunia the night before. The scarecrow buried his head in his hands with a rustle. His head came off, but people were used to that, so nobody said anything.

'Raaaark, he might, as well,' said Razor, from his perch on the left-hand pole of a banner that read "Down Withe Kinges And Suchlike." 'Likes a good head-zapping if he can get away with it, raaark. And he can.'

'Voice of experience there,' said Alditha, getting up and sniffing appreciatively. 'What's got you all riled up anyway?'

Old Tom took off his hat—it's always wise to show deference to a witch, especially when she's lost her hat and might be touchy about the subject. 'Timmoluk,' he said, and the crowd murmured its agreement.

Alditha narrowed her eyes, feeling the prickle of something in the air that was going to make her angry. 'Timmoluk Van Der Buck, sturdy lad from The Sheds?' She blinked, slowly. 'What about 'im?'

It was Verno who plucked up the courage to tell her what had happened.

'I see,' said Alditha, long seconds after Verno had finished speaking.

'Not just him,' said a voice behind her. Odiz came forward. 'Blighter killed my housekeeper, Mistress Fazackerly. Not right. Not right at all.'

The crowd reacted, a wave of shock rippling through them all—Mistress Fazackerly was famous for her pies.

'Raaark, not to mention Harper and Gunkin,' said Razor.

Alditha's head snapped up to him. 'What?' she said. 'Harper? *My* Harper? Is he-? Explain yourself, Mr. Razor and be quick about it.'

'Raark, well, I mean, I'm not sure. Things were going a bit mad when I...Raaark, that is to say, I...'

'You left him behind. *Them*, you left them behind,' said Alditha.

'The world was going nuts,' squawked Razor. 'There were all these things popping up out of the ground, and these weird-looking fellas coming out, saving your presence, friend-' He nodded at Alpha.

'Oh, no,' moaned Celeste. 'The bio-mechs are awake. That means the Sleepers are up, too.'

'What about my *owl*?' demanded Alditha with the patience of salt on a cut.

'Well, I don't know, do I? I know he was left behind with Gunkin. If it's any consolation, this here is Harper's Army, raark. Memorial, y'know? For the brave owl that stood up to my mad master, raaaaark. We're protesting in his name.'

'Consolation?' said Alditha, quietly.

'Oh corks,' Odiz muttered, backing away.

'Consolation,' said Alditha again, just as quietly, but breaking into a sweet smile.

'She's gonna blow,' said Odiz urgently to Celeste and Alpha —he hadn't lived to be an old man by not knowing the signs of a witch about to explode.

'CONSOLATION?' roared Alditha. 'That little owl was worth a dozen of you, Razor Blackwing, and another dozen for best. And you left him to die at the hands of that, that-'

There was a fluttering noise that Alditha barely heard in her fury. If she'd been paying attention she would have noticed that the crowd wasn't looking at her, which, given that she was an angry witch, was remarkable in itself. Then there was the feel of claws on her shoulder.

''s'nice to see you too,' said Harper.

Alditha turned her head. 'Harper Fluffbelly, you are a nightmare. See what you've caused,' she said, more or less out of habit, before rubbing him just at the top of his chest feathers. He turned his neck, and she scratched where he let her.

'*I've* caused?' he asked. 'Seems to me like your *alien* friends there are the cause of all this. Well, them and that loopy wizard.'

'This is Celeste, the girl from the teacup.'

'It really isn't a-'

'And this is Mr. Alpha, who I gather you've met.'

'Met the teacup-girl too.' Harper sniffed at Alpha, then turned his head to look into Alditha's eyes. 'And you're sure they're not going to try and kill me, are you?'

'Yes.'

'Or invade and enslave us all and take food off our tables?'

'Pretty sure, yes.'

'Erm-' said Celeste.

The crowd held its breath as Alditha stopped scratching Harper's neck feathers and turned around, slowly.

'You *don't* want to invade and enslave us all,' said Alditha firmly. 'Do you?'

'We don't, no,' Celeste agreed, gesturing at herself and Alpha. 'But it's not as simple as that.'

'Please,' said Alditha, smiling a little too sweetly, '*do* go on.'

'Oh blimey,' muttered Odiz.

'We were sent to find the Sleepers. There was supposed to be a team we'd call in once we'd found them. A team skilled at re-orientation. The Sleepers were originally on a mission to find an uninhabited planet for us to settle on. They thought they'd found it, then we lost contact with them. Although we figured out part of the story from their last transmission, we now know exactly what happened—there was an accident which forced them into cryo-sleep. If they've woken up cranky on a planet that's not so uninhabited any more…actually, if they've woken up cranky on a planet that's not so uninhabited anymore and met *Skoros* as the first example of what you're like…well, I don't know, the variables are not strictly calculable, but they might well decide to sterilize the planet, take it back to the uninhabited state they found it in.'

'They might *what?*'

'I'm not saying it's right,' said Celeste, 'but it makes a certain amount of sense. From their perspective. Possibly.'

'Oh good, I'd hate to die horribly if it didn't make *sense*.'

'Told you not to trust the aliens, didn't I?' whispered Harper in Alditha's ear.

'So there are good aliens, and bad aliens?'

'Astarians,' said Celeste. 'And of course there are. Aren't there good and bad witches? Good and bad wizards? Good and bad owls? Good and bad everything?' she asked, appealing to the crowd.

'There are only *good* elves,' sniffed Brangle, but everyone ignored him.

'Besides,' said Celeste, 'they're not necessarily *bad* Astarians. They just might possibly want to kill everyone on the planet.'

'If we survive this,' snapped Alditha, 'you and I are going to have a long talk about the meaning of good and bad around these parts, Missy.'

'Oh,' said Celeste, as something struck her.

'Oh blimey,' muttered Odiz, who also hadn't got to be an old man without recognizing the moments when things don't seem like they can get any worse, and then suddenly do.

'There's more?' Alditha demanded.

'Today. It's today, isn't it? Your Midsummer-?'

'Hallowe'en, yes. Why? What's that got to do with- Oh.'

'Will somebody finish a bally sentence around here?' Odiz exploded. ''s'enough to give a fella acute heartburn.'

'Ven Tao, the Gardener,' explained Alditha. 'He pruned the Hedge today.'

'Well yes, of course he did, we all know that.'

'It was doing its *thing* today.'

'Raark, it always does its thing today, dunnit? Very pretty and all that.'

'It's the time when dimensional boundaries are at their weakest,' said Celeste. 'When this world is closest to others. Believe me, it's stupidly hard to get in here safely at other times. You can get in here dangerously, but you'd probably do all sorts of damage to the dimensional integrity if you did that. I think the scout ship only got here by luck.'

'Luck and someone having a faulty grasp of dimensional physics,' Alpha added.

'Here, is there a dimension where there are giant worms and beetles and things, suspended in the sky?' asked Harper.

It was such an odd question right at that moment that people turned to look at him.

'I shouldn't say,' said Celeste. 'But yes, that would make a great deal of sense.'

'Then I reckon the walls between dimensions have been thinning for a while now. Don't...don't ask me to explain,' pleaded Harper, looking up at the sky beyond his visor.

'Harper, darling bird, you know I'm going to ask you to explain.'

'Yes, that was what I meant by don't.'

'If there's been a weakening...' Celeste stared up at the sky, but saw nothing but a blue sky turning pink as the afternoon wore on. She shook herself. 'Yes, if the Hedge flares, it'll be the best chance for the Sleepers to report back to Command. They'll want to report that everything's as it should be.'

'Which means none of us should be here?' asked Harper.

Celeste nodded.

'And you think they could kill us all?'

Celeste looked pained. 'They'd have the technology. Depends how desperate they are to conclude their mission.'

'They've been asleep for nearly seven thousand years,' said Alditha, 'they're probably going to want to get things done.'

There was a cough.

'If we might return to the *small* matter of the wizard who's declared himself our *king*,' sneered Brangle down his nose.

'Don't be a dingbat, man,' roared Odiz. 'Skoros is round the twist good and proper, but he hasn't got his orbs anymore, which means any one of us can take care of him. Any *mage*, anyway,' he amended, before the crowd got any ideas. 'Meantime, bunch of alien Johnnies might blow us all to kingdom come for the sake of a gold star on their "What I Did On Me Holidays" essay.'

Wizards? Thought Alditha. *Talking sense?*

'You lot go blundering up to the castle, he'll pick you off soon as look at you. But without his orbs, I can take care of the loon before he can crown himself king of anything more than his stupid slippers.'

'Meanwhile we go and confront the Astarians,' agreed Alditha. 'And you lot go home,' she told the crowd. 'There will be a reckoning today, for Timmoluk and Mistress Fazackerly. You're all going to be in the square tonight anyway for Midsummer Hallowe'en, but if we can make sure the Sleepers aren't intending to blow us all sky high before that happens, there's no sense you getting in the way.'

The crowd shuffled.

'Raark, fnmarpersarmy,' muttered Razor.

'What was that?'

Razor faced Alditha. 'I said we're Harper's Army,' he repeated. 'We don't have no kings, and we don't need no witches to swoop in and save us all. We're not *useless* you know? We're not *stupid*.'

A small cheer went up.

'I know you're not,' agreed Alditha. 'Course you're not. You're Gardenfolk.'

'I don't know whether this helps,' said Celeste, 'but if the Sleepers decide to sterilize the planet, it'll happen everywhere in a second, so being at home won't save them.'

Alditha's thumbs were itching. 'I sense Fate happening,' she said, disapproving. Witches disapproved of Fate on principle, because things like Fate and Destiny depended on some people being more important than others. Witches thought of themselves as many things—more intelligent than most people, wiser, more likely to be right most of the time. But never more important—they'd sit up with a sick animal, help a dying troll find peace, bring a difficult child into the world and soothe the mother too, all because they could. Witches found their importance in the importance of other people. 'What's more, I have the peculiar sense that I would lose an argument with you lot, so it's one I don't propose to have. Come if you're coming, but do nothing until I tell you. Do you understand me?'

Brangle snorted. 'And why should we take orders from you, madam? You're late to this protest.'

'Witches don't give orders, either, Mr. Brangle. We give suggestions. Up to you if you follow 'em. Just so happens though that today, if you choose not to follow 'em, as is your right, you might condemn everyone in the Garden to death. Your choice.'

And without another word, Alditha picked up Sprat the pixie, and carried him through the crowd, followed by Celeste and Alpha, the crowd folding back on itself to follow her, leaving Brangle at the back.

———————

'Whut do yoo wunt?' croaked Zirca.

'Good question,' said Gamma. 'Excellent question, and we'll come to that. But first, some answers. What's your plan? What do you intend to do?'

Zirca looked into Gamma's eyes, but they gave nothing away. Win or lose, live or die, he knew it depended on his answer. 'The Astarian fleet of spaceships will be here within hours. We were to find an uninhabited planet. I intend to make sure that's what we found before the fleet arrives.'

'To kill *everything?*' asked Gamma. Even in his metallic voice, Skoros' surprise came through.

Zirca grunted, tried to get a breath through the bio-mech's grip. It relaxed a tiny fraction. 'Everyone,' Zirca corrected. 'All non-sentient life will be preserved as we'll need to produce protein. But nothing intelligent will be allowed to share the world with us.'

Gamma was silent for a moment. Then he laughed—a strange sound from a bio-mech. 'So, by killing you right now, I could save my world?' The laugh erupted. 'Skoros, *saviour* of the world, as well as its king. Some might be tempted by that notion.' The fist on Zirca's throat tightened. 'Some might be *very* tempted.'

The fist relaxed again.

'But not me,' he said. 'As far as I'm concerned, the people of this world are cattle to be slaughtered. Do with them what you like. I'll even deliver them to you, like a Midsummer Hallowe'en gift.'

'I ask again,' Zirca squeaked. 'What do you want?'

'It's simple,' said Gamma-Skoros. 'I want one ship. Just one of your giant spaceships. Fully stocked with these toys of yours, these mechanical people, to do my bidding. And plenty of the orbs, they were rather fun. I let you live and deliver you the people of this world for extermination so you can please your masters, you give me the ship, the mechanicals, the orbs, and you let me go. This world was always too small for me. I will find others to conquer. Do we have a deal?'

Zirca coughed as Gamma's hand tightened on his throat again. He managed to nod briefly.

'Say it. I need to hear you say the words.'

'We have an accord,' the Astarian squeaked.

'Good then,' said Gamma-Skoros, releasing his grip immediately, letting Zirca cough air into his lungs properly. 'Oh and-' Gamma tapped him hard on the shoulder. '-just in case you get any thoughts about betraying me once my part of the bargain's completed, you should know I really like these mechanical men of yours. I know how to transfer between them now.'

Delta, who had been silent throughout their confrontation, waved a hand. 'You'll never see me coming unless I want you to,' said the second bio-mech. 'Remember that.'

The bio-mechanical creatures moved away, leaving Zirca to consider the bargain he'd made—and leaving Peridot, unseen, hiding behind the entrance to her pyramid, her eyes wide with fear.

18

In the relative busyness of the Milky Way, the ships went unnoticed. They masked their signals to look like lumps of ordinary space junk, but having come so far, now all they had to do was wait. Wait until the moment was right.

Peridot nipped quickly back into her pyramid to think. Zirca was considering genocide. More than considering it, he'd struck a bargain to deliver it. A clean sheet. An uninhabited planet, just like it was when they'd gone into cryo-sleep, when Venny had been so fascinated with worms.

It felt like just hours ago. Just hours since they'd had that last joking conversation, and now here she was—Venny was dead, the planet teemed with intelligent life, the fleet was on its way, was almost here, and she had little time to make her choice.

It was true, the team had been looking for an uninhabited world for a long time, somewhere the Astarian people could call home again after thousands of years of wandering the universe. Did she have the right to take that dream away from them, for the sake of people she didn't even know?

Would the mission parameters have shifted? Was she still bound by their original mission profile? What was the procedure when an uninhabited planet became an inhabited one while you were sleeping?

Oh Venny…

Everything was strange about her situation, but the strangest thing to her was that she hadn't yet had time to really feel that Ven was gone. It was the blink of an eye from their conversation about worms to right this second, and he'd been dead for nearly seven thousand years—almost as long again as she'd been alive when they had that conversation. It just felt like he was down in the engine room, tinkering and pruning, like she could call his name and her communicator would buzz and there he'd be, cheeky and cheerful and monstrously full of himself as ever.

She couldn't even miss him yet, he hadn't been gone long enough. His death was utterly unreal to her, for all she was trained in reason and logic.

Focus, she told herself. *One problem at a time. Ven will still be dead when the reality of it hits you, and when it does, you might not be able to do what you need to do.*

Right now, the immediate problem was Zirca and his plans. What if she told the others, and they agreed with him?

Maybe I agree with him, she reminded herself. She knew nothing about the inhabitants of this world. Maybe they were worth sacrificing to the mission. Maybe they weren't. She needed more information, but she knew she also needed to share what little she did know with the rest of the crew. If they were all in favour of Zirca's plan, maybe they'd calm the nagging feeling in her mind that it was wrong.

Can't use the comms system, she realized. Zirca would be in the loop. Also, if what this Skoros said was true, she couldn't trust any of the bio-mechs. *Got to get them together the old-fashioned way.*

Resolved at least that far, Peridot went to the back of her pyramid, and took the elevator down into the earth.

When Ven had initiated the cryo-sleep protocol, they'd all obeyed without question, getting to the cryo-pyramids and feeling the thrust as they'd been punched into the ground, deep, deep beneath the surface. They'd already been asleep when the pods had automatically initiated phase two, and unfolded, vapourising earth and soil, replacing them with metal, building tunnels and rooms while the Astarians slept, connecting each of their pyramids together by a network of functional tunnels. The self-building base was a safety mechanism in case of the pyramids being activated on worlds where the surface suddenly became hostile or uninhabitable. While it was in no sense a ship, they could have come out of cryo-sleep at any point and at least lived in the metal world the automatic systems built for them. She reached the bottom of the shaft now and stepped out into the dimly lit corridor. Mali-Juna would be in the makeshift lab. He'd be her first confidante. She moved off down the corridor.

––––––––––––

There are a great many things at which books are superb. As stores of knowledge, they're unsurpassable. As storytellers, they're excellent. As jesters to make you laugh when nothing else can, they're second to none. As table-straighteners, they will happily get the job done. As occasional step-stools, they will grumpily get the job done. Even, in the greatest extremes, if it's them or you, they'll lay down their lives and make a really handy fire, though in those circumstances, they will glower at you as the flames rise higher, as if to say 'Of all the readers in all the world, I had to get you, you ungrateful wretch.'

What they're really not good at is sprinting. Dramm had the boundless enthusiasm of a puppy and kept bouncing ahead of Jasper, losing his balance and falling over, creasing his pages. But he'd get up and close his covers as tight as he could, still impatient, and have to bounce back to the older spellbook to chivvy him along.

Jasper mumbled in his old gibberish language. His pages were old now, and some of them were dog-eared. He had his reasons for not rushing this journey. He didn't need to look at the sky anymore to know what was coming, he could feel it all the way down his spine. The end was coming. The end of everything he knew.

Dramm bounced and flapped and fluttered round his binding, and Jasper slumped, leaning for just a moment on the young spellbook's back to keep him upright. Then he walked on, front cover first, back cover following, to meet his inevitable future.

Alditha held up a hand, and Harper's Army stopped marching as they came to the leg of the square. Not long before, it would have been guarded by a bio-mech, but now it was empty. Eerie. Alditha narrowed her eyes at it, suspecting a trap.

'Harper, and young Master Sprat,' she said, without turning her head either way to address the owl on one shoulder or the pixie who sat on the other, holding tight as she walked, 'I have an important job for you. I need you please to both get down, and go about the people, *quietly* telling them to wait here. I don't like the look of this, and I don't want them rushing in. Do you think you could do that for me?'

'Yes, Miss Alditha,' squeaked Sprat, clambering down her witch's robe and going off into the crowd immediately.

'You be careful, all right? I don't want to lose you again,' Harper warned her.

'Nobody dies here today,' Alditha promised him. 'Nobody.'

'I swear when you say stuff like that, Fate rubs its hands,' muttered Harper, nuzzling his head against her neck. 'Just look out.'

'Are you presuming to tell a witch her business, "General" Harper, now you've got your army?' Alditha deadpanned, stroking his claws with one finger. 'You never did say—why aren't you already dead?'

'I'm an owl, I am.'

'I'd noticed, dear heart.'

'Skilled in the arts of tracking my prey, sort of thing.'

'Ah,' said Alditha. 'You followed Razor when he scarpered.'

'Exactly that. Kept a low profile. Thought he'd go skulking back to his horrible master once the coast was clear. He didn't, he joined up with this lot.'

'I see. Well-'

'I don't know what happened to Gunkin,' said Harper, looking as guilty as it's possible for an owl to look. It's not a look they generally go in for, but he almost managed it.

Alditha chuckled. 'If I know anything about Gunkin Pimplebutt, there's no creature in this Garden more able to look after himself. If you found a way to escape the beardless wonder, I'm sure Gunkin'll turn up in a few days once all the danger's passed.'

'That'd be the danger where no-one's going to die today, would it? That particular, safe as houses kind of danger?'

Alditha smiled a thin smile. 'Missed you, darling bird. Go on, help me out. Keep this lot occupied.'

With a tiny hoot, Harper flew off her shoulder and began to circle the crowd, whispering as he went.

'I'm going in,' said Celeste suddenly. 'They were supposed to be met by an Astarian ambassador, so I'd better go alone. Alpha, you will accompany me though.'

Alditha grabbed her arm. 'You surely don't think you're going to leave me behind?' she asked. 'I know you're too *intelligent* to be thinking anything that foolish.'

Celeste sighed. 'This is a *witchy* thing, isn't it?'

'To be honest, it's more of a "If you're going to kill everything in the Garden, then you've got to go through me first" thing.' Alditha considered. 'So yes, it's a witchy thing.'

'All right,' Celeste agreed. 'Come on then.'

The three of them walked into the silent square, newly decorated with Astarian pyramids, all standing open. Alditha cast a glance at Stone Hedge. It hadn't begun to dance yet, but if you watched it hard enough, you could see the ripples of colour pass through it. Most people would tell themselves they must have been imagining it. Witches, however, didn't do that.

'Alpha? Where are they all?' asked Celeste.

Alpha chittered to himself a moment, then announced 'Five Astarian life signs in subterranean base. Also, six bio-mechs of historical design.'

Celeste breathed out. 'Are they awake?'

'Yes.'

'And together?'

'Three Astarians clustered in laboratory on west side of complex. One in computer room, north. One on the move, to the south. Bio-mechs as indicated.' Without warning, a colourful, three-dimensional plan of the complex appeared in front of them, beaming out of Alpha's eyes.

'Holographic gelatin,' muttered Alditha. 'Handy.'

'Plotting direct route to clustered Astarians.'

A red line appeared in the map, showing their way in and down.

'*Very* handy,' admitted the witch with a certain grudging respect.

Celeste led the way to one of the pyramids, finding the elevator at the back. Soon, the three were speeding down and down through the earth, till they came to a smooth halt, and the elevator pad went *bing*, opening doors on both left and right sides.

'Do you people not believe in stairs?' gasped Alditha, quickly uncurling the fists her hands had become.

'No time,' said Celeste. 'This was all done in a hurry. Emergency protocols,' she explained. 'Originally the pyramids would have been alone down here. The system had to dig its own shaft. Actually,' she added, realizing it as she said it, 'it will only have done that since the pyramid went up to the surface. The pyramid itself will have taken up the space we're about to walk into.' She looked at Alpha's map and chose the right-hand path. 'Come and meet my ancestors.'

'You have evidence?'

Peridot was taken aback. They'd been a team for so long, she'd expected her testimony to be enough to convince them of Zirca's plans. Then again, she supposed, he'd been part of the team all that time, too.

'No,' she admitted, 'not beyond what I overheard. But I met this Skoros, briefly, and he did claim to be the King of the Planet…or *Garden*, as he put it.'

'But to hack a bio-mech? You're telling us something that evolved here while we had a power nap is capable of that?' Mali-Juna was the team's official biologist, and Peridot could see she hadn't convinced him. 'You do know it was only 6.8 thousand years, yes? The life here should be practically the same as it was when we went to sleep. Mosses, trees, worms and insects, nothing in the higher primate range, certainly.'

'I know what it *should* be,' Peridot told him. 'But I spoke to this Skoros. He's a fully developed humanoid. Have you even checked the scans yet?' She traced a line on her headband, and the information appeared in Mali-Juna's mind. His eyes widened.

'That's unbelievable,' he said. 'How is that possible? Sentient vegetables?'

'Told you so.'

'So there's sentient life here,' said Rhodon, the purple-haired climatologist, biting her lip. 'Do we care? Enough to sabotage the mission, I mean?'

'There's *lots* of sentient life here,' Peridot corrected her. 'Lots of massively improbable life.'

'Why d'you think we were looking for an uninhabited planet in the first place, Rho?' asked Mali-Juna, his pale, opal-coloured eyes still looking a little vacant as he digested the information in his head.

'Hmm,' she agreed. 'What does Quarka think?'

'Haven't told him yet,' admitted Peridot. 'Probably whatever Zirca tells him to think. That's why I wanted to get your views first.'

'This is genuine, is it?' Mali-Juna was still having trouble coming to terms with the amount of life in the Garden. 'Still makes no sense.'

'I didn't fake the report, Mali-Juna,' sighed Peridot. 'D'you think I want to throw away my career in an act of mutiny just after losing my only brother?'

The three of them were silent for a moment, remembering Ven. It was new for all of them not to have him there, being bouncy and sarcastic and laughing at their seriousness. Gardeners were often more free-spirited than the other scientists on exploration teams, and Ven had been a classic example of the breed.

Mali-Juna blinked, shutting off the data stream into his mind. 'Right then,' he said finally. 'Let's go stop a genocide. For Ven.'

'And because it's wrong,' said Rhodon.

'That too.'

'Aye aye,' said Alditha. 'They're on the move.' She nodded to the map that Alpha was projecting. Sure enough, the three Astarians from the lab were moving.

'Coming our way,' Celeste agreed. 'Should be able to head them off if we go left at the next junction, then right.'

They moved, and the closer they got to the point Celeste had suggested, the more distinctly they heard voices. When they stepped around the right-hand corner, the voices stopped too.

Alditha gave the three Astarians her customary head nod.

'You're new,' said the boy with white hair and opal eyes. 'How can you be new?'

'I'm not that new,' said Alditha.

'He's talking to me.' Celeste stepped forward. 'Hail, Sleepers. My name is Celeste, I'm the commander of Astarian Scout Ship Gol HuR 87. I've come to find you.'

'You've succeeded,' said Rhodon. 'Well done. Only took you nearly seven thousand years.'

'It's not an easy planet to find,' said Celeste. 'We're sorry for your loss,' she added, remembering what they'd seen happen to Ven Tao in the Tarot Wheel.

'Thank you.' Peridot nodded sadly, assuming that Celeste had merely accessed one of the pyramids' memory databanks and discovered the events of Venny's death.

Alditha looked at the green-haired, green-eyed girl in front of her. She looked exactly like she'd done in the Tarot Wheel. Witches often knew what people were thinking, but this felt different. It felt uncomfortable, knowing she'd actually been inside the girl's thoughts, without Peridot having any idea about it.

'Who's your friend?' asked Mali-Juna.

'Oh, yes, of course. This is Alditha, she's a native.'

'Reeeeeeally?' said Mali-Juna, almost running in his eagerness to take a look at 'a native.' 'That's remarkable,' he said, lifting Alditha's arm and prodding it with his finger.

'Er, I really wouldn't do that if I were you,' Celeste advised.

'What's your name, Mr. White-Head?' asked Alditha, preparing to raise an eyebrow at him.

'Mali-Juna,' said Mali-Juna. 'How long have you been alive?'

'Long enough to know I don't like to be poked and prodded on a first acquaintance,' Alditha told him, poking him back with every word.

'Mmm, yes, no of course not,' he agreed. 'Apologies, Garden person Alditha. Forgive my manners. Peridot, Rhodon,' he said, gesturing to his teammates. 'You're really not supposed to exist,' he said, turning his attention back to Alditha almost without a pause for breath, 'I'm just curious as to how you do.'

'I do very well, thank you,' said Alditha. 'Well rested, are you? Sure you wouldn't like to go back and have another hundred years or so?'

'Mmm, no no. Can't do. The fleet'll be here any time now.'

'The fleet?' yelped Celeste. 'Here?'

Rhodon nodded. 'Zirca, our chief chemist and leader contacted them not long after we woke up. I admit we were all surprised, but it turns out they were already in the vicinity. Said something about receiving an earlier signal. I'm guessing that would be from you?'

'I didn't send a signal,' said Celeste. 'At least, not intentionally. I did lose track of a couple of orbs, but-'

'There you go then,' said Mali-Juna. 'Never, ever lose track of your orbs.'

'Well I know that *now*,' Celeste snapped.

'They're just waiting for the dimensions to synchronise, and then-' Rhodon shrugged.

'Oh, Harper'll be thrilled,' muttered Alditha. 'More aliens. There'll be special "I told you so" banners and everything. Look, Mr. Pokey-Boy, this might be a totally ridiculous question, and I really hope it is, but are you lot planning to kill everything on this planet any time soon?'

Zirca slid his hands into the gloves that were part of the sterile, clear plastic cube in which he held his test tubes. He looked along his line of tubes and selected one that held a clear liquid. He shook it and the liquid turned a frothy, creamy white. As he watched, the froth fizzed, seemed to wriggle, to divide, to shape itself into bodies, each with sharp, snapping teeth at one end. The white frothed faster, climbing up the side of the tube. Then the white turned red as the teeth tore, the blood flowed, the bodies gorged. And then, as though nothing had happened, the redness disappeared and the liquid settled to clear again. He shook the tube a second time. Nothing happened. The liquid had become plain water.

Zirca smiled.

He understood the data about the Garden. He understood where its bizarre examples of life had come from, in so short a time, while they had been asleep. He understood why the Garden had trolls, and pixies, and goblins and witches and wizards and even, for its sins, talking potatoes, mushrooms and trees (and, unbeknown to him, intelligent spell books).

The exploration team was made up of experts in their field, of course, but Zirca knew he was the most crucial among them, because all their fields, all their expertise, depended on his. Mali-Juna's biology came back to chemistry. Quarka's geology came back to chemistry. Peridot's hydrography. Rhodon's climatology. Everything you needed to know about a planet came back to chemistry. That was why Zirca had gone into it in the first place. And chemistry was where the secret of the Garden was hiding.

Ordinarily, if it hadn't been for Ven Tao, that arrogant irresponsible child, there would have been no sentient life in the Garden even now—none except them. When Ven had caused the ship to vapourise, he had inadvertently turned himself into microscopic, organic particles, which had gradually settled into the ground. And there, chemistry had done its magic trick. Astarian body chemistry was special; their appendixes synthesized a chemical called Melazoidin from the food they ate, and Melazoidin's job in their bodies was to create sigma energy. Sigma energy was the most suggestible form of energy in the universe—it could be harnessed, directed by concentration in the brain, and it kept Astarian bodies as 'young' as the rest of the universe seemed to think them. Melazoidin promoted life, promoted healing, and, when expelled through the lungs or the skin, it formed a field, suspended in the air, that allowed what many races thought of as 'magic' to be made. When Ven Tao had vapourised and blended with the soil of the Garden, the Melazoidin from his body had changed the Garden, blade of grass by blade of grass. And then it had changed the things that ate the blades of grass. And the things that ate the things that ate the blades of grass, and so on up a primitive food chain, extending it as it went, making life evolve at many times its natural rate. Now the air of the Garden was thick with a Melazoidin field breathed out from many species, meaning you never quite knew what was going to spring to life next, and meaning there was magic.

Magic was just chemistry if you understood what you were doing.

Zirca understood what he was doing well.

He took a second test tube of clear liquid and pressed a timer-seal into the top of it. It was an artificial enzyme that simply ate Melazoidin. He had finely tuned its structure so it only targeted large deposits of the chemical—he didn't want it eating all the grass and gorging itself on the air. It would eat the Melazoidin, and everything containing concentrations of Melazoidin. And then it would eat itself, before harmlessly dissipating, turning into water and washing away.

He pulled his hands out of the gloves, then pressed a button and saw the rack of test tubes slide sideways through a contamination shield. He picked up the tube and smiled. That presumptuous wizard-king would get his just desserts along with all the other products of Ven Tao's recklessness. He set the timer-seal on the tube and walked out of his private lab, making his way quickly to the elevator that led him to his pyramid. Peeking out, he saw a mob at one end of the street. He turned and walked the other way, a sense of exhilaration pushing him on. At the far end of the square, he found a rock about the size of an orb at the edge of a patch of grass.

Perfect.

He dug a small hole in the grass behind the rock with his hands, hid the test tube with its seal facing down, and covered it back up. Then he stood up and walked nonchalantly back into the square, stopping to look at the mob again, this time with a sense of intense satisfaction.

Soon, he thought, *the mistake of your existence will be undone, and my people will have a home at last.*

He smiled at them, then saw Peridot coming out of her pyramid.

19

Peridot had never thought of herself as a leader. But now, by some process of natural selection, she found herself leading her fellow Astarians, a bio-mech and an indigenous woman up to the surface to confront the person who *was* their leader, which she supposed would mean she'd *become* the leader. That was how things worked—if you deposed a leader, you had to be able to answer the question 'What shall we do now then?' And answering that question meant you were the leader.

They took the elevator up in batches, and Peridot tapped her hand on her leg all the way, wondering how you went about relieving a commander of duty for technically doing his job.

When the new girl, Celeste, and her Garden friend, arrived, the native woman had her fists clenched and her eyes stubbornly open. Peridot laughed despite her nerves. That was it. She'd challenge Zirca, make him stop his insane plan with the Garden king, and now, looking at Alditha, she had her answer to what to do next. It was so simple, so obvious, she couldn't believe she hadn't thought of it till now.

This is why you've never been the leader.

She stepped out of her pyramid. And there he was.

The others followed her in a loose line, spreading out as they got near the boy with the conker-coloured hair and the pinched expression.

Zirca looked from face to face, frowning at Celeste, who kept her face stern.

'I'm issuing Executive Order 514,' he said eventually. 'Things have clearly become more complex here since the original survey team landed. There's life here-' He eyed Alditha coldly. '-where there shouldn't be. The fleet will be here shortly, they can sort it out. Meanwhile, the exploration team is to return to cryo-sleep and await their arrival.'

'Except you're lying, aren't you?'

Peridot had said it before she'd even thought it.

Zirca's gaze hardened on her like frost. 'Lying, Hydrographer Peridot? What do you mean?'

'You're lying on the basis that you don't know I overheard you talking to that Skoros man. He took over a bio-mech somehow. I don't know how, but he did it. And you told him you planned to kill everyone here.'

Zirca frowned, but chuckled. 'Peridot, I think perhaps you have a cryo-sleep hangover. These vivid fantasies of yours belong in a dream.'

'Your hands,' said Celeste.

No-one had noticed Zirca's hands except Alditha, but now they all looked. They were stained with mud.

'Become a Gardener since you woke up, have you?' asked Peridot with an unusual sarcasm.

'What have you done?' demanded Mali-Juna.

Zirca didn't hesitate. He reached out and grabbed Alditha's hand, pulled her to him and yanked her arm up her back. She was taller than he was, but he was surprisingly strong.

'I've done what had to be done,' he snarled, dropping all pretence.

'These *things* aren't life. They're a mistake. A stupid mistake by your idiot brother,' he said, nodding at Peridot. 'How long were we on our mission? Trying to find our people a home. You want to throw all that away for *them*? Hydrographer Peridot, I'm putting you on report for insubordination and dereliction of duty.'

'Commander Zirca, I'm putting *you* on report on a charge of attempted genocide.'

'Attempted,' murmured Celeste. 'What *have* you done, digging in the ground?'

'Stick around, whoever you are,' Zirca snapped. 'You'll find out soon now.'

Celeste frowned, unable to shake the sense that he wasn't bluffing.

A witch gains her importance from the importance of others. But others sometimes gain their importance from the importance of their witch. Harper's Army had been, for a banner-waving mob, obedient, waiting at the end of the long leg of shops and houses. Waiting for their witch to invite them in.

The call would never come. Alditha would never impose on them that way.

Harper, though, had no such qualms. He saw the strange alien boy grab Alditha, yank her arm up her back. 'Alditha.' He took a breath, puffed out his chest feathers, swallowed the panic of his first reaction. It was time for a little owl to be brave.

'SKRRRRRAWWWWK,' he screeched across the crowd. 'Harper's Army. They've got our witch. GET 'EM.'

Without waiting for them, but knowing in his talons they'd follow him, Harper flew into battle.

Odiz heard the singing as soon as he set foot in the castle. His beard seemed to hear it too, and pulled away from his face, as if trying to escape. He smoothed it down his belly and his eyebrows got in on the act, waggling as if alive.

Wizards, on the whole, liked a bit of a sing-song, on the principle that it often led to or was accompanied by alcohol and large quantities of food, and a good night being had by all.

This wasn't that kind of singing.

This was the singing that made the hairs on the back of your neck stand up and want to run away. It was Skoros, singing what could only be a song he invented. A song that sounded like the singer was not at home to Mr. Sanity, or any of his family.

Odiz straightened up from his fighting stance, all three of his remaining hands ready to fire magic. Instead he simply walked towards the direction of the mad crooning. It seemed to be waiting for him.

He followed the singing down hallways and corridors he'd never seen before, the voice getting louder all the time. Soon he came to a large wooden dining hall door, and knew without a doubt that the voice was coming from the room on the other side. Odiz pondered—people thought wizard battles were all about shooting lightning bolts out of your fingertips and the size of your staff, but that was why most people weren't wizards. Wizard battles were about winning, purely and simply yet as deviously as necessary. *Veeraswamy's Silent Fart?* The spell had a certain appeal—it was an undetectable vapour that rendered the opponent unconscious unless they'd read a lot of books about breathing protection spells, or could turn themselves into a swamp dragon at will. It gave you the element of surprise, and–

'So you're here at last then?' said Skoros, breaking off his song.

Odiz cursed silently. So much for the element of surprise. Right. Lightning bolts out of the fingertips it was, then. He said the words of *Caxton's Oblivionator* in his mind, and his hands grew hot. When he felt like he couldn't hold back the power anymore, he went through the door, roaring as the power flowed through him. He shot three handfuls of the Oblivionator at a big iron chair at the far end of the room, where Skoros sat, his arms along its ornate square arm-rests. The Oblivionator screamed through the air, hot and orange, and then-

-Hit an invisible wall that crackled blue around the chair. Skoros' throne was sturdy, but covered in moving cogs and wheels and flashing lights. Odiz goggled at it. There was even a 'crown' of sorts, a metal skullcap which seemed to pulse with the same lights.

'Caxton's Oblivionator? Oh, that is disappointing. I expected something more imaginative from the *great* Odiz. Like the third hand though, I can imagine that comes in-' He chuckled suddenly. '-Handy,' he finished. 'D'you want to do the tedious trading of insults thing, old man, or shall I just kill you now?'

Odiz bristled. 'Oh, can't dispense with the social niceties, y'know? Crucial to the fundamentals-'

He snapped his fingers and three giant cobras slithered from thin air up and over the throne, down over Skoros' body.

'That's more like it,' said the beardless wizard. Then he crooked a little finger, the chair flashed blue for a second, and three dead cobras fell heavily to the floor. 'Y'see, the trouble is, old man, there's magic, and that's all fine and dandy if you want to eat a lot of dinners and throw snakes at people. Then there's what I've got. The Astarians call it bio-mechanics.'

As he gave it a name, he pressed a button on the throne, and compartments opened up all over it. Cogs whirred, pistons pistoned, and thin strips of metal emerged from the throne, covering his toes, his legs, his arms and body, a sudden suit of armour, till just his face was showing. He stood up with a hiss of steam and clanked heavily over to Odiz, gripping the mage's shoulders in his metal-gloved fingers. Servo-power intensified his grip, and Odiz winced as he felt the fingers bite down on him.

'I call it science,' said Skoros. 'You can call it death if you like.'

He smiled, and the armour glowed blue, sending massive bolts of electrical energy into Odiz' body. The mage's third hand leapt up and punched Skoros square on the nose, once, twice, then it began to char and blacken, and fell out of the air.

'Yours,' grunted Odiz, 'not mine.' Against the will of the lightning coursing into him, he raised his hands, grabbed Skoros round the midriff and focused, grunting against the blinding spasms of pain as his beard caught fire and seemed to squeal as it sizzled. His hands glowed red through the blue fire, and he poured the heat of them through Skoros' metal armour, which glowed yellow, then orange, then red.

'Yaaaaaargh,' yelled Skoros as the red-hot metal fused, burning cloth and flesh, sticking to his body, burning *through* his body in places. Wisps of smoke curled up from him, smelling like cooked bacon. Odiz dropped out of his grip and lay panting, recovering on the floor.

Skoros could see nothing through the agony of the melted metal, tried to take a step forward. As he bent his legs, the metal pushed against them, sending new waves of exhilarating pain through him, and he fell. The sensation of landing racked him all over again with screaming sobs, and Odiz rolled over onto his side. His heart was beating too fast, the electric shock had turned him into a chemical mayhem.

'Y'know…Odiz,' gasped Skoros through the pain, 'you're a difficult man to kill.'

'What…what gave it away?' panted the old man.

'I cut off your hands, but still you kept coming, ahh,' Skoros seethed, sucking his teeth to push through the heat as he tried to get to his knees.

''s'called…being a wizard,' said Odiz. 'A proper one.'

'Really?' Skoros panted. 'Let's see how you do…without a *throat*.' He swung one arm around clumsily, grabbing Odiz by the neck. The mage scrabbled frantically, but within seconds, there was nothing to scrabble at—the heat of Skoros' gauntlet pushed through him, burned his skin away, his throat, his breath. Odiz was an old man, but when he died, it wasn't a comfortable, old man's death. Skoros fought the pain with pure, cold satisfaction, seeing his enemy finally drop away from him, head and shoulders parted. Inside the gauntlet, the pain was like nothing he'd ever known, as molten metal burned the skin off his fingers, fusing to flesh and bone.

'Pain…' said Skoros to no-one but himself, to fight the sensation, 'is life. Pain is victory. I will master it. I will be its ruler. I will… endure.'

He began to crawl towards the door, leaving the body of Odiz behind him.

**

'Why did the mission depend on finding an uninhabited planet?' demanded Peridot. 'We all just accepted it, because that was the way things were done. But why? You're the mission commander, you must know.'

Zirca sneered. 'All available research suggests there can only be one dominant sentient species on a planet. To have two or more only leads to inevitable conflict, war, and the destruction of one species by the other. Finding a planet with no other sentient life is the only viable solution.'

'So now you're prepared to reverse engineer the situation? To take life and destroy it, just because you think it shouldn't be here?'

'I'm doing my job, Peridot. Moral philosophy is not your forte, go back to looking at water.'

'You're missing the point, Zica,' Mali-Juna butted in. 'You've seen the data, how can you not have worked it out yet?'

Zirca frowned, but kept a tight grip on Alditha's arm. 'Worked *what* out?'

'They're all sentient,' said Mali-Juna. 'The trolls, the pixies, the goblins, the potatoes, point me out a sentient life form on this planet, I'll point you out a sentient life form living alongside other sentient life forms. No inevitable war, no ultimate destruction, nothing.'

'We call it sharing,' muttered Alditha.

'Wooly-headed idealism,' snapped Zirca, yanking Alditha's arm higher.

'Any minute now, I'm going to get tired of that,' she told him politely.

'You can't argue with the data,' said Peridot calmly. 'All these different sentient life forms are here. Yes, it's unusual in the universe, but that's academic—they're here, and they're the ones that matter because they're the ones you're thinking of destroying.'

'In fact, they're *right* here,' said Rhodon, looking sideways. Everyone followed her gaze. Harper's Army was charging down the square towards them.

'Ha,' snorted Zirca. '*No war, no destruction, nothing,*' he said, mockingly.

'You really are daft as a brush, aren't you?' asked Alditha. 'We've had wars, we're not a perfect people. We've had wars cos the Spooky Enders took Old Michlethwaite the Troll's quarry and that weren't right. We've had wars cos the Cremini Family and the Chanterelle Confederacy couldn't come to terms over spore-spread territories. But we don't have wars to extinction. What'd be the point of that?'

'In your case, I'm increasingly of the opinion that extinction is its reward,' growled Zirca.

'That just makes me better'n you then, don't it?'

The roar of the army got closer.

Then another noise overpowered it. It was the sound of roots ripping through the ground, horizontally, towards the army. Celeste yelped as one went under her feet.

On the far side of the Astarians and Alditha, the roots tangled together, blossomed into a tight wall of soft yellow dandelions, ripened, closed, turned to puffballs of seeds on white parachutes. Then, as one, the dandelion clocks launched towards the racing army, an impenetrable sudden snow of seeds. The army slowed, fighting its way through the dandelion blizzard. Harper and Razor, though, flew above the flurry and prepared to dive on Zirca.

'No,' Alditha yelled, and both birds pulled up suddenly. 'No-one attacks these people,' Alditha explained. 'They're here now, and whether they need a witch or not is up to them, but right now, they're under my protection. Do you understand me, Harper Fluffbelly? Razor Darkwing?'

'Raaark. Did you miss the part where they've got you *prisoner*?'

'I'm nobody's prisoner, Razor Darkwing, you should know that by now. If I wasn't held by Blackheart Bindweed, d'you think the fear of a broken arm is keeping me here?'

'But-?' stammered Harper. 'But then, why?'

'These people have no *home*, Harper. Their home was lost to them a long time ago, and they've been looking for somewhere else to be. You know what home is like—it's warm, and safe, and you can be yourself in all your daftness. Now you tell me how it felt when you and I were at odds, eh? When you felt you couldn't come home to me? These people are *scared*, my wonderful, silly bird. It's not how they treat us that matters right now, it's how *we* treat *them*.'

'That was well said, Witch Alditha,' said a resonant, woody voice behind them. In all the confusion, people seemed to have forgotten the fact that a wall of dandelions had spontaneously been created. The Green Man and Big Red walked up to them.

'Thank you, sir,' Alditha acknowledged, for she knew the dandelion storm had been the Green Man's doing—could *only* have been his doing. She called very few people in the Garden 'sir,' but the Green Man was one of them. 'I hope all is okay between us now…'

The Green Man paused, considering his answer.

'Indeed,' he said eventually with a slow nod of his head. 'Indeed, you *are* forgiven, Witch Alditha.' He extended a curling branch towards the witch and stroked her face. 'A feud between you and I will not help matters, and my kin did not die in vain. And you are right— these Astarians must be *very* scared.'

'I'm not *scared*, you pathetic aberration,' growled Zirca, his eyes growing wild. 'You're all going to be dead soon.'

'Yes, about that,' said Alditha. 'What have you hidden in our Garden, Mr Zirca?'

'You think I'm going to tell you?'

'Well you see, I'm not going to let you get hurt. Now, there are plenty of people who seem to want you to get hurt, for hurting me and threatening to kill us all, and I can see their point of view. But I'm not going to let that happen, and it strikes me that you wanted to nip off back to bed for a bit because whatever you've done, it can't get you in there. But it can out here. So the longer we waste nattering, the more likely you are to die right along with the rest of us. I mentioned the bit about not letting that happen, didn't I?' she asked, checking with Celeste.

Celeste nodded.

'Good. So, there we are. Oh, and one other thing.'

She coughed, and Zirca suddenly found he was holding nothing but a whisper of black smoke. Then, before he could react, his hands were yanked behind him and tied tight with string.

Alditha reappeared in front of him. 'If you're going to break someone's arm, just break it. Don't go for the yanking it up their back option, it just irritates everyone to no good purpose. Now, I'm going to ask you properly.' She fixed him with a firm stare. 'What have you done, and how do we stop it?'

20

'I'm not sure the lad's up to it…' said Big Red to the Green Man, within earshot of where Zirca was still being held prisoner, '…coming clean, and telling us what he's done, I mean. I think he'd rather die along with everyone else.'

'You might be right, old man,' the Green Man replied. 'You'd think he had a *little* sense, though. He looks quite intelligent…and what will he gain from doing it?'

Zirca looked on and scowled. He wasn't going to fall for that one.

'Mayyybe, Mayyybe, but I know a coward when I see one,' Big Red continued, trying hard to goad Zirca into a reaction. 'Forget him, he's not worth it.'

The Green Man paused and scratched his bark-like head.

'I think you're right, old man. For an Astarian, he's pretty lame.'

'Absolutely. There's really no mayyybe about it.'

'Lame as they come, old man.'

Celeste faced Alditha and groaned. She knew Zirca wouldn't be caught that way.

'You had to go giving him ideas about being taken seriously, didn't you?' she said to the witch. 'Didn't it occur to you that might make him even more stubborn?'

Five minutes had passed since the stand-off. The dandelion wall had blown away, but Zirca had resolutely stood his ground and had decided not to say another word. Consequently, everyone had been hastily mustered into search groups, and were combing the area around the square. Even Big Red and the Green Man had been roped in—intent on playing rudimentary mind games with Zirca in an attempt to make him confess.

"If you're going to break someone's arm, just break it." Well, guess what? Turns out the same logic holds true for committing genocide,' Celeste continued.

'He's a strange one, that Zirca,' admitted Alditha.

'Don't know how long we've got or anything. How long till your Midsummer Hallowe'en?'

'Been Midsummer Hallowe'en all day.'

'You know what I mean—how long till the engine, the Hedge, does its thing?'

Alditha looked at the now dark sky. 'Any time, I reckon.'

Celeste sighed. 'He'll have wanted time for whatever it is to have done its work before the fleet got here. Oh. Oh, that's a bad thought.'

'What?' said Alditha.

'We're all assuming we'll know when it happens, like it'll go bang. Maybe it won't—Zirca's a chemist, after all. Maybe it's already happened. Maybe we're already breathing in poison that's going to kill us.'

Alditha frowned. 'No use thinkin' like that. Where there's life, there's a desperate need to kick probability in the shins, as my old mother used to say.'

Celeste joined her in the frown. 'Probability doesn't have shins,' she pointed out.

Alditha smiled. They'd take some getting used to, these Astarians. 'Could be worse,' she said. 'If we hadn't caught him with dirt on his hands, we'd never have known he'd done anything. Would have gone to Midsummer Hallowe'en and not known, and prob'ly have died.'

Celeste's frown deepened. There was something- 'Say that again,' she demanded.

'What?'

'Say it again. There's something...'

'Could be worse,' Alditha repeated. 'If we hadn't found him with dirt on his hands-'

'That's it. I know what to do,' said Celeste. 'Oh, I'm such an idiot sometimes. Alpha was mapping out the underground base, yes?'

'Yesss?' said Alditha, not seeing where the girl's thoughts were going.

'He's a bio-mech. Our job was to find the Sleepers. To find Astarians *and Astarian technology*. Believe me, when we lost track of the orbs, I mentioned that to him more than once.'

Alditha snapped her long fingers. 'And this hoojamaflip that's going to kill us all will be Astarian technology,' she exclaimed. 'You're right, you know, you're a bit of an idiot sometimes.'

'Thanks, I'll remember that when it comes time to save all our lives.'

'Oh, it's come time. Believe me, it's more than come time.'

'Bio-mech Alpha, respond please.'

Her headband glowed almost immediately, and Alpha's voice came through. 'Alpha receiving.'

'Do a local area scan for Astarian tech, report any anomalous readings.'

'Confirmed.'

Sensing new activity, the Green Man and Big Red ran over to them. There was a moment's silence when each of them heard only their hearts thudding—and when you had a heart as big as Big Red's, that was saying something.

'Tree-oid life form known as the Green Man has several Astarian power conversion balls in his possession.'

Celeste shook her head impatiently. 'No, I gave him those.'

'Time-sealed object detected, six hundred metres southwest of your current location, buried one quarter metre beneath a rock.'

'That's it. Acknowledged. Thank you, Alpha,' said Celeste, taking off at a run, followed close behind by Alditha.

They found the rock easily, and, forgetting she had advanced technology to use, Celeste fell on her knees and started digging in the dirt furiously. When her hands found the sleek glass tube, she almost wept with relief. Then relief turned to stomach-churning fear. The read-out was counting down. She had only slipaways—*minutes*, she corrected herself—before the seal disintegrated and whatever was in the test tube was released into the air. Again, she found herself running.

'Peridot, come in.'

'Celeste, acknowledged.'

'I've found it. I don't know what it is, but I've found it.'

'Excellent, well done.'

'Meet me at your pyramid immediately.'

'Why?'

'Time-seal,' she gasped. 'Nearly out of time. Need a bio-chamber.'

'Mali-Juna has those. Or Zirca, of course.'

'Need a guide. Oh wait, Alpha, meet me at the pyramid we were in earlier, immediately.'

'Confirmed.'

'See you both in there,' she panted, 'less than a slipaway.'

Her legs hurt by the time she got to the pyramid, but she didn't stop, running to join the other two, who'd already taken their place on the elevator pad.

'Down, down, down,' she yelled. The pad smoothly began to drop through the earth. 'Can't this wretched thing go any faster?' she muttered.

'Not unless you feel like a long fall.'

Celeste showed the time-seal to Peridot, whose green eyes flashed in alarm.

'Exactly,' said Celeste. 'Just in case you think I'm worrying unduly.'

'We'll make it,' Peridot assured her. 'Not by much, but we'll make it.'

Celeste watched the timer countdown, hoping she was right.

———————

Jasper and Dramm had made it to the square, but were confused to find none of the usual merry-making going on. Jasper had witnessed innumerable Midsummer Hallowe'en celebrations in his time and knew something was wrong. The Hedge had begun to pulse with regular ripples of colour, but no-one was around. There was no singing, no dancing, no endless chatter. They didn't understand—but facing the Hedge, Jasper knew what he had to do. It was nearly time.

He thought back over his life spent in the Garden. It seemed a long time ago since he had first set up home here. Seasons had come and gone like leaves blowing in the wind, and still he remained living, like an old hermit guardian. He had always known that his role in the Garden would, one day, be an important one, but did others realize how important? He didn't think so—not even Alditha. Nor did he imagine that they ever *would* realize, until…well, until maybe he was gone.

He allowed himself the briefest of smiles as he reflected on how he knew the names of virtually everyone living in the Garden—yet found it unlikely that few residents, save Alditha, the Green Man, and some of the mages, even knew of his existence. Such was the life of his kind. It was what it was. There were plenty of other, lesser spell books, after all.

Jasper thought again of Alditha. She had been an exceptional friend to him. He would miss her. He tried to remember all the spells and incantations he had provided for her over the years, and all the spell books he had helped her to train, but the list was immeasurably long, and he had to give up after a few seconds. Feelings and sensations surged through him and lit his imagination like a bright, happy sun. In his bookish mind, he relived the time they had come across a dead scarecrow and brought it back to life using the Spell of the Ancient Fireworm, then danced with it through the Iron Meadows until sunset. Then there was the time Alditha had made a talking bat cake using lemon bats from The Forbidden Cave of Min. What fun they had trying to convince the Grogan Dust Trolls that the cake would not taste of talking lemons, only to surprise them by making it do just that.

Then he remembered when he had first come to know himself— when he had first understood why everything in the Garden was as it was. After all, talking spell books, potatoes and green men weren't an everyday occurrence, not in this part of multiverse anyway. *Ho ho,* he chuckled to himself in spellbook language. *Wait till they all understand.*

Of one thing, he was sure, however—none of these memories would be lost after his inevitable demise. They would all be passed on…to another.

Jasper took a deep breath and inhaled the scents and perfumes of the Garden. Parsley, lilac, sage, pine, new mown lawns, compost, summer bonfires…and the unmistakable smell of…*quantum electricity.* The old spellbook turned again to look at Stone Hedge. The colours were intensifying, branching out further. There was a shimmer just above the Hedge itself…

No time to lose.

Without further thought, Jasper opened his pages and beckoned Dramm to join him. Dramm hopped back, refusing, not understanding what was required of him. His pages ruffled, slowly. In answer, the blood spot emerged on both the elder book's open leaves. Dramm rocked to and fro as if hypnotized—slumped forward a little, then trudged, as only a spellbook can, forward, backing his spine up against the fold of Jasper's pages. Then Jasper slowly closed his pages around the little book.

'Don't be afraid, little one,' said Jasper in the language of books— the words ran across his pages, and into Dramm. 'I give all my knowledge to you. Soon, you will need it.'

'But I *am* afraid, Mr. Jasper,' Dramm replied, shedding a single golden tear onto his cover. 'I don't understand—what is happening? I wish Miss Alditha was here...'

'Don't worry, it's all going to be just wonderful,' Jasper replied, in a way that only spell books could communicate. 'Hush now, and learn...'

The last thing Dramm saw before Jasper engulfed him completely was a frantic girl with a glass tube running into one of the pyramids dotted about the square.

21

'Peridot.'

Peridot closed her eyes and mouthed an Astarian obscenity. 'Quarka, not now.'

'What's going on? Who's this?' demanded Quarka, the Astarian geologist, his blue, almond-shaped eyes staring at Celeste.

'It's Celeste. Command sent her to find us. I'm not trying to be rude, Quarka, but we have to get to a lab, right this minute.'

'What's the hurry? Has Zirca sanctioned your lab time? I'm sure it's not on the rota.'

'We've been asleep for nearly seven thousand years. It's been a little tricky to keep up with the rota. Oh Celeste, go, now.'

Celeste didn't need telling twice, she began to move. Alpha ran with her.

'Wait a minute, somebody needs to bring me up to speed. I haven't been told about this lab allocation. I'm not sure Zirca would approve.'

'I'm absolutely sure he wouldn't,' muttered Celeste. 'One slipaway.

Is the lab near here?'

'Left, left, right, right, left, door on the left. Go,' said Peridot. 'Good luck.'

Celeste took off, and Quarka made to follow her. Peridot blocked his path.

Celeste ran, Alpha following close behind in the narrow corridors.

Left, she checked it off.

Left, she checked the time-seal. Forty spangles.

Right. Twenty-five spangles. *You're not going to make it.* The thought tried to paralyse her, but Celeste shoved it down, deep down inside herself.

Right. You're really not going to make it. She swallowed hard, wasting precious spangles of the last slipaway any of them would know on this planet. *And you know what that means.*

I can't ask him to do that, she thought.

'Celeste,' said Alpha, 'give me the tube.'

'No.'

'Everyone will die.'

'Everyone's not you.'

'Irrational. I am a part of everyone. We will all die. Give me the tube.'

Celeste's eyes were wet, and she clutched the tube tightly in her hand. Alpha reached out his spindly fingers and prised it from her. His chest opened up with a smooth hum—bio-mechs were designed to be entirely self-contained, sealed systems, so they could house data-pyramids if necessary over the long distances of space travel. He placed the tube inside his chest and his body closed back up.

'I…' said Celeste, but the words wouldn't come. The tears rolled down her cheeks though. 'Thank you,' she squeaked.

'Acknowl-'

Alpha stopped abruptly. Celeste didn't know what had happened to him, but she knew it was whatever Zirca had planned to happen to everyone.

She cried.

Alditha made it back to the square to find people already gathering. When the Hedge started pulsing intensely, it was like a hypnotic call; the Gardenfolk came to see it dance.

She spotted Jasper in the front ranks, seeming to watch the Hedge, and wandered over to him.

'Evenin' Jasper,' she said. She never *quite* called Jasper 'sir,' but often wondered whether she should.

Jasper didn't respond. That wasn't unusual—he pretty much lived as a hermit, after all.

'Happy Midsummer Hallowe'en to ya,' she said, touching the brim of a hat that was no longer there. *That needs to change,* she thought. *A witch with no hat is no witch at all.*

Jasper fell backwards suddenly, and Alditha turned back to him in shock.

His pages had turned brown and brittle, and the fall snapped some of them like crackers.

'Jasper.'

Then Alditha saw him. Dramm. Standing still, where Jasper had fallen. He had a mark on both his covers.

A red star with wings.

Celeste had dried her tears and hauled Alpha's body onto her shoulder. She retraced her steps, only to find that Peridot and Quarka were still arguing about her when she reached them.

'How did it go?' asked Peridot. 'Did you-?'

Celeste looked at Alpha over her shoulder.

'Oh, Celeste, I'm so sorry.'

Celeste sighed, nodded, and pushed on.

'Just you wait a moment, Celeste,' said Quarka.

Celeste turned her eyes on him. 'Go back to sleep, Quarka,' she said, the energy drained from her voice. 'You were more use as a Sleeper than you ever were awake.' And she walked on, reaching the elevator pad.

'Celeste, wait, I'm coming with you,' called Peridot. But if Celeste heard her, she gave no sign of it. Peridot only caught her up as the pad began to move.

They travelled to the surface in silence. As they arrived, they saw the Hedge flare with colour and light.

———————

In orbit, the ships of the Astarian fleet sensed the dimensions as they came into alignment. They scanned for the sign they were waiting for. The readings were confused. They set their engines to pick up the sign as soon as transmission was clear. For long minutes, no-one on board dared take anything but shallow breaths. Why did the signal not *come*?

———————

Celeste watched the Hedge with everyone else, but she felt more alone than she ever had. There was something of her missing, an Alpha-shaped hole in her life that she had no idea how to fill, even if she wanted to.

Something nudged her leg and she looked down. It was a book, and apparently, it was alive.

This planet is weird. Even by the universe's usual standards, this planet is just weird.

She stopped and looked at it. The book had the symbol of her own lost planetary system on its cover—the red star with wings, with a halo of planets around it.

'What are you doing here?' she asked, bending down and picking it up.

The symbol rippled as she picked up the book, and colours flowed from the book, flowed up Celeste's arm, over her face, into her hair. Colours that corresponded to the colours of the Hedge as it danced.

'Oh,' she said out loud. 'Oh, I see.' She reached up with her other hand, and in the crowd, the Green Man's pocket unraveled without his say-so. One of the silver balls she had given him—ordinary power conversion balls—flew out of the bag and soared through the air, changing shape as it did so, lengthening, splitting, becoming a tool that no-one there entirely recognised. Of course, it looked *something* like the ceremonial Shears of Destiny the beggars usually used at this festival, but it was altogether a more daunting thing—it didn't glitter or glisten, but it did definitely shine.

Celeste held the book in one hand, the colour still flowing from its pages into her. She caught the flying Shears in the other hand and looked at the Hedge. 'Yes,' she said, as if it had asked her something. 'Yes, I see,' and she began to trim the Hedge—a snip here, a lop there, the colour and the energy aligning, not dissipating as it always did, but growing, becoming more complex, pulsing faster as she worked.

Celeste felt the colour pulsing through her, felt the energy and the dimensions trying to tear her apart, pull her into a thousand million directions, a thousand million realities all at once. She swayed, danced with the Hedge, felt its purpose as her own, lopped, snipped, reducing the variables in the possibility matrix, reducing the pressure of the thousand million directions, focusing on the one, the one she wanted, the one that had the connection-point to *home*.

She worked faster, and faster, the leaves of possibility fighting her, the dimensions pushing back against her work, but the book flooded through her, keeping her moving, keeping her in sync, and she began to win again, the numbers going her way, the colours and realities going her way.

The rainbow of colour and light from the Hedge shot up into the night sky and exploded into a single thick beam of possibility like a huge cosmic firework.

Celeste passed out.

———————

The signal came.

The ships caught it, and those on board whose job it was to move the moment the signal came did their job. They moved.

The ships engaged their drives, and disappeared down a multi-coloured tunnel that hadn't been there but suddenly was.

The space of the Milky Way continued about its business as if nothing had happened.

———————

The Gardenfolk looked up as the beam of multi-coloured light shot into the night sky.

They kept looking up as giant, round hunks of metal popped into existence above them, making plenty of ears pop too. They seemed not to stop until they almost filled the sky. The slick Astarian fleet of spaceships had arrived.

There are lots of them, thought Alditha. *This is not going to be easy.*

As they watched, a hatch on the underside of one of the ships slid open, and what looked for all the world like a giant frying pan began a slow, stately drift down to earth, like the last exhausted snow of winter.

Eventually, it landed outside the square, not far from where Celeste had found the test tube.

Peridot woke Celeste, and they went to greet the new arrival. Mali-Juna and Rhodon marched Zirca along too. Alditha and Harper tagged along, because although no-one had asked them or invited them, Alditha was a witch and needed nobody's permission to be nosy.

When a slab of blackness opened in the side of the frying pan, it was remarkable how few of the welcoming party were surprised. And when four teenage-looking figures—three females and a male—with spectacularly-coloured hair and almond-shaped eyes of vivid glistening shades stepped out in long, ceremonial robes, nobody was surprised about that either.

'Commander,' said Celeste, 'I present the Sleepers. Well, most of them, anyway. One's still underground, probably arguing with himself about the right way to argue with himself.'

The commander, a female named Numiia, whose hair had the warm tones of amber, looked beyond her. 'Life?' she asked. 'We understood from Commander Zirca this was an uninhabited world.' She paused, to admire the frying pan-shaped exterior of the spacecraft, then gave a little smile. 'Nevertheless...life here *would* explain a lot of things.'

'Yes,' said Celeste. 'About that-'

''Scuse me, Your Commanderness,' said Alditha, pushing to the front with the self-possession of witches everywhere. 'Good evening, welcome to our planet...erm, Garden. My name's Alditha and I'm a witch, but don't let that worry you. Fact is, there's life here. All sorts of life, and there has been for generations now. I know you lot were hoping to find an empty planet, and I know why. I can respect anyone who wants to keep themselves to themselves and doesn't want the business of warring with other folk in their lives. But I need to tell you that we don't wage war to the point of extinction on this world, so before you get any ideas of wiping us all out and startin' again, you don't need to be doin' that. We're happy to have you if you want to be here, and if you don't, we'll wish you well and bid you so long. We've only met some of you so far—your Sleepers and Celeste here. But this day, Astarians and Gardenfolk—that's us—have worked together to save this world from danger. So we know that we can do it, and we know that you can do it an' all. You need to know that. You need to know what we're all capable of.'

Numiia stared at Alditha, as if expecting her to pass out from lack of oxygen. When she didn't, Numiia simply said 'Thank you, Alditha. But is there someone who can update me on the circumstances of this "danger" that has brought our people together?'

'I can do that, Your Commanderness. You see-' Alditha began.

'Perhaps I might be allowed to address the Commander,' said a voice from behind them. Celeste gasped—it was a voice she'd know anywhere, no matter how many times people told her that all bio-mechs sounded the same. 'You're alive,' she said.

'Conclusion rational, if obvious,' said Alpha.

'How?' Celeste gasped.

'Chemical only permanently harmful to creatures containing significant concentrations of Melazoidin. Explanations will follow,' he advised, making his way up to Commander Numiia.

The new arrivals huddled with the bio-mech for a few minutes, during which the Gardenfolk began to mutter about missing their normal Hallowe'en festivities, complete with dancing, eating, drinking and the customary midday and midnight fireworks. Then the Commander came forward again and the crowd tuned back in.

'We have heard the account of the events that led to the Sleepers' discovery. We would be prepared to entertain negotiations with your representatives to establish peaceful co-existence on this planet.'

They're a bit full of themselves, thought Alditha, *but they're already getting the idea. That's the Garden doing its thing to 'em. I have a feeling that something amazing and wonderful is about to happen.*

'Bring Commander Zirca to me,' said Numiia. 'And we will be prepared to talk to this Skoros, King of the Garden, whenever he is ready.'

'Begging your Pardon, Your Commanderness, but Skoros has been deposed. We don't have no kings in the Garden. We've never needed 'em, and we don't propose to start now.'

The Gardenfolk raised a cheer at that.

'Very well, then. Choose your ambassadors and send them to us at your convenience.

Well, thought Alditha, *they're here now. The challenge is to make it work.*

22

It was on the news and everything. Reports of spectacular lights in the sky, going down a funnel of colour, hitting the earth. Hitting my garden.

That's the thing about people these days, they're all on their phones, and enough people record things to make them undeniable.

Of course, I don't know what happened. It was like being at the end of a rainbow, and for a while, I thought about digging in my garden for a pot of gold—well, you never know.

But then I thought about that little owl I sometimes see. And I thought perhaps I didn't need a pot of gold that badly after all. Perhaps there are more important things than gold.

Maybe one day I'll go and do the Thing, and see what all the light and colour was about.

But not today.

Alditha sighed as she stirred a pinkish mixture on her stove. It had been a busy week.

She and Celeste had been nominated as ambassadors, Commander Numiia preferring to negotiate through an intermediary whenever possible.

Already, the framework was coming together—the Garden was big, and although there were a lot of Astarians, they were by no means all the same. Some were content, for the moment, to stay in their communities, and settle in spaces where most of the Garden-folk had taken one look and said 'Nah, let's keep going, y'never know what's round the next bush.' Others, many others, were inquisitive about their new home and the people who had lived in it before them, keen to learn everything—history, socialization, food, every-thing. They brought their point of view and their technology, but were keen to experience the Garden and its people on their terms.

Some said it would never work, and stayed in their ships, trying to decide whether or not to wait until the next Hallowe'en and move on, looking for their perfect, uninhabited home, or even their lost plane-tary system.

Things that had never made sense before began to take a shape in the minds of the Gardenfolk. The story of Ven Tao the Gardener was given its details, its history. Alditha chuckled. Even she hadn't realized about Jasper, not even when she'd seen him in Ven's hand in her Tarot Wheel. After Ven's death, the great 'Manual of the Engine-Seers', Jazper 5-9—once an ordinary, all-purpose reference booklet used by the Astarians—had become an intelligent being, living as a hermit in his ramshackle cottage since the beginning of sentient life in the Garden, and no-one had ever realized. No wonder the book had been lost for so long. Though many years ago, Jasper *had* dis-played a red star with wings on an old welcome sign outside his cot-tage—and *that's* where both she and Skoros had originally seen the symbol. Of course, like a raspberry seed stuck in her gums, the Tarot Wheel image of Ven throwing the manual clear of the scout ship had haunted Alditha's subconscious daily until she had understood its significance. And now, Dramm—her little Dramm—had become the new Manual, just as, much to her surprise, Celeste had become the Garden's new Gardener, whatever that meant.

Poor Jasper, he knew he didn't have the strength to see in the Astarians' return she thought to herself, stirring philosophically. *He was such a character and I'll always miss him. I do hope Dramm is up to the job. Only time will tell.*

The Gardenfolk were beginning to see their history as something intertwined with the Astarians'. Some people were even starting to vaguely worship the Astarians as their 'creators' at which Alditha rolled her eyes.

It would be a long journey, bringing the Gardenfolk and the Astarians together properly, but between them, Alditha was confident they'd manage it. Big Red, Sagar, Gunkin, and the Green Man had volunteered to be Garden Marshals and do their bit for the 'new order of things'. Though what a giant blue dragon and a temperamental red demon could realistically do for a race of advanced space beings remained to be seen.

Odiz had been found, of course. The Convocation of Mages had plans to give him the biggest and best funeral in their history—but, as yet, they couldn't lay their hands on quite enough beer to do him justice.

Mistress Fazackerly and Timmoluk had both been buried, returned to the Garden to begin the cycle of life again, feeding the worms and the insects.

Skoros had not been found. That *was* a worry.

So was Harper, who still wore his visor because, he said, the sky was full of worms and beetles and horrid things waiting to break through and eat them all. But Alditha reasoned she had too much to *actively* worry about to do much about dimensional hoojamaflips that weren't, it seemed, about to endanger them any day soon.

There was a loud knock on the door of her cottage.

Alditha frowned.

'Don't-' she called, but there was a ZZZAP and her door disappeared.

'Mr. Alpha, how many times,' she snapped. 'Knocking is *so* much easi-'

Something grabbed her round the back of the neck. Something squeezed.

'Don't make a sound, witch,' said a voice that was half human and half bio-mech. 'Guess what? I'm here to kill you—quite painfully.'

'Well, of course you are.' Alditha grunted, trying her best to escape. 'Wondered what had happened to my favourite wizard.'

The hand let go of her, and Alditha turned to face her assailant.

It looked like an ordinary bio-mech.

Ordinary, she chided herself. It had been a *really* busy week.

She folded her arms. 'Well, what do you want, wizard?'

'To kill you. Naturally.'

'It's been tried—*many* times.'

'Listen, witch—I'll soon be gone from here,' Skoros screamed, though the voice of Gamma. 'I don't need the Garden anymore, I'm destined for greater things.'

'I'm not stopping you leaving.'

'*No-one* can stop me.'

'Well go on, then. Go, if you're going.'

'Ah, but I want to hear you scream before I leave, you meddling witch.'

Alditha blinked.

'Well, that's clearly not going to happen, now is it?'

The bio-mech advanced again. Alditha raised an eyebrow at it. She knew that escape was futile, unless....

'Would it help if I said I was sorry?' she said, stepping back.

The bio-mech stopped. 'Sorry? Sorry for what?'

'For that whole "wet blanket" thing. I mean, I knew you liked me, but you just dithered about so much. I didn't mean for it to become a thing. And then you got all stroppy and dark wizardy, and I never got a chance to tell you I was sorry. So…*I'm sorry.*'

'Why didn't you tell me before?' Skoros asked, half little boy, half bio-mech.

'You never gave me the chance,' Alditha replied, with a sincerity that surprised even her. 'You just *never* gave me the chance.'

There was a thoughtful sigh from Skoros which seemed to lessen the bio-mech's menace for a second. However, any intended thoughts of eleventh-hour romance from the wizard quickly disappeared as the sigh turned into a frustrated, blood-curdling scream, the likes of which hadn't been heard in the Garden for many a long year.

'AARRRRRRRRHHHHHHHHHH.'

Suddenly, the bio-mech lunged, then lunged again—but then was silent for a long moment. Alditha took the opportunity to move out of its way.

Then it hummed with power. 'Bio-mech Gamma-Omega-Delta, reporting. Location anomaly. How did I get here?'

'That's all right, Mr. Gamma. I...I don't think you were yourself.'

It hadn't taken Alditha long to confirm her suspicions. Minutes after her run-in with Gamma-Skoros, a shuttle had left the Garden for one of the big Astarian ships. Minutes after that, the big ship had broken orbit. It had punched a hole in reality without a dimension drive or a Stone Hedge or a Gardener to help it along.

Good riddance, she thought. Skoros leaving was a weight off her shoulders, but it had given her a whole new set of things to worry about.

When Skoros left, his ship caused a rupture of the dimensions above the Garden. Nobody knew about it until a giant worm dropped out of the sky to land in Spooky End and quickly burrow its way under the surface of the Garden. Celeste had explained what it meant—the barriers between the dimensions were thinner than they'd suspected. That meant the Astarians who had returned to their ships and hoped to leave couldn't be allowed to go—at least not until more was understood about the damage that could be caused by their popping through dimensions willy-nilly. It also meant that when a brave, if sometimes melodramatic little owl told you the sky was full of worms and beetles, occasionally—just occasionally—you'd better listen.

Alditha looked up at the sky, which still looked like any other Garden sky she'd ever seen. She couldn't see the other dimension up there, not with all her witchcraft. It was only Harper who could see it, and people were starting to listen to him more and more and labelling him 'The Seer of the New Garden.' Well, he *was* an unusual owl, for sure.

Either way, Harper certainly *did* have aliens in his garden now. And, in many ways, maybe it *was* his garden after all.

It'll go to his head, she thought, smiling softly.

The road that lay ahead of them would be harder now that the Astarians who didn't want to be there had no option but to stay. They'd come an immeasurable distance to find a home.

Now they've got to live in it, for better or worse, thought Alditha. She pondered, then stopped it and shrugged. *That's what home means, after all.*

THE END

Jude Gwynaire was born in the UK and lives in Suffolk, with his family, where he combines a love of writing with that of music and composing. Drawing inspiration from history, folklore, and the natural world, Jude has written science-fiction and fantasy stories for children and adults. *Aliens in my Garden* is Jude's first published novel.

Twitter: @judegwynaire

Website: www.judegwynaire.com

Lightning Source UK Ltd.
Milton Keynes UK
UKHW01f1843250918
329518UK00001B/206/P